To: Julian

With every good
wish for Christmas
and after!

Eleanor Sandy

November 1977.

GOLD SCOOP

GOLD SCOOP
Sandy Gall

COLLINS
St. James's Place, London, 1977

William Collins Sons and Co Ltd
London · Glasgow · Sydney · Auckland
Toronto · Johannesburg

To Africa

in all her savagery and splendour

and to all my African friends who
made this book possible.

First published 1977
© Sandy Gall 1977
ISBN 0 00 221355 9
Set in Plantin
Made and printed in Great Britain by
William Collins Sons and Co Ltd Glasgow

I

Alastair Playfair obeyed instructions and did up his seat belt. The engine took on the plaintive note which denotes half power and that landing is imminent. Although he could see nothing in the darkness, he knew from the angle of the plane that they were banking over the lake and approaching the runway. The airport lights suddenly came into view and they began to lose height. Someone at the back of the cabin was trying to be sick into one of those paper bags. There was a bump and the tyres squealed. For a moment the plane swerved from side to side as if the pilot was not completely in control. Then he steadied the aircraft and they taxied in without further incident.

Playfair was one of the first off. The tropical night advanced to meet him, hot and humid. A big white moth with ruby eyes clung for a second to his shoulder before vanishing into the darkness. Playfair walked across the tarmac, carrying his typewriter, noting the soldiers lounging round the terminal with automatic weapons slung from their shoulders. They eyed the incoming passengers suspiciously. In front of the building what at first sight appeared to be two huge catherine wheels spun against the darkness. They were naphtha flares, hissing like old gas lamps, and round them revolved hundreds of moths, beetles and other denizens of the African night. Every so often one would get too close to the naked flame, scorch its wings and hurtle to the ground like some fragile meteor. But for every one that fell, there were always a dozen more to take its place. Playfair stepped through the door and up to the desk. A sleepy immigration officer checked his passport slowly and with a hint of arrogance. Playfair explained that he had come from Mombasa, that he was resident here in Kawawa and confirmed the entry in his passport declaring that he was a journalist. Finally the African shoved the passport back at him wordlessly, indicating he was free to make his way to the baggage point, and the airport bus. It was past midnight and not surprisingly there were few passengers; one Asian family, some Africans, one other European and himself. The bus rattled off along the lakeside on the fifteen-mile trip to the capital. They met hardly any traffic and on their left, the huge expanse of the lake, dimly reflecting a dying moon, showed no sign of life. Playfair had heard that the fishermen would not go out at night now. Like everyone else in Kawawa, they were frightened.

The driver dropped Playfair and his bags at the Grand Hotel, an unprepossessing brick pile in the centre of the town. In the old days it had been called the Imperial, but naturally those days had gone, and with them any pretensions the place had had to colonial splendour. The hallway was dark and the night porter asleep. Playfair woke him by dropping his suitcase. He jumped.

'Good evening, Mr Playfair, there's a cable for you.' He handed over the flimsy green envelope with a yawn. It was a routine message from Playfair's office. He crumpled it up and put it in his pocket.

'How are things?' he asked the night porter. The man's brown eyes flickered apprehensively round the empty lobby. A cockroach ran boldly across the floor.

'There was some shooting again last night.' He licked his lips nervously.

'Kadongo's men and the Palace again?'

The Indian nodded.

'Any casualties?'

'Three or four, I heard.' His eyes never stopped moving. 'Royal bodyguard that is.' He came round the desk and picked up Playfair's case. They walked to the lift, and went up in silence. The tension between the Palace and one section of the army led by Major Kadongo was common knowledge, but it was only in the last few days that it had really come into the open. There had been two or three shooting incidents recently but this was much the most serious.

The Indian opened Playfair's room – 201 – and carried in his case. Playfair gave him a coin and said goodnight. It was a small suite: sitting room, bedroom and bath, Playfair's current home and office combined. As the room smelt stuffy, he walked over to the double windows and opened them wide, listening to the silence. The town was asleep. It was after one . . .

It seemed only a few minutes later that he awoke with a start.

The loud bang still echoed in his sleep-fogged mind. He looked at his watch: five o'clock. He lay for a moment or two listening; a dog barked in the distance; suddenly he noticed a peculiar smell in the room. He got up and went cautiously to the open window. About a hundred yards away, a small cloud of white smoke, sinister in the half-light, was rising from the roadway and drifting towards him. He was still puzzling why anyone should want to fire a smoke grenade at the Grand Hotel, when a thin, high-pitched scream made him drop to the floor; there was a loud bang just outside the window and shrapnel pattered against the palm trees. Kneeling behind an armchair, Playfair waited for number three – they always came in threes. This time it was much closer, just below the window. The blast made his windows rattle furiously and the palm trees took another peppering. Playfair heard a crash behind him in the bathroom and went to investigate.

A large chunk of jagged metal lay in the bath. It must have flown in through the open window, sliced its way through the thin partition wall and dropped tamely into the bath, only slightly chipping the enamel. It was still warm. He went back to the window and looked out across the road, beyond the palms and blue gums, and suddenly understood. Over there about half a mile away, hidden by a screen of trees, was the Palace. Whoever had punctured his bathroom had undoubtedly been aiming at that, but was not a very good shot. Round the Palace the trees stood motionless in the pearly mist of an African dawn. Nothing moved on the broad tree-lined streets. Only a pair of kites circled in the pale sky. It would be hot in an hour or two, for he could feel the first prickles of sweat on his skin. The palm fronds began to make a dry rustling noise. Soon, when the breeze got up, they would start their daily St Vitus' dance.

Playfair rang and ordered breakfast and then dressed in a lightweight safari suit. As the room boy came in with his paw-paw, scrambled eggs and tea, the shooting started again. He could hear the deep boom of a heavy machine-gun, and the lighter rattle of automatic weapons, then the measured thump of a mortar. A puff of dark smoke rose above the trees. They were obviously mortaring the Palace itself. He was just finishing his eggs when the phone rang.

'Hallo, Playfair here.'

9

'Thanks for the call.' It was a girl's voice, cool, mocking.

'Arabella! I was just going to call you. I didn't think you'd be up yet.'

She was obviously peeved he hadn't rung her. Quite frankly, he had forgotten in the general excitement, but couldn't very well admit it.

'With all that banging and thumping? You must be joking. I thought I was going to be blown out of bed.'

'Someone's taking potshots at the Palace, but I can't see from here. What's the view like from the top floor?'

'I think the Palace is burning. You can see quite well from the balcony. Do you want to come up?'

'Thanks, I'll be right with you.'

Playfair walked to the end of the corridor and took the lift to the fifth floor where Arabella had a large corner room with a balcony. She had shared with another girl from the High Commission but she had gone home and Arabella had stayed on alone. Alastair Playfair had arrived three months ago as resident correspondent for *Worldwide News*. They had got to know one another through a row in the hotel dining room. Arabella had booked a table for her boss, the British High Commissioner, and the head waiter had given it by mistake to Playfair, whom he knew as a regular customer and generous tipper. When the High Commissioner had arrived with his party and Arabella, Playfair and a number of noisy colleagues were already installed. There had been an argument, with Arabella icily furious, and another table had to be found for the High Commissioner. Next day, Playfair, his gallantry not altogether unaffected by Arabella's blonde beauty, had apologised; so disarmingly that she had relented and even agreed to discuss the matter over a drink. Since then Playfair had found himself rather intrigued by the girl with the amethyst eyes.

Arriving outside number 512, Playfair knocked and announced himself. There was a quick footstep and the door swung open to reveal a tall brown-skinned girl in well-cut cream trousers and an open-necked silk shirt that matched her eyes. Her mane of blonde hair was tied in a pony tail. She offered her cheek.

'When did you get back?'

'About midnight.'

'How was the trip?'

She led the way to the balcony where Playfair could smell freshly-made coffee.

'Not too bad. They want me to stay on for another three months. They think it's going to be very newsworthy here, as they put it.'

'They could be right. Look.'

The view from Arabella's balcony was indeed excellent. They could see the roof of the Palace over the top of the trees, and one corner of it seemed to be on fire. The smoke that Playfair had seen from his window on the first floor was now much thicker and blacker, and was floating towards the centre of the town. The thump of mortars and the rattle of small arms was louder and angrier. Through the trees Playfair could see army vehicles moving towards the front gate of the Palace. In the lulls between mortar salvoes they could hear the whine of heavy tyres, probably armoured cars.

'My God,' said Playfair, 'it doesn't look too good for our friend King George. Have you talked to your boss?'

Arabella gave Playfair a cup of coffee and shook her head. 'No, I couldn't get through to him.' The High Commissioner's house was only a few hundred yards away from the Palace.

'He might get a mortar in his front garden, with any luck.'

'Alastair, that's a cruel thing to say.'

He grinned. Sir Harry Crumb, the High Commissioner, had the reputation for being a bit of an old woman.

The telephone rang. It was the switchboard wondering if Mr Playfair was with Miss Cavendish.

'Just one moment, sir. I have a call for you.'

'Mr Playfair?'

'Speaking.'

'Ah.' The voice sounded breathless. 'This is Kamanga here from the Royal Palace.'

For a moment Playfair was nonplussed. Then he remembered. A rather stiff and formal political adviser to the King. A man who had always seemed rather colourless and pushed into the background by some of the King's more ebullient courtiers. Playfair acknowledged that of course he knew him, and asked what he could do for him.

'Can I have a word with you privately, Mr Playfair? It is

extremely urgent.'

Playfair looked at Arabella.

'Where are you?'

'Downstairs.'

'Right, come to room 512, fifth floor. Take the lift to the top floor and I'll meet you there.'

Arabella had been standing close enough to hear the conversation.

'Sounds as if the King has sent him.'

'Could be he's in so much trouble he wants to tell the world.'

As if in confirmation, the smoke from the Palace was still climbing towards the sky. Playfair walked to the lift and waited. It arrived with a clank and a jolt. Kamanga freed himself from the clutches of the mesh gates. He had glasses and a small beard and carried a briefcase. He was clearly exhausted and shaken but still dignified.

'Come along,' said Playfair, leading the way to the corner room. 'We'll talk here.'

Arabella was waiting with a cup of coffee, but Kamanga was too agitated to give her more than a passing glance.

'His Majesty sent me,' he began with a gulp. 'He is besieged in the Palace, under attack by a group of mutineers led by Major Kadongo.'

'How do you know it is Kadongo?' Playfair's voice was neutral.

'We know, but His Majesty will give you the details himself. Since the situation is critical he demands . . . er . . . requests your presence at the Palace as soon as possible. He thinks that if the world is alerted speedily the final disaster may yet be averted.'

'Is the Palace surrounded by Kadongo's men?'

'We can get in the back way.'

'Right, then let's go.'

Arabella's fingers squeezed his arm.

'Oh, I'd like to bring my . . . friend if that's convenient?'

'Of course. I have a car.'

They were in and out of the lift, across the lobby and in Kamanga's car within two minutes. The town, usually frantic with cars, buses and bicycles at this time of the morning, was almost empty. They made good time in the small blue Volkswagen. At one point when they crossed the main boulevard that ran up the hill to the Palace, Playfair noted that two or three armoured cars were parked in the middle of the road, their machine-gun snouts pointing towards the entrance. He could see several figures in uniform standing beside the vehicles. Was it his imagination or was one figure markedly bigger than the rest? Was that Major Kadongo personally directing operations? It would be typical of the man. But it was only a glimpse and then they were past and turning and twisting through a maze of dusty streets that lay behind the Palace. They emerged in the lee of a high wall and followed it for a hundred yards or so. Finally Kamanga pulled up beside a small gate. It would have been easy to miss behind the trailing branches of a glossy-leaved mahogany tree.

Kamanga took a pistol from the briefcase and rapped smartly on the gate. Someone inspected them through a spyhole, then a key turned and a nervous-looking Palace guard waved them inside. Playfair and Arabella followed Kamanga in and found themselves looking down the barrel of a Bren gun. The guard behind it was dug in between the roots of the tree overhanging the entrance. Arabella stood rigid. Playfair squeezed her arm: 'It's alright, he's got the safety catch on.' But he would not have bet on it and the soldier looked very young and very jumpy. Gently, Playfair eased both of them round, out of the line of fire. Kamanga had finished a brief consultation with the guard on the gate and beckoned to them to hurry. They crossed an open park-like space dotted with big trees and flowering shrubs. The papery blooms of the bougainvillea blazed in red and purple profusion. But Playfair and the girl were so intent on their mission that they barely noticed.

The Palace was really an inter-connecting jumble of large African huts with thatched roofs, and a European-style mansion at the centre. Servants, lowly officials and a host of tribal hangers-on occupied the outer quarters. Here and there they passed a crater where a mortar had fallen and one or two of the trees showed signs of blast. But it was not until they came to the Palace proper that Playfair saw just how much damage had been done. The wing nearest the main entrance had received a direct hit. The roof had collapsed and the interior of the rooms was heaped with rubble and smoking wreckage.

Kamanga hurried them on. Every so often they came across a group of frightened-looking Africans who fell silent as the little party passed. The atmosphere, Playfair thought, was already one of defeatism. It showed clearly in those dull faces and mournful eyes.

They were now in the royal quarters. A few guards stood at the entrance to a much wider corridor and their feet fell on a thick carpet. Kamanga stopped before an imposing, polished wooden door, and knocked.

There was a muffled reply. Kamanga swung the door open, and they walked into a big airy room almost English in its atmosphere. Playfair's eyes were drawn to the walls; everywhere were photographs of the King as a young man: standing in front of his Cambridge college in rowing clothes; in the College Cricket team, and even one of him hunting. He came towards them, older and less self-confident and Playfair took the outstretched brown hand and introduced Arabella. The eyes lit up with interest for a moment. In happier days, the King's well-known gallantry would not have stopped there, but now it was a rather frightened monarch who waved Playfair into the armchair beside him. Arabella sat discreetly behind.

King George had been educated, trained and some would say, ruined by the British. It had been a traditional and privileged progress; public school, Cambridge and then Sandhurst and the Guards. En route, so to speak, young King George had got to know the West End of London and its pleasures and that could have been his downfall. Too many hours spent in night clubs with the more effete members of the minor aristocracy may have blunted his instinct for survival. At any rate, Playfair reflected, he seemed to have been out-manoeuvred by an energetic young barbarian with a few soldiers at his back. But then, many greater kings had come to grief in similar fashion.

'Thank you for coming so promptly, and for bringing your charming companion.' He made a little bow with his head in Arabella's direction.

'Your visit is the only agreeable thing that has happened today. Well, you heard the shooting, and you have seen the damage to the Palace. I think we have managed to put the fire out but one wing is totally destroyed.'

'We saw it, Your Majesty,' said Playfair, 'but what actually started the shooting?'

'I will tell you the story from the beginning. But, forgive me, I am forgetting my manners.'

He got up and walked over to a cabinet against the wall, pulled open the door and peered inside.

'I'm afraid things are rather disorganised, we only seem to have whisky.'

He poured out three large measures into different-sized glasses and carried them back across the room. Neither Playfair nor Arabella felt like whisky at that time in the morning, but did not wish to offend the King who certainly looked as if he needed a stiff drink.

'The present crisis began about a week ago when my Prime Minister announced that he intended to make Major Kadongo the new Chief of Staff of the army. I opposed this for various reasons and gave the Prime Minister instructions to nominate someone else. To my intense displeasure, the Prime Minister went ahead all the same and made the appointment. My reply was to dismiss the Prime Minister yesterday morning – did you know that?'

Playfair nodded: 'I heard it on the radio.'

'Well, I dismissed the Prime Minister and countermanded the appointment of Major Kadongo.' The King took another draught of whisky and wiped his lips.

'Then I had a visit from an officer who is entirely loyal and who brought me some extremely disturbing news. This was in essence that Major Kadongo is involved in treachery on two counts.'

'What, precisely?'

'Plotting a *coup* – and trying to embezzle a great deal of money.'

'Really! What money?'

'You have heard of the Simba rebels?'

'Of course.'

'You'll remember that they set up a rebel state in the old Congo, and terrorised the north until the mercenaries attacked Stanleyville and drove them out?'

'I recall it very well.'

'It's some time ago now, and the weeds grow up very quickly in Africa. But when the rebels were chased out of their temporary capital they took with them one very interesting piece of booty; a king's ransom in gold.'

'Gold? That rings a bell.'

'There were lots of rumours about it but the full story never came out. Anyway, it was called the Simba Gold by some of the more sensational London papers. It was in fact part of the former Belgian Congo's foreign exchange reserves, which the rebels had simply – liberated, as we would say today.'

'How much in terms of cash?'

'About ten million – sterling.'

Playfair whistled and looked at Arabella.

'Yes, a lot of money. Well, after the fall of Stanleyville the rebels and the gold disappeared. It was thought that most of them had been killed and that the gold had either fallen into the mercenaries' hands, or else found its way, with some . . . er . . . reductions, back into the coffers of the state where it rightfully belonged.' The King took another swallow of whisky. 'But the truth was very different.'

Playfair leant forward, unable to contain his excitement.

'A couple of months ago, one of my intelligence people found out that the Simbas, or what was left of them, had gone to ground not far from our border, and had their gold with them.' The King swirled the whisky round in his glass. 'The matter was clearly rather delicate, and I did not wish to get involved officially – for obvious reasons. But I did not like the idea of these people being so close to our border. They were dangerous men and there were suggestions they might stir up trouble . . . so, perhaps I shouldn't be telling you this, but . . .' He looked out of the window and shrugged. 'I contacted a group of people in South Africa, soldiers of fortune you might say, and retained them to get rid of the Simbas once and for all.'

'And get hold of the gold, no doubt?'

The King had the grace to smile. 'I must say it did cross my mind.'

'And Kadongo was on to all this?'

'Apparently. There must be a traitor in the Palace. I think I know who he is, but it is too late now. Of course, I had no idea he was plotting behind my back until this officer came to see me.'

'But why did Kadongo not wait until you had recovered the gold for him?'

16

'For one very simple reason. Last night I gave orders for his arrest. Unfortunately the officer entrusted with this vital mission . . . bungled it.' The King bent over and put his hands to his face in a sudden gesture of despair.

There was a knock on the door and Kamanga came in. He crossed to the King's side and whispered something in his ear. After a moment the King got up and held out a hand. Playfair noticed it was shaking.

'I have just heard that the mutineers are bringing more men up in front of the Palace. It looks as if they are going to make a frontal attack. I think you and your . . . charming friend had better go, Mr Playfair. Thank you for listening and,' his grip emphasised his words, 'please tell the world the truth of what is happening here.'

'I will do my best. Good luck, Your Majesty.'

They left him standing by the open window, listening, a frail figure, about to be engulfed by the rising tide of war. Kamanga led them out by a different route. He explained that the Palace was surrounded and that they would have to go by the 'emergency exit'. This turned out to be a tunnel. They reached it through a kind of outhouse, which was unguarded. Kamanga took a torch from a shelf and led the way down a flight of wooden steps.

'Mind your heads,' he cautioned.

The torchlight flickered on the red earth walls. Their feet made practically no sound on the soft ground, and the air was cool. They walked in silence and Playfair, holding Arabella's arm to guide her, started counting his paces. He had just reached two hundred, and judged they were some way beyond the outer wall of the Palace when Kamanga stopped and turned left. Another flight of steps led upwards. Kamanga struggled with the trap door at the top. Finally, with Playfair heaving too, it swung back and released a cascade of fine red soil down the backs of their necks. They were in another outhouse or toolshed. Playfair could make out a hoe and a couple of rusty pangas, heavy chopping knives, in a corner. Kamanga began to open the door. It gave with a piercing squeak suggesting that it had not been used for a long time. They were suddenly bathed in a brilliant green light, as if they had just swum to the surface of the Green Grotto. Playfair and Arabella screwed up their eyes after the gloom of the tunnel. Slowly the world outside took shape as a banana grove, a profusion of pale green leaves and here and there bunches of reddish-skinned fruit.

Kamanga lifted his finger to his lips and listened hard for a few seconds. Then he told them to wait and disappeared into the silence.

Playfair inspected Arabella. She had a dirty smudge on her cheek and her hair was festooned with cobwebs. She wore no make-up, only a natural tan. He had just noticed she wore no bra when Kamanga's solemn face appeared round the door.

'Come quickly, please.'

They followed him through the banana grove in single file.

The Volkswagen was waiting by the side of the dirt road. There were a few mud-walled houses farther down, their thatched roofs only just higher than the banana trees. Kamanga drove quickly and in silence, taking a roundabout route through the African quarter to get to the hotel.

As they shook hands, Playfair heard the renewed thump of mortars exploding across the valley. It sounded as if Kadongo was making his final attack.

2

That night word came that the Palace had fallen. Major Kadongo, the reports said, personally led the final assault, but the King had escaped by a secret underground passage. Arabella was kept late typing telegrams at the High Commission. Playfair worked in his room, filing to London the whole story of the interview with the King, the scene at the Palace and the reports of the King's escape. He was able to give a vivid description of the underground tunnel.

It was the type of story that newspapers love – a *coup d'état* and a king deposed – plenty of action and an eye-witness report. Playfair knew that he had a scoop and that papers around the world would print his story on their front pages. He was the only resident correspondent in Kawawa and, although his colleagues in other capitals in the rest of Africa would pick up the story from the radio and other sources, his would be far and away the most authentic. His only concern was that he might not get his story out. But Major Kadongo was too busy at first to bother about the cable office. It was only much later that night that a truck full of soldiers arrived at Telegraph House and arrested the night staff at gunpoint. But by then, the world had the news, and in London reporters were already being alerted to fly out to cover the story. One of them in fact arrived on the last plane from Mombasa that night. He was Roger Straight, one of the real old hands in Africa. He rang Playfair as soon as he reached the Grand. Playfair offered to show him his copy. Straight, who worked for the *London Daily Campaigner*, accepted gratefully. With the time difference between Africa and home he might just make the last edition.

Half an hour later, there was a tap on Playfair's door. It was Straight, returning Playfair's messages.

'That was quick. Did you get through?'

'Well, I rang Mombasa and got our stringer to forward it. He has a tape recorder, so you can dictate at normal talking speed. He transcribes it on to cable forms and sends it round the corner to the cable office. His flat is bang next door.'

'Probably just as well,' said Playfair. 'The switchboard told me a few minutes ago that there is some sort of trouble down at the cable office. I think the army has been paying them a visit.'

'Ah.'

Straight accepted a whisky and lowered his six-foot-four frame into one of Playfair's chairs.

'Quite a night. Cheers.' He took a deep swallow. 'Looks like curtains for the king.'

'Yes, poor bugger. I shouldn't think he's enjoying his forced march through the bush, knowing that Kadongo's men are on his heels.'

'What do you think the chances are of his own people rallying and fighting back?'

'Not very high. They're not a warrior tribe, as you know, the Wawa, and they haven't any arms apart from the odd elephant rifle. Kadongo has the armoured regiment completely under his thumb, and that's the key to the situation. He'll have all his chums in the top posts by now. Jock Thompson, that old crook, was saying as much at lunchtime. The Wawa won't like it, but there's not much they can do.'

The African night outside the open windows was velvet soft now. No sounds came except the cicadas. The air on the little balcony was warm and scented with the sweet smell of frangipani. Playfair could almost see the big waxy flowers in the darkness below. He sighed.

'One sometimes forgets what an African night can be like. Why does one seem to spend one's time reporting bloody wars?'

'Well,' said Straight, 'when this is all over you must come down and spend a few days with me in Mombasa. We'll go down the coast and catch some sail fish. Ever tried it?'

Playfair shook his head. 'No, but it sounds marvellous.'

'When you see them jumping ten, twelve feet out of the water, with that great sword of theirs, that's really exciting. And the boatman shouts '*Piga! Piga!* Strike, bwana, strike!' That is one of the most exciting moments you'll ever have.'

'I'd love to do it,' said Playfair getting up. 'I've always been mad about that coast. It has lots of romantic memories for me. Nyali, Mnerani, Zanzibar too, in the old days. That fantastic smell of cloves you get as soon as you step ashore. I wonder what it's like now! Pretty bloody, I should think. I wonder what's happened to the Zanzibar Hotel?'

Straight laughed. 'A rest house for East German commissars, I should think. Well, see you in the morning. I should think all the boys from Fleet Street will be here on the first plane. Wild at being scooped. Goodnight, Alastair.'

Next morning, as predicted, the East African Airways morning flight disgorged a full complement of press men. They came off the plane in ragged order, toting typewriters and briefcases, their tropical suits crumpled, their faces bleary from the long overnight flight from Gatwick, blinking in the un-accustomed glare. First in line was Bill Broadside, his shock of hair sticking out wildly at all angles. He had a habit of wiping his nose with the back of his hand and sniffing in a rather disparaging manner.

The African Immigration Officer eyed him insolently. 'What paper?'

'*Daily Examiner.*'

'I warn you not to make any trouble here, Mr . . . William.'

'The name is Broadside.'

'Eh?'

Jabbing a rather dirty forefinger on the open page of the passport, Broadside said, 'The name is William Broadside.'

The Immigration man went on blandly as if he had not heard. 'I am warning you, Mr William, we do not want any British spies here.'

Broadside lit a cigarette and muttered to his companion in the queue: 'Bolshy bastards.'

The Immigration Officer continued his examination of the document with maddening slowness, finally stamping it and pushing it back across the counter.

'Remember what I said, Mr William, or you will make trouble for yourself.'

Broadside trudged through to the Customs hall, puffing his cigarette and muttering to himself. Half an hour later he was installed with his colleagues in the airport bus. It would take them about an hour to drive along the lakeside to the hotel. They were all hot and tired but chiefly thirsty. Only the thought of the cool bar at the Grand revived their jaded spirits. On arrival, Broadside did not even bother to go to his room. He sent up his bags and strode straight to the bar. There, clinging to it like a couple of castaways, were Playfair and Straight.

'Hallo, you two bastards,' Broadside shouted in his gravelly voice. 'Hard at work as usual, I see.'

'Wondering when you would get here,' said Straight.

'Ah, balls,' growled Broadside. 'Stop being so bloody pleased with yourselves and buy a man who's been travelling all night a drink.'

Johnny, the Goanese barman, took the order. A large gin and tonic for Broadside, beer for the others. The bar was suddenly full of journalists. They brought a breath of alien vitality, a florid cosmopolitanism into the water-tight European society of bank managers and tea planters. The barman was swamped by demands for gin and whisky and local beer called Tembo which came in enormous bottles, with an elephant on the label. The switchboard was suddenly humming with incoming calls from London and New York. The newly-arrived contingent hurried from bar to switchboard and back again with the speed and persistence of a company of ants on the move. And in between times, they crowded round the 'experts' represented by Playfair and Straight, and pumped them for information.

During one of these exchanges, one of the porters from the front desk leant over Playfair and handed him a message. It was from the Ministry of Information and said that Major Kadongo would give a press conference at noon. A loud buzz filled the bar as the word was passed round. One photographer still in his thick London suit tapped Playfair on the shoulder.

'Who's this bloke Kadongo then?' he asked.

'He's the bloke wot's in charge.'

'Oh, I thought that was King George,' said the newcomer.

'He was,' said Playfair, patiently, 'but he was overthrown yesterday. That's why you're here,' he added with heavy irony.

'Oh, thanks, mate, I'll just go and get myself sorted out.'

'Christ,' said Playfair. 'Who's that?'

A few minutes before twelve, Major Kadongo arrived at the hotel with a cluster of officers. He made a triumphal progress through the lobby to the dining room, where he mounted the dais used by the band and surveyed the room with the self-satisfied air of a conqueror. His huge chest strained the buttons of his British-style battledress tunic.

'Gentlemen,' he began, 'I have an important announcement to make first of all.' He waited, a smile of childlike simplicity playing over his features.

'I have, as of this morning, assumed the rank of Colonel. Full Colonel.' The smile became more cherubic.

'Who promoted you?' It was Broadside's gravelly voice. Kadongo's smile flickered off momentarily, like a faulty bulb. Then it returned.

'Maself. I promoted maself. As Major Kadongo, I was Chief of Staff. As Colonel Kadongo, I am still Chief of Staff and head of the army.' He chuckled, a deep rumble. Round him his officers also chuckled and slapped their thighs.

Straight, his thin features disdainful, tilted his moustache at Kadongo. 'What has happened to the King?'

The chuckles stopped and a crafty look came into Kadongo's eyes. 'The King? What about him? I think he is still the King.' Again the big man chuckled and his sycophants bent double with amusement.

'Did you personally order the attack on his Palace?' Playfair interjected.

'Attack?' The big man made it sound as if it would be the last thing he would dream of doing. 'Attack on the Palace? Now, let me tell you gentlemen of the press what happened yesterday.' His face was screwed up in the effort of concentration, his skin glistening blue-black under the artificial lighting.

'Yesterday's attack on the Palace was made by rebel elements in the King's bodyguard, mutineers, gentlemen. When we heard the shooting, I immediately ordered three scout cars to the Palace to give the King any protection he might need.'

He paused, his eyes crafty. 'It was in the course of this operation, ah, that we were in action, ah, against the mutineers, and that several of my men were killed and wounded. And it was during this operation, carried out in support of the King, of course, gentlemen, that the Palace was damaged, despite all our efforts to save it.'

'I understand the King had ordered your arrest?' All eyes swivelled to Playfair. Kadongo's brow wrinkled up in disbelief and then anger. The deep-set eyes looked suddenly red. 'That is a lie,' he snarled. 'A dirty lie. This press conference is now closed. I have work to do.'

There was a commotion and the huge figure barged out, followed by the comet's tail of suddenly grim-faced officers. At the door Kadongo turned and gave Playfair a malevolent stare. For a moment his bulk filled the doorway menacingly. Then he was gone.

'Wow, that was a real dirty look.' Straight grinned. 'I've never seen a press conference break up so smartly.'

'*Persona non* bloody *grata*, that's Playfair.' Broadside laughed hoarsely. The Africans present filed out silently. Only one, Sam Murowa, the editor of the local evening paper, came over to Playfair. 'He is a dangerous man to cross, you know, but I'm glad you asked the question. How did you know that the King had ordered his arrest?'

'The King told me so himself yesterday.'

Sam whistled. 'We had heard the story too, but not from quite such an impeccable source. The King made only one mistake. He failed to get hold of him.'

'And Kadongo did not give him a second chance.'

'That's what I mean when I say he's dangerous.' Sam gave a little laugh. 'Well, I must be getting back to the office. Take care.'

'I don't know about anyone else, but I feel like a drink.' Broadside's voice sounded familiarly thirsty.

The bar was a cool dungeon with deep pools of shadow. A handful of local white residents sat in one corner, a few Africans in another. One white sat at the end of the bar, talking to Johnny who was serving him. Playfair spotted him and tried to avoid him, but he was too late.

'Hallo, Alastair,' he boomed, 'come and have a drink. Johnny, ask the bwanas what their poison is.'

There was no way of escaping his all-embracing *bonhomie*. Playfair introduced his friends. 'This is Jock Thompson. He knows more about Kawawa than anyone else. Lived here for twenty years, worked for the last three British Governors and then for the King since independence. Married to a local lady of great charm.'

'Worse luck,' Thompson grinned, displaying a few broken and stained teeth.

'Now you'll be working for Kadongo, eh?' growled Broadside.

'Not on your life,' said Thompson. 'Now what are you boys going to drink?' He pointed a large grimy forefinger at each man in turn, while Johnny noted the order: Playfair did not exaggerate when he said Thompson knew Kawawa better than anyone else. There was no one in the former Colony he had not worked for, advised, spied on, bribed or been bribed by in those twenty years. He was at home in the half-world where corrupt whites meet corruptible Africans: he belonged.

'How well do you know this chap Kadongo?' asked Straight.

'Too well,' Thompson replied. 'He looks a great big idiot, but in fact he's very fly. Don't fool yourself. He'll have all those ministers who opposed his appointment as Chief of Staff out of the way in a jiffy. In fact, some seem to have disappeared without trace already. Give us another beer, would you, Johnny? Make no mistake, Kadongo intends to run this place. In fact he already does run it. Now he's got rid of the King there is no one to stand in his way. He controls the army and whoever controls the army controls Kawawa. He has his own men in all the key positions. The head of the armoured regiment is one of his men, and the head of the Military Police is an old school friend. They both come from the same village in the bush on the banks of the Nile.'

'What makes him tick?' asked Broadside.

The Scotsman took another pull of beer and wiped his forehead with a dirty handkerchief. 'Well, he does have some ideals, whatever one may think of him as a person. He is an African Nationalist in his own rather curious way. He has a sense of national and personal pride. But he's a savage, let's face it. He doesn't mind getting rid of people who stand in his way. But then there are plenty of leaders in Africa like that.' Thompson had a soft north-east of Scotland burr. 'On the credit side, he admires many things about the British. After all, we taught him all he knows. Without us he would still be running round naked in the bush.' He took another long draught of beer and motioned Johnny to set them up again. 'But there is something else as well. He is in a hurry to get rich, like so many African leaders. As you know, Kawawa is not a particularly wealthy country. And suddenly, a huge amount of money has fallen into his lap. You've heard about the gold?'

Playfair nodded. 'You think it's true, then?'

25

'I do. I think it's completely true. Of course, it was only a question of who was going to get his hands on the gold first. Either the King or Major, now Colonel, Kadongo. I think one is probably just as much of a rogue as the other in that respect.'

'But has Kadongo actually got his hands on the gold yet?' Playfair persisted.

Thompson shrugged. 'I really don't know. But if the King has been forced to flee from his Palace, and Colonel Kadongo is giving the orders, it can only be a matter of time.' He stood up. 'I must go, lads, or I'll get into terrible trouble with the wife.' He grinned then became serious again. 'As I was saying, lads, don't underestimate this Kadongo bloke. He's a dangerous man and there are some pretty nasty stories told about him. So go canny.' He waved in friendly salute, hitched up his dirty khaki shorts and made his way out of the bar, a jaunty, scruffy figure with a gift for survival. He would probably need it, thought Playfair as he watched him depart.

That night, Playfair paid a call on Arabella. She was sitting reading by the open window, dressed in a flowered top and long pale blue skirt. Her fair hair was tied with a matching velvet bow. Her eyes, as she raised them from perusal of some report on Kawawa coffee exports, were the shade of purple the Mediterranean sometimes takes on in the evening. But, Playfair thought, not for the first time, underneath those almost conventional English good looks lay a very different personality.

'Hallo, you look very sensational tonight.'

'How sweet of you, Alastair. I'm commanded to have dinner with the High Commissioner and other heads of mission.'

'Very grand stuff.'

'I don't know about that, but it will be interesting to see their reactions to the take-over.'

'I should have thought you'd been up to your neck in that all day.'

'Yes, I suppose I have been, but we don't seem to have had any blinding flashes of inspiration.' She stood up and he got a whiff of perfume. 'Let me get you a drink. Whisky?' Arabella held out a long glass of whisky and soda. Her hand was brown and firm.

'By the way,' he said, 'I don't suppose you've been able to confirm the King's story?'

'About the gold?'

'If he really did hire a group of mercenaries, the word ought to have got around by now.'

'I think we did do a telegram on it. I'll try to find out for you. I really must go, or I'll be late, and you know how worked up Sir Harry gets. But stay and finish your drink.' Her cheek brushed briefly against his lips. Playfair finished his drink. He put down his glass, switched off the light and pulled the door behind him. It locked automatically.

3

Two days after his *coup* Colonel Kadongo announced that he would make a public appearance in Independence Park. The announcement was made at the last minute for security reasons, but a crowd of several thousand Africans soon gathered. At the entrance to the Park, the statue of a former Governor brooded over the scene. Africa is full of statues to its great men: Stanley in Kinshasa, his arm outstretched over the Congo rapids; Rhodes in Salisbury; Livingstone in Zanzibar . . . Playfair could not remember the name of the first Governor of Kawawa. He wondered how long it would be before the locals pulled down this reminder of their colonial past. But for the time being, two or three small boys were benefiting by using His Excellency's legs and arms as vantage points. By three o'clock, Kawawa police and troops had encircled the Park and a guard of honour was drawn up at the gate. In the middle of the ground, the bandstand had been draped with the green, black and crimson Kawawa flag, and a red carpet awaited the tread of the new chief.

Only twenty minutes late, there was a whine of sirens, and a roar of exhausts as the motor cycle escort arrived in their shining white helmets and gloves. Then came a Land-Rover full of bodyguards and finally, in a big, black Austin Princess, with the hood down, the Colonel himself. The crowd, now probably four thousand strong, cheered and waved. One group of women, no doubt tribal supporters, started a high-pitched howling. Colonel Kadongo looked pleased. He stepped from his car in smartly-pressed battledress and slowly walked up the red carpet to the bandstand where a lectern had been prepared for him. After a few squeaks and groans, his voice came bellowing over the loudspeaker system, to reverberate over the roofs of Kawawa.

'Friends. I am very happy to see you here today. I have good news for you. We have rid the country of some people who were just out to enrich themselves and who cared nothing for the well-being of the people. Well, we have changed all that. From now on, Kawawa will be a truly democratic country, and we will put the people of this country first . . .'

Loud cheers greeted this remark. The Colonel mopped his gleaming brow with a large red handkerchief. The small group of foreign correspondents, an island of tropical-suited whiteness in a sea of negritude, were taking notes.

'Yes, my friends. I am going to stamp out corruption wherever I find it and see that you all get better schools for your children, higher wages and longer holidays . . .'

More cheers . . .

'Together, we are going to make Kawawa the number one country in Africa, and the world . . .!'

The audience was now shouting enthusiastically. One man darted out of the crowd and started capering in front of the bandstand in a tribal display of admiration. The bodyguards moved towards him menacingly. The speaker's face took on a sombre expression. 'But one word of warning, my friends. Although we have won a great victory, there are still dangers. There are still some of the old bloodsucking élite in hiding. We did not get them all. And they may try to sabotage our great revolution. Listen to me carefully.' He paused for effect and looked round the now silent crowd. 'We will track down all our enemies, and destroy them. Make no mistake about that.' The crowd growled.

'But we will respect our friends. And I want to say today . . .'

As he rambled on, Playfair looked round. He wondered how many Wawa proper, tribesmen, supporters and relatives of the King were there. He guessed very few. Colonel Kadongo had made no direct reference to the King. He might as well have never existed. On the other hand, who was the Colonel afraid of? He had brought a small army of guards with him. They stood about watching the crowd suspiciously, big men mostly, with tribal scars etching their blue-black cheeks. Playfair had heard that Kadongo had formed his own unit, the armoured regiment, almost entirely from Nubian mercenaries, tribesmen from the Sudan border. They had a reputation for exceptional cruelty. Kadongo, ranting in the vernacular now, was telling the crowd things he knew they wanted to hear.

Then, suddenly, the speech was over. The big man was wiping his face and beaming at the applause. The ululating cries of the women near the dais gave the proceedings a note of triumph, as if Kadongo were some hero returning from a great victory over an enemy. In a way, Playfair supposed, that was how many people in the crowd would see it. With a last wave and rapid phrase or two of farewell, the new ruler of Kawawa left the dais, his bodyguards trailing behind him, and strode towards the waiting Austin Princess. The driver, an old-style colonial chauffeur, in peaked cap, held the door for the new boss. The springs visibly sagged as they took Kadongo's weight.

Playfair and his friends, Straight and Broadside, had only walked a few yards, and the Austin Princess was still moving slowly through the crowds towards the main entrance when they heard a bang. It was not very loud and could have been a back-fire. Then the big car accelerated, horn blaring, and one of the bodyguards started to shoot. Playfair and Straight walking slightly ahead heard the bullets whistling over their heads. They dropped to the ground. The crowd started running. Some women near the main gate, whether hit by gunfire or just terrified, started screaming. Through the flying legs and rising dust, Playfair watched the bodyguards' Land-Rover, stop twenty or thirty yards from the gate. A soldier with a machine-gun began to swing it round towards them. Playfair could see it coming, but felt powerless. Straight was shouting: 'Watch out, they're going to shoot. Get behind the tree!' This was to Broadside and a man from *The Times*, who were both standing looking towards the gate. Africans were fleeing on all sides, women with babies on their backs running pigeon-toed in blind terror past them. The machine-gun began to traverse the field.

Playfair, head down in the dust, peered over his crossed arms. People were falling screaming. He saw an old man cut down as he ran slowly towards the army, waving his arms weakly. A small boy was hit in the legs. The bullets smashed into the leaves of the big blue gum six to ten feet above the ground. Playfair pressed his face to the earth. He hoped they would keep shooting high. It stopped as suddenly as it had begun. An officer, standing beside the Land-Rover was shouting and waving his arms at the machine-gunner. The engine revved and it drove slowly away. There was no sign of the Austin Princess.

The four or five journalists picked themselves up cautiously – there might always be some trigger-happy *askari* still around – and went to inspect the damage. Between them they had counted ten dead and twenty-five wounded by the time an ambulance and truckload of Military Police arrived.

'I think this would be a good time to leave,' said Straight. 'Before these monkeys in the white hats start picking people up for questioning.'

They all started walking, purposefully but not too fast, towards a side entrance. Small groups of silent Africans were also heading in the same direction, some of them at the trot. They passed one or two wild-eyed soldiers hurrying towards the Park, but no one stopped them and they were back at the Grand in half an hour.

At the door they met a photographer called Jimmy Jarvis. He was swathed in cameras and camera cases, his shirt open to the waist and a bruise on his forehead. He was a tough Cockney with a big reputation as a war photographer.

'You want to look out for these Military Police,' he said.

'Black snowdrops?' said Straight. 'Why, they been bothering you?'

'You hear the shooting?'

'Yes, we were there.'

'So was I. I was at the gate. Old Kadongo was just driving up when this bloke threw a grenade. They tore him to pieces double quick. I got some good pictures. One bloke was shot in the head right next to me. Then just as I was leaving, these MPs arrived and started knocking me about.'

'Why?'

'No reason. They didn't say anything. They just started hitting me with their rifle butts. Then this officer bloke came up and told them to fuck off. Lucky he did.' He grinned. 'Anyone feel like some tea? I'm just going to get rid of all this junk.' He humped his camera bag off the ground and went up the steps.

That evening, Arabella asked Playfair if he would run her up to the High Commission. The events of the past forty-eight hours were still being catalogued and relayed to London, but she was non-committal about the details, and Playfair knew there was no point in pressing her. If there was something vital he should know, he felt sure she would tell him, although he was equally sure that she would never tell him anything that came under the heading of an official secret. He knew how stubborn she could be. And she had a highly-developed sense of duty. They drove through the empty streets. Despite Kadongo's attempts to generate a feeling of normality, most Africans were staying at home after dark. Unlike a European city, where you can live next to someone for years and hardly know anything about them, in an African town, as Playfair well knew, the sense of community is as developed as in a village. And so news and rumour travelled fast. Changes of political atmosphere communicated themselves rapidly – what the European settlers in their rather patronising way called the bush telegraph. Well, the bush telegraph was telling the inhabitants of Kawawa to stay at home, and they were obeying its instructions.

A bright splash of light ahead announced the High Commission. Playfair drew up at the floodlit, half-open entrance, with the Royal crest over the door. A guard sat just inside.

'Shall I wait for you?' He could only see her outline against the light.

'Don't bother, I'll get a lift back. If I'm not too late I'll buy you dinner at Ernesto's.'

'What a good idea. Don't be too long.'

As Playfair turned out of the gate, he saw something moving in the darkness on the far side of the road. His headlights swung round to pick up the figure of a man, dressed in a dark suit and tie. He signalled, requesting a lift. Playfair slowed down automatically, his thoughts still on Arabella and the slight, delicious smell the warmth of her body had left in the car. Normally he would not have stopped for an unknown African by the side of the road at this time of night: there were too many *kondos* – hold-up men – about. He was about to put his foot down, when the man appeared at the window, slightly breathless.

'Excuse me, are you going into town?' The voice was educated. Playfair's eyes searched the darkness behind it.

'Yes, I am. Do you want a lift?'

'I would be extremely grateful.' If he was acting, he was doing it too well to be a common thug.

'Okay, jump in round the other side.'

As he crossed in front of the lights, Playfair saw the man's dark jacket was torn. He got in beside him, his musky African male smell obliterating the faint presence that Arabella had left.

'What are you doing out here on a lonely road like this? Car break down?' Playfair let in the clutch smartly. The man, still breathing heavily, said with dignity, 'I will tell you, and once again I am very grateful to you, sir. By the way, did I see you at the Royal Palace yesterday?'

'Ah, yes, you probably did. Do you work there?' Playfair changed up to top.

'I did. I was His Majesty's security adviser.'

'Were you?' Playfair tried to keep the sudden interest out of his voice. 'Why aren't you with him now? Isn't he making what you might call a rather difficult journey?'

The African beside him sighed. 'Yes he is, a very dangerous journey, travelling by night and hiding by day. Luckily our own people will look after him. My brother, who was my deputy, has gone with His Majesty. He asked me to stay behind to carry out a mission . . . But tonight they came to my house, and I was only just able to escape. I managed to get away across the fields and I thought at first I would go to the High Commission. But then I saw one of the new ministers going in to see the High Commissioner, I suppose, and I didn't want to be recognised. This man knows me. So I decided I would have to go back to the town. Then I saw you driving in.'

'Well, glad to be of use.' Playfair slowed down. They were now nearing the centre. 'If I drop you at the hotel, will that be alright?'

'Yes, a little way from the entrance. But there is something I want to tell you. It may repay in a small way your kindness. You are a journalist are you not?'

'That's right.'

'Tonight, just before the police came to my house, a friend came to see me. Maybe they followed him, I don't know. He was arrested on the day of the attack on the Palace, and taken to M'lolo Prison.'

'Where's that?'

'Just outside the town, on the main north road.'

'Go on.'

'He saw about fifty bodies being brought in. The prisoners were made to bury them.'

'Bury them, where?'

'Right there, in a part of the prison. In the grounds.'

'Did he see this or just hear about it?'

'He saw it himself. He had to help unload and bury some of the bodies.'

They had stopped at the hotel, a street light lit the man's face. He was trembling.

'Some of them he recognised. They were Palace people and some of them had been . . .' his voice faltered, '. . . hacked to death.'

Playfair's hands gripped the steering wheel. 'How did your friend get out?'

'He was lucky, they didn't know who he was. They wanted more cell space, so they released him.'

'Did he say who was doing the killing?'

'The army, the Nubians. On orders from Colonel Kadongo. He is getting rid of all the old Palace people who might represent a threat to him.' The light gave the man's skin a sickly look. His hand was on the door handle.

'I fear it is only the beginning . . . Goodbye.' He got out and walked quickly away.

A police car was coming towards them up the wide and practically empty street that ran past the Grand. For a moment Playfair thought the car would stop. But his late passenger turned sharply down an alley, and the car cruised on. Playfair got out, locked the doors and went inside. He felt exhausted. It must be the heat and the humidity. He went to his room and lay down for an hour . . .

He was fast asleep when the phone rang. It was Arabella, asking if he was ready to have dinner.

'I'll be with you in five minutes.'

Playfair reached the lobby first. As he sauntered from the lift past the desk, he noticed two Africans talking to the night manager. They were in the little office behind the counter and bending over something. Playfair strolled up to the desk and asked the porter if there were any messages for him. The man turned and looked in Playfair's box. Playfair saw that the two Africans were examining the hotel register. One of them looked up when Playfair spoke. He was dressed in a long fake leather coat. His eyes were hostile. The night manager looked as if he were frightened of them. As Playfair turned away, his mind clicked: special branch. Why would they be studying the hotel register? No doubt checking up on some undesirable guest. Still, he had never seen it done quite so blatantly before . . .

He heard the sound of high heels. Arabella came across the hall smiling, wearing a yellow dress and some exotic perfume. Playfair gave her a kiss on the cheek and sniffed appreciatively.

'You look as nice as you smell.'

'You are good for my morale, Alastair. Come on, this is on me tonight.'

They walked across the warm dusk of the square, almost empty of traffic now. Ernesto's was more of a snack-bar than a proper restaurant, but the pasta was good – by African standards – and he did have genuine Chianti.

Ernesto greeted Arabella with his usual professional gallantry and took their order with a flourish and a smile, but he seemed uneasy. When Playfair asked him what was wrong, he merely shrugged and muttered something about the 'usual problems'.

'Something to do with the new Government?' Playfair persisted.

'Shhh.' Ernesto looked round nervously. 'Be very careful what you say in public now, my friend.'

During dinner, Playfair mentioned that he had seen the special branch men inspecting the hotel register, and then repeated the conversation with the man he had given the lift to. Arabella wrinkled her brows.

'Fifty dead seems a lot. We haven't heard anything like that as far as I know, but then I'm not sure we're very anxious to listen to that kind of story.'

'Very few people in your position ever are.'

When they reached the hotel Arabella put her hand on Playfair's arm. 'Come and have a nightcap, there's something I want to tell you.'

They walked across to the desk to get their keys. The special branch men had gone.

'What did they want, those policemen?' Playfair asked the night porter. The man shook his head.

'Please, Mr Playfair, better to forget you saw them.'

'Were they looking for someone in particular?'

'They were checking the names of all . . . foreigners.' The man seemed reluctant to say it.

'You mean people like us?'

The man looked around nervously and then nodded.

'But, please, Mr Playfair, do not tell anybody what I said, please!'

Playfair could see the sheen of sweat on his forehead.

'Don't worry. We never discussed it. Goodnight.' Arabella and Playfair walked to the lift and went up to the fifth floor in silence. Arabella opened the door and switched on the lights.

'Help yourself to a drink, Alastair.'

'What can I get you?'

'Nothing, thank you. What did you make of all that?' Alastair went to the drinks cabinet and poured himself a glass of *fine Champagne*. Arabella got it duty free at the High Commission. He swirled it round gently in the glass.

'I think it may just be a routine check. After all, with a new régime in power, it's not altogether surprising. They want to know who's who and where, in case of a possible counter-*coup*.'

Arabella gave a slight shiver. 'I don't like it. I think I will have a small brandy after all.'

Playfair handed her a glass and raised his own with a smile. 'Maybe we're all being too jumpy. Cheers . . . what was it you wanted to tell me?'

'You asked me to find out if the King had really hired a private army. Well, it is true apparently. The office knows the whole story. Our military attaché was up on the other side of the border a couple of weeks ago.'

'Straying a bit wasn't he?'

'He was on holiday in the Ruwenzoris. He's keen on birds. Don't laugh. When he was there he came across this strange bunch of people masquerading as a big game safari.'

'How did he know they weren't?'

'Well, he knew some of them. They were well-known mercenaries, or ex-mercenaries.'

'So why shouldn't they have been on a legitimate safari?'

'We checked with Pretoria. The South African police confirmed that they had picked up a would-be recruit and he spilled the beans, names and everything.'

'Did he say who the leader was?'

'Someone called MacGregor.'

Playfair whistled. 'Dick MacGregor? I used to know him years ago in the Congo. A real hard case. So he's in the Ruwenzoris just over the border, is he? Very interesting . . . Did this recruit know who MacGregor was working for?'

'No. All he knew was that he was going to be paid a lot of money.'

4

When MacGregor heard on the BBC World Service that King George had been driven from his Palace and was hiding somewhere in the bush, in fear of his life, with Kadongo's men after him, he experienced a moment of rare elation. With the King out of the way, nothing stood between him and ten million pounds of gold. From his discussions with the King's ADC he knew that only a handful of close aides had been let into the secret of the mercenary operation, and he guessed that most of them would either have been killed in the fighting or would be with the King in the bush.

MacGregor decided to head straight for the Simba hide-out. His number two, Major Jeremy Gibson, who had made a recce of the area a month before, led the way. They walked up the hill overlooking the farm and studied it through binoculars. The place looked deserted, with no smoke rising from the farmhouse, and no sign of life apart from a few goats that were browsing round the front door and walking in and out of the house. After watching for a quarter of an hour, MacGregor turned to Gibson who was lying in the grass beside him. 'That's an empty building if I ever saw one.'

'They might have got word of our approach and be sitting waiting for us.'

'You mean they might have set us up for an ambush?' MacGregor raised his glasses again. 'We'll make the attack as planned at first light tomorrow. No point in taking any risks.'

They moved in quietly before sun-up. Some buffalo they disturbed went crashing away through the undergrowth. MacGregor waited anxiously, peering into the shadows. The noise would have frightened any terrorist within miles. A bird called querulously, woken from its sleep. They closed in from two sides, with a backstop placed on the road on the far side of the farm in case anyone should try to break out that way.

The house grew out of the morning mist. They could hear a tap dripping, and a door swinging on its hinges. A mercenary crept across the grass and lobbed a grenade through a window. After what seemed a long pause – it was only five seconds – a big orange ball blew out the front door. The base plate of the grenade made a dull whirr as it went over their heads. MacGregor led the way into the house: it was quite silent and, as he had thought all along, empty.

In the living room a dozen or so empty beer bottles stood on a table. MacGregor blasted each one to smithereens with single shots, the vindictive expression on his face suggesting that he would have preferred to have been shooting Simbas instead.

The farm had obviously been derelict for years. Apart from the rusty equipment which had belonged to the previous Belgian owner, the Simbas had left behind only a few cases of small arms ammunition, a couple of broken AK 47's and a jeep minus three wheels.

'No signs of any gold,' Gibson reported after he had inspected the farm buildings. 'If there was any gold, they must have taken it with them. And what's more they left a few days ago.'

MacGregor held a *post mortem* in the wrecked living room. Someone had found a couple of cases of warm beer, opened them and stood them on the table. While the mercenaries drank noisily, MacGregor went through the options.

'Major Gibson says they have to go via the Mutukulu crossroads, so we'll head that way as fast as possible and see if we can pick up their tracks. Depending on the result, we'll decide whether we make the hotel our base, right?'

Gibson nodded.

The Land-Rovers turned north and the red dust from the murram roads swirled up into the blue sky like so many battle pennants. MacGregor was used to setbacks. Every soldier was and he was still very much a soldier at heart.

As they climbed the long escarpment that led to the crossroads, MacGregor's thoughts turned to the desert. Not that the terrain here was at all similar but the sense of pursuit and the openness of the country reminded him of North Africa. He had fought in the war there as a young subaltern, and after that everything had seemed tame, especially stockbroking in London.

So he had emigrated to South Africa and there, among the sugar planters of Durban, he had found a niche and made a small fortune. But when the Congo war started in the early sixties, Dick MacGregor could not keep away. He recruited a small band of ex-army toughs and drifters and went off to fight for Moïse Tshombe, the Katangese businessman turned politician who tried to take on the United Nations. When Tshombe was defeated, MacGregor and his men went home: fewer in number, but richer. For all his faults Tshombe was a good payer. MacGregor moved to the Cape and bought a wine farm. He seemed to have settled down and become a solid citizen. But when the call came from King George, he did not take long to make up his mind. And when he heard that there might be ten million pounds' worth of gold at stake, he caught the next plane to Nairobi. There he met the King's ADC and, after lengthy negotiations, got the terms he wanted: one million pounds, cash down, against delivery of the gold.

The convoy slowed down. The Mutukulu crossroads presented a picture of utter emptiness. Any tracks they could find were so old as to be meaningless. It was another five miles to the Mountains of the Moon Hotel so MacGregor decided to head for there: maybe they would have some information.

The country began to change. The dry, sparse scrub of the African bush dotted with flat-topped thorn trees, gave way to lusher savannah. Finally from the top of a small ridge, they looked down on a great shimmering expanse of water, silver far out in the middle and ruffled blue round the edges.

'Edward,' said Gibson, 'lots of elephant and hippo up in that corner. Used to be anyway. There's the hotel.' He pointed to a clump of trees on the edge of the lake, pale-leaved blue gums and wispy casuarinas. Sheltering in this pool of shadow was a long, single-storey house with white walls and a red corrugated iron roof. Round it, and scattered among the trees and shrubs, were a number of rondavels, circular huts with mud and wattle walls and thatched roofs. The place looked tidy but deserted. In the far distance, if you knew where to look, you could just see the peaks of the Ruwenzoris, the Mountains of the Moon, piercing the clouds.

The sound of the Land-Rovers bumping up the rough drive

brought movement. A door with mosquito-proof netting opened and a small cranky-looking individual appeared. MacGregor walked up to him and held out his hand. 'I'm Dick MacGregor. Jeremy Gibson you already know.'

'Boenens,' said the old man. 'Gaston Boenens. From Antwerp. I did not expect you so soon. Not that we get many tourists at Mutukulu these days.' His English was Flemish-accented but good. MacGregor noticed that half of his teeth were missing.

'No, I'm sure you don't.' He smiled thinly. 'Not that we're exactly tourists, as you can see.' He waved his hand vaguely at the tough-looking bunch of men who were climbing down from the vehicles, stretching themselves and lighting cigarettes. Boenens was chattering away.

'I told Monsieur when he came to see me the other day,' he nodded in Gibson's direction, 'that the hotel is closed. I don't want any of those *macaques* coming in here as if they owned the place. I turned out a minister the other day. He wanted a room for the night, with his white girlfriend. *Imaginez-vous*, here where King Baudouin once stayed. I told him he would have to pay in advance. He didn't like that. He threatened to have me arrested. But I told him: *"fous-le-camp"*. No money, no bed. He didn't like it but he went. *Sale macaque.*' The old man cackled malevolently, showing his broken teeth.

'They did that with their gun butts when they celebrated their independence.' He spat. 'Anyway, that is why I don't run the place as a hotel any more, it's a jam factory now!'

'Jam factory?' asked MacGregor baffled.

Boenens pointed inside the verandah door. There, sure enough, on a table, stood a dozen pots of jam.

'*Ananas*,' said Boenens. 'Pineapple . . . and *fraise*, how do you say in *Englisch*? Strawberry? And lots of other kinds. Madame Boenens makes them, and very good they are too. So you see, we are a jam factory. But for you gentlemen . . .' he lowered his voice although no one else was near . . . 'You are army, eh, *mercenaires*? *Bon* . . . you can stay here. As long, gentlemen, as you respect my house and there are no *bagarres* . . . *comment dit-on* . . .? no rough stuff.'

MacGregor, who had listened quietly, his pale blue eyes expressionless throughout, said with complete authority: 'There will be no rough stuff, Monsieur Boenens. Of that I can person-ally assure you. And if you have any complaints, please come straight to me or to my adjutant, Major Gibson.'

He moved to the door and shouted: 'Sergeant-Major MacLean. Come here a moment, will you?' Heavy boots climbed the steps and a shadow filled the doorway. Sergeant-Major MacLean, six foot five, and the best part of twenty stone, stood to attention. His face looked as if it had been chipped out of granite and when he spoke, it sounded as if two boulders were being ground together by some Hebridean storm.

'Aye, surr. What can I do for you?'

MacGregor told him that they would stay there for a few days and that there would on no account be any drunkenness, fighting or unruly behaviour of any kind. And above all no looting. Any man found looting would be shot.

'I will tell the men, surr. Have no fear.' He measured the Belgian with his terrible eyes and strode out. They heard his heavy tread descending and his shout for attention.

'*Quel géant.*' Boenens was impressed.

'A bad man to cross, I can assure you.' Even MacGregor would have thought twice about it. Outside they could hear MacLean delivering his message in his harsh voice.

'. . . The curnel says that anyone found looting will be shot. But let me tell you that first, I will personally break all the bones in his body with my ane two hands.' There was silence for a moment. Then a derisive laugh from Lorenzo.

'Ah'm watching you, Eytie, boy.' The laugh turned into a cough. 'Alright. Get that vehicle unloaded. Dismiss.' The formalities over, MacGregor went straight to the point. 'We had very bad news this morning, Monsieur Boenens. When we went to call on our friends . . . the Simbas . . . at the farm, we found the place deserted. Not a soul in sight. What happened?'

'*Ah, c'est vrai. Les salauds . . .*' Boenens burst into a torrent of French and then stopped himself. 'They went three or four days ago. I heard only last night, from an Indian friend who does business with them.'

'Why?' MacGregor's voice was so quiet it hardly carried across the room.

Boenens shrugged. 'I don't know. No idea. But they must have heard something that frightened them. Perhaps they heard that the Major had been making enquiries. They have their spies too, you know. But all is not lost, gentlemen. They have only gone as far as Bomi.'

'Bomi? Where's that?'

'Only twenty-five kilometres the other side of the border.'

There was silence for a moment then MacGregor spoke: 'You haven't been indiscreet, have you, Boenens?' The old man's face went white then red. He blustered: 'Of course not. Indiscreet? How do you mean? *Nom de* . . . as if I would tell those *macaques* anything. You must be crazy, *mon Colonel*.'

Neither MacGregor nor Gibson looked impressed. They both continued to watch the Belgian with cold eyes. Gibson spoke for the first time:

'You didn't mention my visit to one of your Indian friends?'

'*Non*. Absolutely not. I swear.' The old man was nearly in tears.

'Forget it,' said MacGregor. 'Now tell me about Bomi.'

Boenens gulped and wiped his face with his handkerchief. 'As I say, just the other side of the border, on the edge of the lake. I have asked a friend of mine to come in this evening and give us the latest information. He is an Indian businessman. He often travels down to Bomi, in fact he's there now. I asked him specially to find out what had happened to the Simbas. I guessed you would want to know. He should be here about seven. Excuse me a moment . . .'

Boenens hurried from the room. MacGregor looked at Gibson. 'What do you think. Is it a doublecross?'

Gibson as always took his time to answer. 'It could be. I wondered that myself. But . . . I don't think so.'

'Why?'

'Because he really does hate the people who knocked his teeth out. Perhaps I didn't tell you, but they also killed some of his staff and helped themselves to his possessions.'

They heard a step and the door opened. Boenens, still rather flushed, came in carrying a bottle which he held up triumphantly. 'Colonel, I presume you are as Scottish as your name suggests. Well, specially in your honour, I want you to taste this. I only remembered just now that I still had it. It must be the last bottle of malt whisky in the Congo. I imported it when I had a Scottish *milord* and his party here before Independence. They had come to shoot elephants. They drank a lot of whisky, *ah oui, sans blague.*'

Boenens poured generous measures and raised his glass. 'Death to all Simbas, Colonel, and good luck to your enterprise!'

MacGregor raised his glass and drank. He felt some explanation was needed. 'Monsieur Boenens, I was over-hasty just now, but we are playing for high stakes. As you guessed, we are former soldiers, although now we are just private citizens. However we consider it our duty to settle some old scores with our Simba friends. Even if it means going to Bomi to get them.'

Boenens nodded and refilled the glasses. 'It will not be difficult. I can get you a boat if you want. And by road you can get there in a couple of hours. It is a small place, no one ever goes there. It is really much more a part of the Congo than of Kawawa. You could go there and see . . . your friends, and be back here and no one would be any the wiser.'

'Good. This is all strictly between us of course.' He drained his glass. The others did the same.

'I will tell no one, not even my wife,' Boenens swore. 'You are my guests. Stay as long as you like.'

That night, Boenens arranged a special dinner in honour of his 'safari' guests: trout from the cold stream that flowed from the Ruwenzoris, roast guinea fowl that he had shot himself in the bush behind the hotel and fresh pineapple. To mark the occasion he went down to the cellar and produced some claret.

'Mine must be the only wine cellar that's left in this God forsaken country. You might as well drink it. There's no point in keeping it for those *sauvages.*'

MacGregor, Gibson and MacLean ate together in the dining room, waited on by Boenens. The other mercenaries ate in the kitchen under the supervision of Madame Boenens. Instead of claret they had beer, except for the two ex-Legion Frenchmen. They had wine as a matter of course.

The meal completed, Boenens produced a bottle of brandy and glasses, and left MacGregor and his companions to their planning, promising to announce his friend as soon as he arrived. Half an hour later there was a tap at the door and Boenens ushered a rather frightened-looking young Indian into the room . . . MacGregor was at pains to put him at ease. 'Come in, come in, we would like your help. Don't worry, no one will ever know we talked to you. We don't even know your name. Just let me ask you a couple of questions. Are the Simbas still there, in Bomi?'

'I saw them this afternoon, you know. 'Bout three o'clock. Sitting in the hotel . . . dr . . . drinking . . . be . . . be . . . beer.' He had a bad stammer. Maybe it was fright.

'How many?'

The Indian's dark eyes reflected. 'Mebbe ten or so. Twelve maximum.'

'Armed?'

'Im . . . p . . . p . . . possible to say, you know, they were in civvies.'

MacGregor questioned him closely about the layout of Bomi, establishing that the small police station was opposite the Simbas' hotel, called inappropriately enough, Grand Hotel du Lac. Finally MacGregor asked him if he had seen a large vehicle belonging to the Simbas. The Indian nodded. 'Yes . . . it's an . . . am . . . ambulance actually . . . with doors that close at the back.'

'Ah.'

MacGregor sat up in his chair, and Gibson gave a sigh of comprehension. Only MacLean remained immobile.

'Is it guarded?'

'Yes. One man, in plain clothes.'

'Armed?'

'I couldn't see.'

MacGregor got up. 'Well, thank you very much. You have been very helpful. And we won't forget it. By the way, don't tell anyone you spoke to us.'

As the door closed behind the Indian, MacGregor turned back excitedly to his companions: 'Using an ambulance is clever. You can lock it up and keep everyone away. Tell any snoopers you've got a case of typhoid inside. What do you think, Jeremy?'

Gibson considered his notes. 'It'll have to be tomorrow night. If we leave it any later, we risk them being gone, or having a couple of platoons of Kawawa troops to deal with.'

MacGregor nodded. 'I'll settle for tomorrow night.'

Outside, the moon was riding high, casting a silver flare on the dark water, which they could just see through the trees. The night was full of lake music, the deep baying of bullfrogs and the buzzsaw of cicadas. A small breeze bent the casuarinas in a sleepy ballet. Africa, often so cruel, was being prodigal of its beauty . . .

5

Next day at the jam factory was a busy one for the mercenaries. The enormous figure of Jock MacLean, closely shadowed by Lorenzo, the mechanic, was to be seen striding up and down the little quay in front of the hotel, supervising the overhaul of the strike force, a sturdy old lake steamer with an ancient diesel, the *Lady Peggy*, and two small motorboats. The local owner of the *Lady Peggy* had been made happy with a handful of fivers. Although he may have wondered about the *bona fides* of the *mzungu* tourists, he wasn't going to be difficult when business was so bad. And they were repairing his boat for him.

The Land-Rovers were drawn up under the trees, well camouflaged. All weapons were being cleaned and stacked inside the rondavels: and with the temperature in the high 80's, most men wore only bathing trunks or shorts. Even so, MacGregor became nervy when he saw two canoes paddling past about a quarter of a mile offshore.

'Jock,' he bellowed. 'Sergeant-Major.'

'Aye, surr.'

'Who are those buggers in the canoes out there?'

The big man shaded his eyes with a huge hand. 'Fishermen, most like, surr. Don't think they're much of a threat.'

'Old man's getting jumpy,' he said to himself.

'Well, keep your numbers down out there. Tell anyone who's not actually doing a job of work to get out of the bloody light.'

'Very good, surr. You, MacNab, you're doing bugger all. Scram back to the hotel and get some beer on ice for when I come in.'

'Okay, Sarge. And ane for mesel.' MacNab, a tiny South African Scot, grinned a cheeky Glasgow grin and dodged away. He was a firstclass fitter. Wife-trouble, as he called it, had originally prompted him to seek a change in the Congo. Not that he was averse to making a bit of money too. MacGregor had picked up MacNab when he was recruiting for Tshombe.

As he stood in the shade of the big trees watching Jock and his men at work, MacGregor turned over in his mind once again the personal qualities of the men who would be put to the test tomorrow. The Scots, he was sure, would be alright. They were a group within a group, a team within a team. He turned and strolled back to the hotel. A few mercenaries were having an early lunch. MacGregor stood quietly in the doorway and scanned the room.

The two Frenchmen sat together in the corner. They were both former Legion officers, who had fought against De Gaulle for the OAS and had had to leave Algeria in a hurry. Before that they had served in Indo-China, where so much of the Algerian bitterness was bred. They were both extremely competent career officers, and considered themselves a cut above the other mercenaries and indeed MacGregor himself. From Oran they had gone to Johannesburg, where they had operated a night watchman business. This had turned out to be lucrative, but the call to arms was still too strong for them to resist. When Mac-Gregor had offered them the chance of accompanying him, they had jumped at it. Now they sat quietly, neat and starched, as if they had been in a Legion mess, with a bottle of wine in front of them. They had either bribed, bullied or quite possibly charmed old Boenens. They were, reflected MacGregor, capable of anything.

Then there were the two Italians. A big, slow northerner called Aldo, who had been one of MacGregor's original team, and had later worked on the Kariba dam: and the excitable Lorenzo. He was a firstclass mechanic, able to repair anything from a transistor radio to a bulldozer with a pair of pliers, an old bully-beef tin and a piece of wire. But he was a liability in the firing line. As liable to shoot one of his own side as one of the enemy.

'I don't want Lorenzo anywhere near me when the shooting starts, and certainly not behind me.' It was one of MacGregor's standing jokes, and Gibson, who had joined him, obligingly smiled.

'He'll be armed strictly with a spanner and the toolbox.'

MacGregor's eyes went to the other tables. A young, public school Englishman called Simon Graves, attracted by what he thought was the romantic side of mercenary life; Piet Hendriksen and another Afrikaaner, van der Merwe, from the Platteland, in trouble with the police for beating up *kaffirs* back home; a Dutchman, who had done everything, including working in the South African gold mines, a couple of Greeks, and an Irishman, Paddy, who was wanted all over the place for confidence tricks on gullible widows. He was the joker of the party, of course, liable to burst into song at precisely the worst possible moment, MacGregor thought sourly. But a good cook.

The door opened and in came Klaus Wagner. Despite the fact that he was bare to the waist, he still wore round his neck the 'Iron Cross, second class' that the Führer had pinned on him in 1945, just before the fall of the Fatherland. The Führer's hands were trembling, Klaus said, but his eyes were as hypnotic as ever. He had been fifteen at the time, a Nazi Youth *Werwolf*. Since then Klaus had been in the fighting business all his life, in the Legion mostly. After the fall of Dien Bien Phu, he was one of the few to get away. Apart from the Frenchmen, he was perhaps the most complete mercenary soldier of the lot.

'Klaus is okay,' MacGregor said.

'If we can rely on anybody, it's him.'

After dinner that evening, MacGregor gave his briefing . . . An hour later, the mercenaries, impressed despite themselves by MacGregor's professionalism, got to their feet.

'Piece of cake,' said the young Englishman, Graves.

'*Evidemment*,' said one of the dapper Frenchmen. '*Les Simbas, c'est pas la même chose que le Vietcong.*'

This, he obviously considered, was a very minor operation. And so it seemed, except for the reward.

The moon, in its last quarter, was low in the sky when reveille went at two a.m. No bugle, but far more effective, the skirling pipes of Sergeant-Major Jock MacLean. He appeared, silhouetted against the sky, a wild figure clad in the kilt which he donned only for battle and special festive occasions.

Muttering and cursing, the mercenaries rolled out of bed and, in the near dark, fumbled for their clothes. Boenens brought coffee and fried eggs for anyone who could eat them. MacLean managed three, but his commander could only swallow a cup of black coffee. Like most of them, he had slept badly.

Outside, the lake was dark and very still. As the two motorboats and the lumbering *Lady Peggy* moved off quietly through the reeds a few flamingoes, sleeping with heads tucked under their wings, took fright and flapped away. Two hundred yards out, MacGregor, straining his eyes in the half-light, started to turn away from what looked like a small island. Suddenly it moved, throwing up a trunk and exposing the big tusks of a lone bull elephant. With an angry squeal and much splashing it wheeled away from the little flotilla.

When they were a good mile out, MacGregor swung north to follow the line of the shore. He looked at his watch, 0310. They would be on station in an hour. The others ought to be moving away any time now. Yes, there they were. He could just see the faint glimmer of their tail-lights as they set off in column. Behind MacGregor came the second speedboat, working well so far, and the big dark shape of the *Lady Peggy*. The only sounds were the beat of the engines and the hiss of the dark lake water under the bow. Bomi was not in sight yet, but the horizon showed a faint lightening. Like the morning of the world, MacGregor thought. And so far as peaceful.

The land force was meanwhile climbing slowly up through the savannah towards the ridge that ran like an escarpment west of the lake. A lot of elephant were feeding quietly on either side of the road and at one point the convoy stopped to allow a small herd led by a bossy old cow to cross. They had four calves with them, one a baby. The old cow fretted at the side of the road, lifting her trunk to scent any danger, until the last calf was safely over.

'No kwestion as to who has pree-ority,' said Wagner in his heavy accent.

Gibson let in the clutch as the last of the herd trotted off into the bush.

'They can be very *kali*, those old cows. Worse than an old bull, every time. I know. I've shot plenty in my time.'

Near the top of the escarpment, they rounded a bend to find a dark shape on the road. Creeping closer, Gibson flashed his headlights. A big female rhino scrambled to her feet and backed off, her big horn pointed menacingly towards them. At her side, almost out of sight, was a very small calf. They had been lying in the warm dust of the road and they did not want to move. Gibson revved the engine. The mother backed away, and then lunged forward in a mock charge. Gibson sat tight. He was certain she would not charge, but if she did, for any strange reason – because she was wounded, possibly – she would make an awful mess of the Land-Rover. This was a problem they had not foreseen. Impatiently, Gibson glanced at his watch, which showed 0330, and revved the engine harder. Still the rhino would not budge. Her tail against the tall grass at the side of the road, she pawed the earth and held her ground.

'Damn and blast,' exploded Gibson.

Wagner slapped the side of his door, bang bang. The big rhino snorted but did not move. Gibson felt behind him and located his Armalite M16. Not a sporting rifle, but at this range lethal against anything. He switched on his headlights and took aim. The shot shattered the morning stillness. The rhino seemed to leap in the air and somersault backwards into the long grass, knocking the calf flying. Gibson waited ten seconds. A bird flew off protesting harshly. Silence descended again, broken only by the low throb of the idling engines. Nothing moved in the long grass. Gibson cut the lights and said curtly, 'Let's go.' He gunned the engine and spun the wheels. He did not mind shooting a man in battle, but having to kill an animal like that in cold blood made him feel sick.

'You had to zhoot!' said Wagner. He touched his Iron Cross for luck.

Force B climbed the escarpment without further incident and drove cautiously down towards the Mutukulu border post. It showed no lights and no signs of life. Not even a dog barked.

Gibson braked at the barrier. Wagner jumped out, his automatic at the ready, and swung the single pole upright. Leaving it open he climbed back in and they drove quietly past. The two other Land-Rovers followed at thirty-yard intervals. Wagner looked back: 'No signs of anybody moving, *mon Commandant.*' Although German, his long service in the Legion had given him the habit of addressing his officers by their French ranks.

They drove on. The same glimmer that MacGregor had seen on the horizon was slightly brighter now. They reached the crossroads a little early and waited at the side of the road, lights off and engines cut. Gibson longed to smoke but restrained himself. Round them the bush trembled with a million invisible existences. Day was coming.

A mile offshore, MacGregor took stock. They were five minutes from the rendezvous. The second speedboat was giving trouble, the engine kept misfiring, and he had told it to drop astern. It would only be needed if by some mischance the *Lady Peggy* was put out of action. When he judged they had reached the right spot, MacGregor throttled back his engine and let the motorboat glide to a standstill. Behind him the bulk of the *Lady Peggy* loomed close. He could see the massive figure of Jock MacLean standing in the bow, like some plundering Norseman, his kilt fluttering at his knee. Even MacGregor conceded it was a weird sight in the middle of Africa. He looked towards the shore. Two lights were visible, but whether they were house or street lights, he could not tell. One could be the police station. He listened. Nothing. Only the lap-lap of the water against the side of the boat.

His watch showed 0409. His eyes went anxiously to the horizon where the sky was becoming a very faint duck-egg green. The escarpment, where he could imagine Gibson sitting at the crossroads, waiting like him, was still dark. A flight of duck went winging past, MacGregor could hear their pinions whistling as they flew in dipping formation. It reminded him of early morning flighting in Scotland when he was a boy. He could still remember the keeper, old Angus, telling him to hold his fire, not to bother about the duck, but to wait for the greylag. 'Remember, laddie,' Angus had said, 'hold your fire.'

And now he was holding his fire for, well, less noble game. He checked his thoughts and spat into the shimmering water. As he looked up, a pair of headlights flashed, died, flashed again a second time, a third time, and then cut out.

'Right.' MacGregor's voice was a harsh whisper. 'This is it.' He eased in the clutch and the motorboat began to surge forward trailing a bubbling luminous wake, leaving the *Lady Peggy* to lumber along behind. MacGregor crept in until the jetty loomed abruptly out of the dark. MacNab was ready to fend them off, but they still brought up with a bump that threw Lorenzo into the stern.

'Stay here, Lorenzo, and wait,' MacGregor ordered. He leapt out with MacNab behind him, both of them armed with lightweight M16's. They could see two pairs of sidelights coasting down towards where they imagined the police station to be. MacGregor and MacNab ran towards them through the trees. On the right they could make out the dim outline of a fair-sized building which must be the Grand Hotel du Lac. It had no lights showing. They came out of the trees and on to a hard dirt road. The blue light ahead would be the police station.

MacGregor slowed to a walk. He could see some figures just ahead. He used the password. 'Goldmine . . .'

Gibson's voice came back: 'Operation Goldmine under way.'

MacLean was struggling with someone. MacGregor saw his hand rise and strike and the man fall. As he did so he groaned in a surprised way. By the time MacGregor reached him, MacLean was wiping a knife on the man's shirt. He was an African and he was dead.

'He jumped us just as we came into the police station yard,' said the big Sergeant-Major. He stooped and retrieved something, and handed it to MacGregor.

'Colt 45. Looks like old *Force Publique* issue. This must have been one of our Simba friends.'

Wagner came bustling up. 'The ambulance is there, *mon Colonel*. The key fits *gut*, we are in business.'

'Good, let's go. Jeremy, you follow us out. I'll ride with Wagner.'

MacGregor couldn't repress a smile of victory as he walked towards it. In the half-dark it looked like any other ambulance. A regulation British Leyland three-tonner, probably ordered by the Belgians before Independence and simply 'liberated' by the Simbas. MacGregor patted it affectionately and tried the back doors: locked. And as he got into the passenger seat, he could see nothing behind him because the window in the partition was covered from the inside. If the gold was there, it was not visible. MacGregor tested the partition with his hand. It was solid. He toyed with the idea of smashing the small window, but it offended his orderly mind and he simply said, 'Let's go.'

Wagner hauled the wheel round and they lumbered out of the yard. The ambulance behaved like all three-tonners, slow and noisy in bottom gear.

They began to swing left through the police gateway. Fumbling for the switch, Wagner by mistake turned on the full headlights. The powerful beam lit up the façade of the Hotel du Lac. A burst of fire came from it. High and behind, MacGregor thought automatically, as he squeezed down in his seat.

'Get going,' he shouted to Wagner, but he needed no urging. The German's foot was flat down on the floor. A longer burst followed, the bullets this time making a ripping sound against the side of the ambulance, as if it had been a paper bag. One bullet went through the windscreen. It starred but did not shatter. MacGregor poked his Armalite through the window and fired short bursts at the flashes from the hotel. Then they were out of range, roaring up the main street of Bomi, crashing gears and swinging from side to side like a runaway elephant. As they groaned up the escarpment, Wagner shouted: 'Dis bloody truck veighs about a hundred tons. It vill hardly move.'

'That's the gold, you fool Kraut,' MacGregor shouted back.

He was leaning right out of the window, looking back down the road. There was a lot of fire going into the hotel from one of the Land-Rovers. He could see the tracer. Then he heard the boom of the heavy fifty-calibre machine-gun on the *Lady Peggy*. Jock must be giving them the works.

Suddenly the shooting stopped and he saw the lights of the Land-Rovers coming after them. As they reached the crossroads the waiting rear guard flicked on their headlights, and then, recognising MacGregor, put them out again.

They stopped and MacGregor jumped out. The lights of Gibson's party came round the corner and flooded them in brilliance.

'Put your bloody lights off,' MacGregor shouted angrily.

'Sorry, Colonel, didn't want to run you over.'

'What's the damage?'

Gibson lowered his voice. 'Lost Constantinos, I'm afraid. He got it in that first burst. And van der Merwe is hit in the leg but only a scratch.'

'What about the boats?'

'Still afloat. The *Lady Peggy* did most of the damage. We let them have a couple of grenades through the window just to make sure they were all awake for breakfast,' Gibson laughed.

'Well done, Jeremy. We'd better get out of here. Everyone ready? Right, home, James.'

Wagner, his Iron Cross swinging on his chest, gave the gold wagon full pedal.

Dawn had turned Lake Edward flamingo pink. A lioness was

54

padding along in the dust at the side of the road. She paid no attention to them. She too had made a kill.

The operation itself had taken less than half an hour and they were back at Boenens' jam factory before the dawn had faded. The old man was as excited as a child, dancing round MacGregor jabbering questions until he was told to 'bugger off' and make some coffee for the troops.

He disappeared cackling madly, summoning his kitchen staff with shouts and curses.

The Land-Rovers were driven round the back of the hotel, under the blue gums, and camouflage nets thrown over them. Kawawa had a small air force and MacGregor did not want to have his transport strafed from the air. The ambulance was parked at the far end of the building, close up against MacGregor's quarters. MacLean, who had arrived half an hour after the road party, came up to MacGregor to make his report.

'Alright Jock?'

'Aye, surr, we gave them a real blasting.' His chuckle sounded like a fall of scree down a hillside.

'Did you take any return fire?'

'Only a bittie, surr. Unfortunately, they got young Graves through the head with a lucky shot. That's when I turned the fifty-calibre on them mesel. I think half the hotel fell down after that.' His laugh rumbled. 'That's fixed the Simba laddies for good an' all.'

'Okay, Jock.' MacGregor looked at his Sergeant-Major's kilt. 'You had better get dre . . . er . . . changed and report for the de-briefing in ten minutes. Put MacNab on to guard the ambulance, will you? And see that he's properly armed.'

'I will, surr.' MacLean gave a salute and went off, kilt swinging.

After the de-briefing, MacGregor got Lorenzo to unpick the lock on the back of the ambulance. It took him only a minute or so. Inside, stacked from floor to roof, and covering about three-quarters of the ambulance's floor space, were row upon row of ammunition boxes. MacGregor turned with a snarl to MacLean. 'Get some tools and open these up. Fast!' His voice cracked with impatience.

Gibson stood, saying nothing, staring at the ammunition boxes as if mesmerised. Each one had stencilled on it: FABRI-

MacLean was quickly back with a hammer and chisel. With a grunt, he swung down a couple of the boxes, drove the chisel under the lid of one, and prised it back with a squeak of nails. On top, folded, was a thick sheet of greaseproof paper. For a moment, no one seemed capable of moving. Then MacGregor bent forward, reached out and ripped the paper away. Underneath, packed tightly together, butter yellow, smooth and dully gleaming were, not ingots of gold . . . but rows of bullets.

MacGregor stood for a moment as if he had been punched under the heart, half stooped forward, breathing noisily. Then he started to swear: 'You son of a bitch . . .' His face had gone as grey as the paper. Only his eyes were alive in that dead grey face, and they blazed with a wild expression. 'Open every box, every bloody blasted box, do you hear?' His voice rose to a scream. MacLean had opened a couple and was starting on the third.

'Hey, wait a minute.' MacGregor came forward. 'Maybe it's underneath . . .' He took one of the boxes and tipped it over on its side. Out of it spilled a shower of bullets, but no gold. MacGregor kicked the empty box furiously against the side of the ambulance. 'Empty those others,' he ordered. But the result was the same. Each box contained what it said it did: rifle ammunition, .300 calibre, as supplied to all NATO forces, and nothing else.

'Christ,' said MacLean, the chisel dangling limply from his hand. 'We've been screwed.'

'Jock, you're a bloody genius.' MacGregor's voice was a lash of irony. 'Now open the rest of them . . .'

An hour later, MacLean stood back, steaming with exertion like a tropical jungle after a thunderstorm. Round him lay a litter of wooden boxes and ammunition and the wreckage of MacGregor's dream. There was a long silence. MacGregor stood hunched and shrunken, staring at nothing. Finally, he looked accusingly at Gibson. 'Well, what the hell's gone wrong, Major?' Gibson looked unhappy but kept cool. His voice was as smooth and reasonable as ever. 'I would say either the Simbas did a swop, and have hidden the gold somewhere. Or else, someone did the swop for them . . .'

'Meaning?'

'Well,' Gibson coughed, his manner like a teacher explaining a difficult problem to a rather obtuse child: 'the Kawawans could have got in before us and taken the gold, leaving the ammo in its place.'

'I think it's much more likely the Simbas have hidden it somewhere.' MacGregor paused. 'I'll tell you something else. Just occurred to me. I think they *were* waiting for us. They probably didn't expect so many of us. But they opened up pretty fast and pretty accurately. Anyway, that doesn't matter now. The point is, where's the gold?' A nerve jerked at the corner of his right eye. Gibson looked at him calmly: 'It could be anywhere, by now, anywhere in Kawawa.' For a moment MacGregor stared at him as if sheer will power could discover the answer. Then he shrugged. 'Come on, let's all go and have a drink and see what we can salvage of this bloody operation.'

6

In Kawawa there was high excitement. The radio had just announced that an 'important enemy' of the people had been captured by an army patrol near the Ruwenzori border and that the prisoner was being brought to the capital under close arrest. Several other members of his party had been killed in a skirmish. The announcement was followed by martial music which was then faded down while the public were exhorted to be on their guard. The timing was perfect as far as Colonel Kadongo was concerned. For this was the day of his official investiture as head of the revolutionary council and he was about to promote himself General.

He had decreed a holiday and organised a procession, led by a band that owed much of its style to the old King's African Rifles. The drum-major, resplendent in a lionskin, strode along at the head of his bandsmen, a brave sight in white tunics and trousers, the brass spikes on top of their solar topees glittering smartly. After the band came Kadongo's special guard known as the Tembo battalion, preceded by their mascot, a baby elephant. It ran from side to side as the mood took it, giving its attendant a busy time and somewhat disrupting the precision of the marching. Behind it walked a small boy with a bucket and brush, whose job it was to sweep up if the little elephant forgot his manners, which he frequently did.

Finally, creeping along in low gear, came a trio of Land-Rovers, the first and last packed with malevolent-looking armed guards, the middle one bearing the benignly-smiling figure of General Kadongo, his buttons flashing as his tunic bulged with pride in the occasion. His smile never wavered, not even when the baby elephant, frightened by some particularly discordant blast, turned tail and fled through the ranks of the guardsmen, towing its unfortunate attendant behind it.

The 'oompah' of the brass faded away up the hill, disappearing altogether when the procession reached the Parliament

58

building, erected by the British in the days when they still thought the Westminster model could be exported to Africa. The main doors were wide open and the hard African light flooded into the big central chamber. A dais had been installed beside the Speaker's chair, and it was this that General Kadongo now mounted, as if it had been the turret of a tank. Opposite him sat the foreign diplomats who had been unlucky enough to be posted to Kawawa. They perspired generously in their morning coats and striped trousers, all except for a very fat Nigerian in a loose robe who looked indecently cool.

On Kadongo's left sat the Kawawan dignitaries, worried-looking ministers, civil servants, judges, academics and a handful of Asian industrialists, furtively trying to assess their new ruler. Kadongo had found a Victoria Cross somewhere, and added it to the chestful of medals he had taken to wearing on every possible occasion.

'He's getting to be a bloody African Goering already,' Broadside sneered.

The press had been squeezed in below the gangway and off to one side. They sat, hunched together, hot and cross, their notebooks open and ready for the platitudes which they confidently expected to flow. But instead, there came an unexpected diversion. A wild-looking figure had emerged from the shadows behind the dais and was striding down the aisle towards the centre of the chamber, causing the diplomats and their wives to draw their knees aside sharply as if at the approach of a leper. The newcomer was small and skinny, but some inner magnetism drew the eye and held it. He was dressed in a full-length cloak of monkey skins, which swirled and flapped as he walked, revealing that he was virtually naked underneath, unless you counted some daubs of red and white paint, and a string of necklaces made of lion's teeth and claws. The outfit was completed by a Davey Crockett cap made from the black and white skin of a colobus monkey, the tail hanging down over the old man's shoulders, and swinging from side to side as he capered up the steps to the dais where Kadongo waited.

'Who the hell's that?' Broadside whispered to Playfair.

'I think it must be Mulango, Kadongo's witchdoctor. He looks a joke but I'm told he's quite sinister.'

By now the wizened figure was standing in front of the

General, his hands reaching out towards him but not actually touching him. He stood like that for a moment or two and then slowly turned to face the audience. Every eye was on the strange figure, as he began to speak in some unknown language.

'What's he saying?' Broadside wanted to know. Playfair shrugged. 'He's not speaking Swahili, must be some tribal language, probably Luri. That's what Kadongo speaks, and I think they're from the same tribe.'

Now Mulango was beginning to chant, in a high-pitched quavery voice.

'Trying to cast a bloody spell over this lot, is he?' snorted Broadside. 'Look at the General, will you?'

Playfair craned his head to see. Kadongo sat like a man in a trance, bolt upright, his eyes wide, as if listening to a revelation.

Gradually Mulango worked himself up into a frenzy. He threw back his monkey skins and danced to the edge of the dais, the sweat pouring off his face and neck and running down on to his skinny chest, smearing the painted symbols. The lion claw necklaces flapped and rattled up and down and the monkey tail headdress twined and untwined round his wrinkled neck like a snake. When it looked as if he might lose his balance altogether and plunge into the laps of the nervous spectators sitting immediately below, Mulango stopped in mid-paroxysm, his chest heaving. Then he turned and beckoned to Kadongo. The huge figure rose as if hypnotised and walked slowly towards the witchdoctor, bowing his head as he approached. With trembling fingers, the old man unfastened the largest of the lion claw necklaces, and reaching upwards shakily, clasped it round the General's neck. He chanted some incomprehensible phrases, and capered another few steps.

'First time I've seen a president installed quite like that!' Broadside growled. Somebody laughed, and drew reproving glances from a group of Kawawan officials. Kadongo stepped forward slowly and stood at the front of the dais, the lion claws clinking against his row of medals. There was an awkward pause as if no one knew exactly what to do next, and then a group of officers, Kadongo's praetorian guard, sitting next to the dais, began to clap. Slowly, the other Kawawans took their cue, and finally and rather self-consciously, the diplomats joined in. General Kadongo stood for a long time, rigidly at att ention, looking like a man who was under a spell ...

Anyone who was outside the HQ, as it was always called, at six that evening would, as usual, have seen the floodlights go on and would have been able to observe how the sentries patrolling the perimeter wire paced slowly from pools of light to shadow and back again. He would have noted that the front gates were closed and that a sentry stood beside them with an automatic balanced on his hip. In the unlikely event that a casual passer-by had been there at eight, he would have seen a Land-Rover drive fast up the hill and stop at the gates with a squeal of brakes. He would have observed an urgent conversation between an officer in the Land-Rover and the sentry, after which the gates swung open and the tail-lights of the Land-Rover disappeared up the driveway. What no one outside the HQ would have seen, however, is what took place at the front door where the vehicle stopped. The same officer jumped out, walked quickly to the back and gestured two soldiers out. They were both armed with light machine-guns, and with their free hands they dragged out a heavy object which at first sight looked like a sack. It was only when the sack reached the ground, and was made to stand that it became recognisable as a man. His hands were tied tightly behind his back and his head hung forward on his chest.

The officer snapped an order and the guards prodded the prisoner forward towards the house. By this time the front door was wide open, the light streaming out and illuminating the scene for the benefit of the group standing in the doorway. The prisoner, half supported by the guards, had almost reached the door when one of the group stepped forward and, drawing back his arm, struck the bound man full force in the face. As he fell, the group started to kick him. They obviously enjoyed it. A muffled scream rose from the ground. Then the guards got hold of him and dragged him to his feet and through the doorway. But there was no one else to witness that or the way the moon shone with indifferent radiance over the HQ.

Inside, General Kadongo was in excellent form. He had discarded his uniform and was lounging at ease in a brightly-coloured, loose-fitting garment like a Roman toga. He was drinking beer, his skin gleaming blue-black under the artificial light. Round him in a semi-circle were half a dozen cronies. He did most of the talking, the others listened. Occasionally one would make a joke, and the great man would utter his slow jovial laugh. In their conviviality, they did not hear the arrival of the prisoner. The door opened and an aide came in. He leaned over the General and whispered in his ear. Carefully, General Kadongo put down his glass of beer and sat up. The jovial smile melted slowly from his face and was replaced by an altogether more cunning expression – half grin, half scowl. It was an expression that those who knew him well had come to fear. He looked round the expectant faces. 'Gentlemen, this is indeed mah day.' The big lips formulated the words with relish. He took his time. 'I have just heard,' he jerked his head at the aide standing respectfully behind him, 'that that friend of ours has just arrived here at the HQ. That long-lost friend . . . of ours.' He began to laugh, a slow heave that lifted his shoulders and shook the couch he sat on. His followers watched him with sycophantic but slightly apprehensive smiles. They were not quite sure what was coming next. The big man brought himself under control with difficulty. He wiped his eyes: 'You'll never guess who that long-lost friend, that deah friend is . . . heh . . . heh . . . heh . . . will you? Well, ah will tell you! It's our old friend, our disappearin' friend . . . King George . . .' The laughter vanished as the General stood up. In a second his mood seemed to change from great good humour to towering rage. He roared to the aide: 'Don't just stand there. Bring him in. Immediately.' The others were all on their feet now, a pack of dogs that scented the kill. The room had fallen silent, except for the General's heavy breathing, and a faint babble of sounds from some distance away in another part of the house. Then they heard footsteps, shouts, the door opened and the prisoner was flung rather than marched in. His chin was on his chest, and his shirt was spattered with blood. His hands were still behind him, bound so tightly that they pulled his arms back like a marionette. He stood swaying and would have fallen if the guards had not gripped him. The General moved slowly forward and towered over him. His voice was falsely humble. 'Your Majesty. Welcome back to Kawawa. We have missed you, all your friends.' He gave a terrible chuckle. 'King George!' he almost spat out the words. 'Say something, your Majesty!' His voice had risen to a roar, like a bull elephant trumpeting in rage. 'Greet your new President! Speak to your new master, you dog!' He spat full in the King's face. By what must have been a supreme act of will, or a reflex of old pride, the King lifted his spittle-wet face slowly to his tormentor. The once handsome features were almost unrecognisable. The eyes were swollen and blood-shot. His mouth was cut and some of his teeth were broken. His hair was matted with sweat and blood, his chest heaved painfully. He was obviously very near the end of his physical and mental resources. He just had the strength to look once at Kadongo with eyes that held only scorn. But he could not speak and, after a long moment, exhaustion overcame him and his head fell forward on his chest.

For once the General seemed at a loss for words. Then his fury burst. 'Take him away,' he screamed at the guards. 'He is a traitor! Take him to Mulango! He will know how to deal with a traitor!' He advanced menacingly, but the prisoner was already being hustled away. The door slammed, leaving the General standing in the middle of the floor, his face working while his subordinates stood like sheep at the far end of the room, huddled together for protection.

It didn't take long. Within half an hour Mulango appeared, capering and gesticulating like an evil baboon, his monkey skins swinging obscenely. He said something to the General who stood in the middle of the room, a glass of beer in his fist. He peered over Mulango's shoulder. The witchdoctor cackled in his high-pitched voice and waved. Two men came forward, bending under the weight of something heavy. They carried it between them, as if it had been a side of beef on a platter. As they came into the full glare of the light, the General gave a strange, high-pitched cry and threw up his arms as if warding off a blow. The two men stopped, and as the witchdoctor danced round them, the General's cronies crowded round the grisly spectacle. It was the head of King George of Kawawa, the eyes still staring with the same expression of contempt that they had displayed for Kadongo so recently. There was a moment of shocked silence and then someone stepped forward and closed the lids over those contemptuous eyes.

As he did so, the General seemed to go berserk. One huge fist flailed out, sending the dish and the bloody head spinning across the room. Another blow felled one of the men who had been

63

carrying it. Mulango backed away, half stooping, chattering like a monkey, his skins swinging; the *claque* backed away out of reach. For a moment it seemed as if the General would kill them all with his bare hands. Then he turned and stormed from the room and they heard him go crashing down the corridor, shouting incomprehensibly, like a rogue elephant on the rampage.

Next day, when the General had recovered from the excesses of the night, and the witchdoctor had thrown the bones foretelling that he would triumph over all his enemies, Mulango had a question: 'Tell me about the gold, master. The Simba gold. Where is it now? Did King George get it?'

The General chuckled. 'No, he tried but failed. I, Kadongo, was too clever for him.'

'So what happened?'

Kadongo was relaxed. He started to talk easily, in their own language. 'When the Simbas came to Bomi, they asked for our protection. They said they were being chased by the white mercenaries. They were frightened they would be killed and they asked us to help them. I said we would. They also said they had an ambulance with a lot of valuable medicines in it. This puzzled me a little. I asked one of my officers to have a look in the ambulance – secretly of course.' The big man laughed. 'He did, and found a lot of boxes. They looked like ammunition boxes but when he opened some of them . . .' the General paused and enjoyed the expectancy on the old witchdoctor's face . . . 'he found, what do you think . . . old father?'

The old man screwed up his face. His head jerked. 'Gold?' he whispered. 'The Simba gold?'

'Yes. You are right.'

The General stood up and paced the room excitedly. 'Every box contained gold, millions of pounds' worth. A fortune!'

'So,' prompted Mulango. 'What did you do, my son? Did your officer drive the ambulance down here?'

'We were cleverer than that. On my instructions two of my brothers went up that night. They took with them the same amount of ammunition, the same kind, from army stores. When the morning came, little father, they had the ammunition, and we had the gold.' He gave a great shout of laughter. An aide, startled by the noise, put his head round the door. 'Get out!'

bellowed Kadongo. The man's head disappeared as if it had been cut off.

'But,' wheedled the witchdoctor, his hand caressing his necklaces, 'why did those fools of Simbas let you do all this without protest?'

'Ah.' The General looked smug. 'We told them the vehicle must have a mechanical inspection. We would have to take it down to our servicing depot, a few miles from Bomi. When we returned it, they were suspicious, but they found nothing. After all, we simply put our bullets in their boxes . . .'

'And their gold in our boxes,' Mulango cackled. The General nodded. 'Yes, little father. And I did something else, a stroke of genius. I told the Simbas that they could keep their medicines! But as a general security precaution, purely routine, you understand,' he chuckled, 'we would have to seal them up as if they were in bond, put wire clamps and lead seals on them, as they do in the Customs. They would remain unopened as long as they were in Kawawa. When they left, we would remove the seals.'

'Brilliant, my son.' The old man rattled his necklaces. 'I always knew you would be an honour to your tribe.' They both began to laugh, the witchdoctor hobbling round the room in a victory jig, while Kadongo lay back helpless in his chair.

They were still laughing when the phone rang and the adjutant broke the news about the attack on Bomi. Kadongo's first reaction was one of triumph. He had outsmarted the mercenaries and the gold was safe. Then abruptly, as was his way, his mood changed and he started to rant:

'How dare those devils attack me, attack Kawawa, like that? We are an independent, sovereign country. They must be taught a lesson!' He smashed his fist on the table. Mulango crouched in a chair in the corner, his old eyes glittering with thoughts of revenge. Kadongo seized the telephone and demanded to speak to his Chief of Staff. When the voice came on at the other end of the line, the General seemed to lose all control. His face became huge and ugly with rage. His thickened voice bayed at the unfortunate man and his great hand looked as if it was trying to strangle the telephone.

'Why did you allow these mercenaries to pass the border unopposed?'

The voice at the other end started to stammer an explanation but was shouted down.

'Why was Bomi not better defended? Why did you have no intelligence? And after all that, you allowed them to escape scot free?' The unseen voice stammered and squeaked. There was a pause. Then the General continued in a much quieter and more ominous tone. 'I shall give you one last chance, Colonel. If you do not do better in future, I shall have to replace you.' He put down the phone gently.

'Fools,' he snarled in Mulango's direction. 'They need constant watching. If you leave it to them, they will let the mercenaries walk right into the capital itself next.' The thought seemed to make him brood, heavy-browed for a moment or two. Mulango twitched his skins. When he had Kadongo's attention, he drew his finger across his throat. 'Perhaps it is time for our friend too to be taught a lesson?' He chuckled, his eyes glittering like a lizard stalking a fly. Kadongo frowned. 'Not yet, little father, but maybe soon. I will give him one more chance.'

The telephone rang. Kadongo listened for a few seconds and a slow smile spread over the heavy features. 'Those mercenary devils fell for it. They drove the ambulance away, over the border.' He laughed softly. 'They were after the gold, no doubt about that.' His mood was sunny again. 'Imagine their faces when they discovered what was in those boxes! Thousands of rounds of ammunition!' He threw back his head and gave a guffaw.

'Are you sure the "sick man" inside our ambulance is safe?' Mulango still sat cross-legged in the corner.

'Absolutely sure. He arrived here yesterday. He is now in the safest place in Kawawa, in Africa come to that. Yes, little father, we have been too clever for them.' He struck the table a friendly blow.

There was a knock on the door and Colonel Takeo, the General's closest aide, and about the only man who was not afraid of him, came in. He was a blood brother, a member of the same tribal age group. Takeo was slim and sharp-featured, eyes set close together, deep scars on his cheeks. There was something sinister about him. He saluted.

'According to intelligence reports from Bomi, the enemy are

still in the area, within a few miles of the border.'

The General nodded. 'So?'

'They may launch another attack, especially when they find they have got the wrong ambulance, or rather the wrong patient aboard.' He smiled so that his tribal scars caught the light and gleamed.

'Send the Commandos up to Bomi. Tell them to block the main road and stop any movement on the capital.'

'Yes sir. Right away. There is one other thing.'

'Well?' the deep voice rumbled.

'Internal security.' Takeo's eyes glittered. 'As you know, General, there are a lot of potential spies in the capital. All sorts of foreigners . . . No doubt the mercenaries have their agents here, sending them information on our troop movements. I think we ought to take some temporary, er, precautions . . .'

'Such as . . .?' The big man seemed slow to take the point.

Takeo coughed. 'As interior minister in Your Excellency's cabinet, and therefore responsible for law and order, I would like to see some of the more dangerous of these . . . spies . . . put under preventive detention.'

'You mean arrest the Europeans?'

'Yes, sir. I think it is essential to safeguard Your Excellency's safety, and that of the revolutionary council's programme. We do not want to be sabotaged by the imperialist old guard at this stage.'

Mulango, from his corner, spat and nodded agreement. General Kadongo frowned in concentration. 'Very well; arrest all those spies hanging about in the usual places. In the hotels, in the bars, and anyone found near military objectives. Anyone in the Bomi area who is behaving suspiciously . . . anyone . . .'

As the litany continued, the old witchdoctor sat hugging himself in his monkey skins, his head nodding agreement.

Early next morning Playfair received an anonymous telephone call saying that the King had been beheaded by Kadongo's witchdoctor after arriving bound and beaten at the General's HQ. The informant's voice was African, and sounded both educated and very frightened. Playfair's first reaction was one of disbelief, but by the end of the morning, after checking with a number of sources, Asian and European, and a guarded call to Arabella at the High Commission, he was convinced it was true.

He ordered sandwiches and beer to be sent up to his room and wrote the story over lunch. He had just filed it by telephone to Nairobi – he no longer trusted the cable office – when there was a knock at the door.

'Come in,' he called.

The door swung open and an African with short greying hair, a small moustache, and empty eyes stepped casually into the room. He looked round for a moment or so.

'Yes?' said Playfair still sitting at his typewriter. 'What can I do for you?'

The African's eyes came to rest on a pile of papers beside the bed. 'Ah,' he said, 'I just wanted to ask you a few questions.' And then by way of explanation: 'I'm from the special branch.'

He did not proffer any credentials. Playfair debated whether he should ask to see them, and thought better of it. The man looked like a cop.

For a moment Playfair felt the panic rise in his throat. Then he got up and stood at the foot of the bed. The man was leafing through a pile of papers, mostly English papers, and some cuttings on Kawawa.

Damn, he thought, how bloody silly to leave them lying around for any suspicious fool to read.

The empty-eyed African walked to the wardrobe and inspected that; went over to the wash basin and fingered the razor and toothpaste.

'Looking for something?' Playfair asked as nastily as he could.

The man ignored him, finished his inspection in his own time and then came to rest in the middle of the room. He looked speculatively and rather mournfully at Playfair. 'My boss would like you to come and answer a few questions. It won't take long,' he added casually.

'How long?'

The African shrugged. 'Not long. But you had better take some of your things with you, just in case.'

Playfair wondered if he should throw him out, tell him to go to hell. But there would be others downstairs. He might be armed. Half angry, half frightened, he gathered his razor and wash things, zipped up his airline bag, picked up a paperback and slipped it into his pocket.

68

'Right.'

Mournfully, the African gestured towards the wardrobe. Playfair shook his head.

'No,' he said, 'What's the point of taking all that?' The other shrugged again and gestured to the door. He wanted Playfair to go first. Of course, they always did. Playfair opened the door and made his way to the lift. He pressed the button and waited for the light to appear. He wondered if they had also picked up Roger Straight and the rest of them. The lift came and they got in. The door closed with a sigh and the African pressed 'G' for Ground. They were on their way.

7

Up in MacGregor's camp in the Ruwenzoris, the mercenaries were in mutinous mood when they learned that the raid on Bomi had led to a haul of several tons of ammunition but no gold. After a lot of shouting and impressive use of the Sergeant-Major's muscle, the meeting calmed down sufficiently for MacGregor to make himself heard.

'I am sending Major Gibson and MacNab to Kawawa to make a recce and establish exactly what has happened to that . . . ambulance. We have information that the gold was last seen heading in the direction of the capital. When we find out the exact whereabouts, we will plan accordingly.'

MacGregor's voice was curt, as if daring anyone to argue with him. But the questions were not slow in coming: 'And what happens if ze Major comes back without having found ze bloody ambulance?' It was the cynical voice of ex-Commandant Thoreau.

'Then we pack up and go home.'

'What about the money?' It was Lorenzo, a pained expression on his face, and his palms turned upwards in supplication.

'You will get the basic rate you were guaranteed should the operation not come off.' MacGregor took the offensive. 'But look, let's not have a *post mortem* before there's a corpse. Nobody expected this to be a pushover. No one was led to believe that it was a piece of cake. You all came into this with your eyes wide open, you all took a chance. So don't start bull-shitting me at this stage in the game.'

Jock MacLean glared intimidatingly over his commander's shoulder, threatening anyone who disagreed with instant retribution.

'I want everyone to relax for a couple of days: go swimming, sunbathe, do what you like, within reason. But no one is to leave the grounds of the hotel. Is that clear? Security is all important at this stage of the operation. I don't want anyone shooting off their mouths, understood?'

'There's no one to shoot them off to in this God forsaken hole, is there?' It was the Dutchman, Van Kemp, who spent a lot of his time talking to Boenens and his wife in Flemish.

'You don't seem to have done so badly. Never out of the kitchen.' The other mercenaries laughed and MacGregor knew he had won.

'One final word. Just in case the Kawawans decide to play silly buggers, I have ordered the Sergeant-Major to set up a road-block at the top of the hill, and to mount a guard on the lakeside. We don't want to be caught with our pants down. Right, any questions?'

'Yes, how long before we know the results of the Major's recce?' Sergeant Wagner was standing up.

'It's impossible to say, but I would hope he'll be back in three days, four at the most, and that we'll have the information we need soon after that. I don't want to say too much at this stage, and I don't want to raise people's hopes unnecessarily, but we do have some good contacts in Kawawa . . . in other words the Major is not going out completely blind. Anything else? No? Alright then, dismiss. By the way, I've asked Madame Boenens to lay on something special tonight for you boys, so I hope you enjoy your dinner.'

There was a faint cheer and looking much less bolshy than at the start of the meeting, the 'boys' filed out, sniffing appreciatively the smells that were coming from Madame Boenens' kitchen. She was cooking roast wild sucking pig, a local speciality, formerly reserved for clients like the King of the Belgians.

After the meal, MacGregor and Gibson strolled under the blue gums towards the lake. Fire-flies punctuated the warm darkness with green flashes.

'How long is it since you saw Thompson?' asked MacGregor. They could see a handful of tiny lights half a mile or so out on the lake. The local fishermen were cashing in on Boenens' 'safari' guests.

'Oh, not since we were last in the Congo. I should say seven years. He did write to me once, telling me he was setting himself up in Kawawa as a tour operator and asking me to think of him if I had any safari clients.'

'And did you?'

'Well, I did send one party up and ask him to look after the arrangements. It all worked well enough, but shortly after that we dropped Kawawa from our list. Too much buggering about by the local Parks people, who were all Africanised by then. And there was also a security problem, too many bandits with guns running around.'

'That army's been out of control for as long as I can remember,' MacGregor said. 'Never been properly disciplined, like the Congo, in fact. Any idea what he's doing now?'

'Well, I gather that thanks to his African wife and his farm and so on he's making out alright. I don't know what his relations are like with this new bloke Kadongo, but I'll soon find out.'

A fire-fly flew just in front of them, its green recognition light glowing and fading.

'Well, take care, Jeremy, I need you back all in one piece and MacNab too. And I need the most precise details of where that stuff is. And then we'll think of how we get our hands on it.'

'If it's in some barracks, it's going to be tough.'

'I know, that's what's worrying me. Or he might have it locked away in the old HQ. That would be worse. The whole thing is damned tricky. I obviously tried to gloss over it as much as possible at the briefing, but I would personally rate the odds three or four to one against.'

'I'm afraid I agree.' Jeremy Gibson sighed.

Together they stood on the edge of the water, listening to its gentle lapping and watching the pinpricks of light where the boats rocked up and down. The lights drew the fish towards them, presumably, MacGregor reflected.

He wished he were a fisherman, for a moment, doing something predictable and relatively simple. If the fishing failed, it was not your fault, it was a matter of luck and weather, temperature and current. And there was always hope for tomorrow. They turned and walked back in silence towards the hotel, hardly a light showing among the trees. MacGregor had ordered a blackout after the raid.

'Goodnight, Jeremy, and good luck. I think you're going to

need it.' They shook hands rather formally.

Gibson and MacNab set off early next morning, driving the oldest Land-Rover. No point in getting the best one pinched, MacGregor said. They avoided the Bomi crossing and instead headed south for fifty miles to where there was another small frontier post. They passed through without incident, although they noticed that their papers were examined with much greater care than usual and the formalities took twice as long. Gibson's passport said he was a big game hunter. They drove all day and it was already dark when they reached Kawawa.

Near the market, Gibson remembered, had been a small Indian-owned hotel called the Taj Mahal. Bloody ridiculous name, he thought, but it would come in handy. They made two circuits of the market before Gibson located the right street. It was still there, looking if possible even more dilapidated than he remembered it, the raw concrete discoloured, the windows none too clean, the sign above the door broken. They parked outside, and Gibson went in alone to see if there were any rooms.

An Indian with obvious authority, whom Gibson took to be the owner, appeared and personally conducted the formalities.

'Yes, sir, plenty of rooms, very few tourists at the moment, you know. Situation not too settled. Here on business are you, sir?'

'Yes,' admitted Gibson, writing. 'I run safari tours and I haven't been here for some time. Wondered if the hunting round Kabolo is still any good?'

'Plenty of game, I think, sir, but I'm not sure about the lodges. Some of them were closed down.'

It was too late for Gibson to go to the Ministry now. He would go through the formality of applying for a game licence tomorrow. His immediate priority was to get hold of Thompson. He hoped he was still around. He asked for the local telephone book. No Thompson. It was either out of date or Thompson did not have a phone. Unpleasant thought. The affable Indian proprietor came to the rescue. 'Thompson, sir. Jock Thompson, isn't it? Braemar Farms? I know him very well, sir. I have his number in my office . . .'

Thank God for Thompson's notoriety, thought Gibson. The Indian was back a minute later with the number. Gibson dialled and listened to the number ringing. It took a long time, but finally an African voice answered sleepily. There was shouting in the background. Finally a hoarse but unmistakably European voice said: 'Yes, what is it?'

'Is that Jock Thompson . . .? It's Jeremy Gibson of Trans-African Safaris here . . .' There was a long pause, and then the voice came throatily down the line. 'Jeremy Gibson? Old Gibby? Why, you old bastard, what the hell are you doing in this bloody town . . .?'

Gibson laughed. 'Trying to do a bit of business, you might say . . .'

'What, safari business?'

'You could call it that . . . I'd like to have a chat . . .'

'Where are you in Christ's name?'

'Taj Mahal.'

'Taj Mahal? That bloody flea pit? Business can't be too good.' His laugh crackled down the line. Gibson looked round to see if the proprietor had overheard. If he had, he was being very discreet.

'Give me half an hour, and I'll be round to see you.'

MacNab appeared, having carried the bags up himself. Gibson led the way into the bar. It was empty except for a Goanese barman dozing under a slowly revolving fan. Gibson rapped the bar and the Goanese woke with a start. He ordered beer. They drank slowly. They were on their second when a hoarse voice said: 'Some blokes got nothing to do all day except guzzle beer.' A disreputable figure stood before them in baggy shorts, grubby white shirt hanging out over his belly, brown socks and sandals. His blue eyes were red-veined, but the smile was broad.

'Well, well, you old rogue. Not any thinner, I see,' said Gibson, clapping him on the shoulder. 'But no doubt even more prosperous. This is Mac. What'll you drink, beer?' Thompson took a long swallow and then wiped his mouth with the back of his hand.

'Me, prosperous? You must be thinking of someone else. I'm lucky if I make ends meet, and it's not getting any easier, I can tell ye that.' He took another swig of his beer and put the glass down empty. 'Set them up again, Frank, there's a good lad.' He turned the blue-red eyes mischievously on Gibson. 'And what brings you here to bonny Kawawa after all these years, Gibby boy? Nothing honest I hope?' Another shout of laughter blew a gust of beer across to MacNab who was sitting quietly on the other side of Gibson.

Gibson talked, plausibly he hoped, about the safari business, and said he would be making a licence application. Thompson winked disparagingly.

'It's all gone to hell. Lodges not properly run, game frightened off, poaching rampant, Christ, it's a mess, Gibby, I'll tell you that frankly. A bloody mess. And the longer this kind of *shauri* goes on the worse it'll be. If I were you I would forget it. What's wrong with Kenya and Tanzania? Even Mozambique would be better than here. Unless you want to see your clients ending up at the side of the road with their wallets empty and their throats cut.'

Gibson looked around anxiously. But Thompson was scornful of his caution: 'Everyone knows the score, don't worry.' He consulted his watch and directed a speculative eye at Gibson.

'What about some curry? I know a little place near here. Is Chaudhri's open, Frank?'

'Yes, sir, best curry in Kawawa, sir. Shall I book you a table?' Thompson nodded and when he was gone, said: 'We can talk better there, if you want to talk that is. And the grub's good.'

Frank slipped behind the bar. 'All fixed, sir. Table for three whenever you like.'

Outside, Thompson rolled on impressively in front, talking about himself. As he had promised, the restaurant was not far. It was also very small, very crowded, and at first sight very dirty.

Gibson made an involuntary gesture of withdrawal, but Thompson took his elbow and said: 'It's alright, we'll get a room at the back,' and thrust his way between the crowded tables.

A small, wispy Indian materialised in front of them. Thompson shook his hand.

'Hallo, Chaudhri, got our table?' The little Indian turned and led them through the crush. They were the only Europeans in the place. Everyone else was Indian, and all were chattering like starlings. The noise and heat were terrific. Chaudhri led the way to a small room at the end, empty apart from a table covered with a grubby cloth, and ushered them in as if it had been the Royal Box.

'Bring us beer and some of your hottest curry,' Thompson ordered. 'None of that rubbish you give to the tourists. Oh, and how about a clean tablecloth? My friends are fussy, even if I'm not.'

The little Indian grinned and disappeared, chattering rapid instructions to the waiter.

Beer and tablecloth appeared as if by magic, and the food did not take much longer. As the door closed behind the waiter, Thompson turned to Gibson. 'Well, what do you really want? You can speak freely here, it's quite safe.'

'You know about the raid on Bomi?' Thompson nodded.

'Well, we did that.' Thompson said nothing but his eyes stayed on Gibson's face.

'We had been led to believe that the Simbas had a load of gold in that ambulance. We got the ambulance alright, but when we opened it up, we found not gold, but ammo. Crates of it.' He gave a short laugh. There was a discreet tap at the door and one of the young waiters came in with more curry. MacNab looked carefully out of the door. Chaudhri was hovering in the background. Otherwise the diners were all intent on their own plates, and the noise was deafening. The door closed and Gibson resumed.

'By the way, this is bloody good curry. Well, as I was saying, we came away empty-handed. Someone had got their hands on the gold before we arrived. It's not in Bomi, we're certain of that. We think the Kawawans have it, but where?' He leant back and looked speculatively at Thompson over the rim of his glass.

There was a long silence. Then Thompson asked: 'What's it worth?'

Gibson had expected this. 'A share in the proceeds.'

'What does that mean?'

Another long pause, while Gibson took another swig of beer. 'A hundred thousand. Fifty thousand down for finding out where it is, and fifty if you help us to liberate it.'

Thompson lit a black, Kivu cigar and blew out smoke. Gibson coughed, and Thompson pushed the box over towards the other two. 'Try one, they're nae sae bad.' MacNab took one, but Gibson waved the offer away and lit a cigarette. 'Well, what's your answer?'

'I'll tell you straight. This is not my line of country any more.

If I start sniffing around too much someone is going to get suspicious. And Kadongo wouldn't like that. It's not very healthy around here these days for people the General doesn't like.' He took another puff at his cigar. 'But it's a very tempting offer. I'll see what I can do.'

Gibson looked cross. 'See what you can do? You'll have to do better than that for that kind of money. I can't go back to Mac and tell him you'll see what you can do. Can I?'

Thompson laughed, showing his broken, yellow teeth. 'What the hell do you expect me to say? I don't know where the bloody stuff is. In all probability, the General is sitting on the bloody lot up at his HQ.'

He blew out another cloud of smoke. There was a tap at the door and Chaudhri appeared with a bottle of brandy and three glasses. Behind him they could see a couple of Kawawan officers in battledress.

'They want to know who's in here,' whispered Chaudhri, pouring out the brandy. 'I think they're MPs.' The two Kawawans were whispering together and peering at them suspiciously. Thompson got up and went to the door of the private room. He shouted a name Gibson could not catch.

'What are you doing here? Trying to get a free curry?' His loud laugh broke the tension. One African smiled and immediately came over. He shook hands with Thompson, but kept looking at Gibson and MacNab. Jerking his thumb over his shoulder Thompson explained that his friends were big game hunters who wanted to arrange a safari in Kawawa for some clients. That seemed to allay any remaining suspicions, and after a few more minutes, the two officers departed.

Thompson came back into the room, wiping his face with a dirty handkerchief. Chaudhri was still there clutching the brandy bottle and looking relieved.

'How long had they been there?' Thompson asked.

'Only a few minutes, you know, but they wanted to see who was in this room. I think someone must have told them there were Europeans here.'

'So they were snooping around!' Gibson looked slightly tense round the eyes.

'Oh, just curious,' said Thompson. He turned to Chaudhri. 'Give us a spot more brandy and bring the bill, there's a good untouchable.' The little Indian poured the drinks with a happy grin and left the room.

'You see what I mean?' asked Thompson as soon as the door closed. 'These buggers are always sniffing around, wanting to know who's who and what's what. I'm running a risk being seen with you characters. They know me, and they know I play according to the rules. More or less. I have to. I have my farm here and my wife. This is my home, man. I've nowhere else to go. I can't afford to take risks.'

He lit another black cigar. Chaudhri flitted in with the bill.

'God, they kill you with kindness,' Thompson groaned. 'Look at this bill. It's only about ten bob a head despite all that booze.'

'Let me get that, it's the least I can do,' said Gibson.

Thompson waved him away and put down a note. 'You'll have to do a lot better than that,' he mocked. 'Double your offer and you've got a deal.' He blew smoke at Gibson.

'You've got a bloody cheek. How do I know you won't sell us out to your Kawawan friends in the first place?'

Thompson was angry. 'Don't be damned silly. I may not be a lily-white virgin, but I'm not a crook. Make it two hundred thousand pounds and I'll get you the information you need. And help you get the loot. Without Jock Thompson, Gibby my lad, you won't have a hope in hell.'

Gibson pretended to ponder. 'Alright . . . I might agree to that although I don't know what the old man will say when I get back. Probably have me court-martialled. But what exactly are you offering?'

'That's better.' Thompson was smiling now. 'Look, I can find out where the stuff is. It'll cost me a bit of money, of course, but that's routine. And it might take a few days. You won't want to stay that long, will you?'

'Not bloody likely.' Gibson was emphatic.

Thompson laughed his dirty laugh. 'Thought not. Well, I'll send a messenger, a young Indian friend of mine, a nephew of Chaudhri's by the way, who often goes up that way on business. He goes round all the *dukas*, selling hair straightener, beauty preparations, all that junk. Where are you exactly on the other side?'

Gibson told him about Boenens' hotel.

'He's still there, is he, the old bugger? Must be eighty if he's a day. Oh, aye, I know the place, although I haven't been there for years. Okay, I'll send Ginwallah. That's his name, you dope.' He glowered at MacNab. 'I'll send him up as soon as possible to the Ruwenzoris . . . Verbal message, okay, no incriminating notes from old Jock Thompson. And you send me back whatever you want me to know. Phrase it carefully so I'll understand, but no one else will. And just a few words. But he'll remember, he's carried messages for me before, and he's a bright lad.'

Thompson rose quite steadily to his feet. The heat in the little room was intense. The curry and the brandy made a formidable combination. He held out his hand to Gibson. 'Is that a deal?' Gibson nodded. They walked out through the now empty restaurant. Chaudhri's smile was still in place. Outside, a slight breeze made the evening pleasantly cool. Thompson put his hand on Gibson's shoulder. 'You know, if you try this stunt, I won't be able to stay on. There will be the most almighty rumpus and they'll round up everyone with a white skin. I'll see the wife is alright, beforehand, and I'll come out with you, if you've got a seat to spare.'

'We certainly have and a gun as well, although I hope you won't have to use it.'

'It won't be the first time,' Thompson said. When they reached the Taj Mahal, he held out his hand. 'I must be going, or Black Beauty will think I've been misbehaving.'

Gibson watched him walk off into the night, his dirty white shirt sticking half out of his trousers, and realised that an awful lot depended on that disreputable, swashbuckling figure.

8

As they dropped down silently in the empty lift, Playfair noticed the bulge under the special branch man's jacket that denoted a shoulder holster. He had heard a lot about Kadongo's goons, but this was the first time he had met one of them. Stepping out into the lobby of the hotel, Playfair looked around hoping to see someone he knew, someone to signal to. Two tourists, who looked like Americans, were standing at the desk, the man holding out some air tickets. He wanted to call to them, to attract their attention in some way, but his escort, perhaps anticipating such a move, gave his arm a little push. Playfair caught sight of two Africans in open-necked shirts and fake leather jackets standing waiting on the far side of the lobby. They both wore dark glasses and were looking in his direction.

His escort nudged him again, nodding his head in the direction of the side entrance. Playfair looked over towards the porter. If only he could catch his eye.

'My key,' he said. 'I'll just leave it at the . . .' The special branch man moved remarkably quickly, blocking the way to the desk. He held out his hand.

'Be very careful, my friend, give me the key.' He laid it on the nearest corner of the desk. The porter had apparently noticed nothing, and the two men in dark glasses were half way across the lobby by now. The special branch man nodded again towards the side entrance. Obviously they did not want him to cross the main lobby and leave openly by the front door. Playfair shrugged and stepped out into the blinding sunshine, the three Africans so close behind him that he knew he had no hope of escape. 'The bastards,' he thought, 'they have me completely at their mercy. No one saw me leave, no one knows where I am.'

The special branch man and the two goons walked Playfair quickly across the courtyard towards a waiting white Peugeot saloon, and pushed him into the back seat. He noticed a sheet of newspaper on the floor and as he climbed in, his foot tripped on something hard. Playfair found himself looking down at the cold black barrel of a machine-gun. He sat down as if he had been punched in the stomach. This was beginning to look very different from the routine investigation he had at first imagined.

The special branch man sat in front, and the two goons with the sunglasses squeezed in on either side of him. The car reversed noisily, turned, and swerved towards the gate. The driver swung left and they climbed fast up the hill away from the hotel.

The man who had arrested Playfair turned and said to the two in the back in Swahili, 'These British are criminals . . . bandits . . . godless.'

'Yes,' one replied, 'they're utterly godless.'

Playfair realised with a shock that they were Moslems. Not only was he an enemy because he was white, and British, but because he was an infidel as well. And he knew how intolerant Moslems could be of people who did not share their faith.

They drove fast uphill for about ten minutes, finally turning into a narrow road. At the end of it the driver swung left-handed into a gateway. It was obviously a military camp of some kind. An armed sentry with a red and white Military Police armband came round the barrier and looked inside the car. The special branch man snapped something which made him step back, salute and then swing up the barrier. They swept in, still travelling fast and stopped with a jerk at what looked like the main guardroom.

'Out!'

Playfair climbed with some difficulty over the machine-gun, and was pushed towards the guardroom. A few soldiers in full battle gear, carrying heavy weapons, stood about curiously eyeing the new arrival. Inside, two corporals sat behind a plain desk, like judges on the bench. There was a rapid flow of Swahili as the escort dumped Playfair's airline bag on the desk. One of the corporals turned it upside down, showering the contents over the surface. The other turned to Playfair. 'Sit down!' he barked.

Playfair looked round. There was manifestly nothing to sit on.

'On what?'

Someone hit him from behind, just above the ear, with what felt like a crowbar. For a moment he thought his skull had split. It was true, you did see stars. Then through the pain and sickness, a small ember of rage began to burn at the back of his brain.

'On the floor, *mzungu*,' the corporal spat out the term of abuse for a white man.

Playfair slid slowly down on to the cold concrete floor. His head was hammering rhythmically now. Out of the corner of his eye he could see the end of the cane that had struck him. He decided that this was perhaps not the time to demand to be allowed to telephone the British High Commissioner.

The second corporal was writing laboriously in what looked like an exercise book. 'Passport,' he growled.

'There, on the table,' said Playfair, pushing the corner of the blue book with his finger. He saw the cane swinging on the edge of his vision and hastily withdrew his hand. What did it say on the inside cover, in that copperplate script? Allow the bearer to pass freely, without let or hindrance . . .? Such assistance and protection as may be necessary? He managed an internal sneer. Slowly the big corporal itemised: 'One passport, number 3500637, EAS 250.00, one handkerchief, one Kawawa press card, number 312, one Air Travel Card . . .' The cane-wielder approached.

'Take off your shoes and socks.'

Without turning his head, Playfair complied swiftly, stiffening himself for another blow. It did not come. He regarded his bare feet. A hand snatched away the socks and shoes. They went on the inventory. Playfair remembered that they always took away your shoes and socks in the quite sensible belief that a white man could not run very far without them. The two black corporals finished the inventory. One of them got up, his heavy boots scraping the floor.

He gestured to Playfair to get up and follow him outside. Two or three soldiers were lounging in the shade. The corporal beckoned to one who came forward slowly, lightly swinging a thirty-calibre machine-gun. Playfair was six foot two, but the guard could give him at least two inches, and must have weighed fifteen stone. He poked the machine-gun muzzle towards Playfair in a gesture that could not have been described as friendly.

'Go,' he said in Swahili, and gestured vaguely with his head across a patch of grass.

The buildings behind the guardroom made an L-shape; on the far side of the grass square Playfair could see an archway. He turned and started to walk in his bare feet. The first blow in the small of the back took him totally unawares. The heavy machine-gun drove forward like a battering ram, the muzzle biting into the flesh. Playfair gave an involuntary cry of pain and surprise.

'Run, you bastard,' the guard grunted in Swahili. Playfair began to run, and as he did so, he thought desperately. 'Is he making me run so that he can shoot me in the back and then say I was trying to escape? Shot while trying to escape, the old euphemism for legalised murder?' He ran deliberately slowly. The second blow was so violent that it nearly knocked him over.

'Aggggggggghhhhhhhh.' It helped slightly to cry out. The pain bit into his back like a wild animal. He ran faster, half expecting the roar and crunch of the bullet that would throw him headlong like an empty sack and be the end. He could hear the big guard pounding behind him, hear his breathing, but not judge exactly how close he was. They were running down a road, past a group of grinning soldiers. They shouted encouragement to the guard. Barbed wire, what looked like cells . . . They came to a fork. Which way . . . ?

Playfair half turned and, as he did so, the guard let go again, on or near the spine it felt like. Playfair gasped as if he had been bayoneted. Would he fire now? They were running up a path. Playfair could see some buildings at the top. His back shrank from the pain that would explode again. But then they were abreast of an officer, and he was being told to halt.

'Sit down! Quick!' The machine-gun aimed at his face, but stopped a couple of inches short.

The officer walked towards him. He was swinging a heavy wooden club, which he raised as if to strike. Playfair, gasping, knew he had to stop the first blow. Otherwise he might not come out alive. That club could split his head like a rotten turnip. He rolled sideways and started speaking, fast, in Swahili.

The club stayed up, and then slowly sank down to the man's side. He was a major, and amazingly was prepared to listen. He waved the guard away. Playfair made an effort of will. The great thing was to seem reasonable and rational, show no fear and indeed behave as if this were the most normal situation in the world.

'Major, I fear there has been a complete misunderstanding. I was detained in the Grand Hotel by a special branch officer who asked me to answer a few questions. I am a journalist. I work for a highly important international organisation. I am a friend of Kawawa, and well-known to many of your leaders.'

He decided to play his ace, and hoped it would not be trumped. The big guard was still glowering in his direction, the machine-gun still held at the ready, but some distance off. On the other side of him, a captain, short and with a moustache, had come up to join the group. His right hand rested on the butt of his service revolver.

Playfair fought to keep the shake out of his voice. He listened to it coming out, surprisingly strong and relaxed. It was like listening to yourself speaking in a nightmare. He looked the major in the eye.

'Major, in all seriousness, I know and am known to your great leader, General Kadongo himself. I am sure that if you were to contact his office and give them my name, Alastair Playfair, they would confirm that I am who I say I am.'

Urgency made his Swahili unusually fluent. A subtle change came over the major and his friend with the pistol. The major stopped swinging his club, and slipped it behind his back. The other dropped his hand from the pistol butt. They both looked less aggressive. The major spoke a few words, low and quick, in some dialect. The other nodded. The major now spoke to Playfair, more reasonably. First he told him to get up, then he wanted to know how long Playfair had been in Kawawa, what he had reported, where he had been, and where had he met the General? Playfair told him and he seemed satisfied. The major pointed and they began to walk towards a line of huts. In the few moments it took to get there, Playfair realised they were old British Army huts, cement-walled and with corrugated iron roofs. The major and the captain stopped and spoke softly. They seemed unable to make up their minds about something.

Playfair glanced at the huts. The doors were all shut, there was nothing remarkable about them. He noticed that the end one was marked C19 – the next one C20 and so on.

Suddenly the major pointed to C19. A soldier had appeared with a large bunch of keys. He marched up to the door of C19 and went through the elaborate ritual of opening it. The major and the captain stood back.

The opening was taking a long time. The soldier had the wrong key. He extracted it and tried another. The major snapped something peremptory. Playfair had an acute sense of nakedness. He felt exposed, like a man on a bare plateau with no cover, trying to hide. He suddenly realised that he wanted, he actually wanted to go through that door. Inside, it would be safe, he told himself. There would be fewer risks of being shot, out of hand, like a mad dog. At last the door was open and he was being pushed inside. The guard pointed to where he was to go, the far end of the room, and he started to move. As he did so, his eyes took in the new situation. The floor was bare concrete, the walls too. Immediately on his left two soldiers sat on the floor – legs out. Guards or prisoners, he wasn't sure. Next to them were three Africans in civilian clothes, their eyes muddy with fear. In the far corner, what looked like a bundle of rags stirred. It turned out to be a soldier, his uniform covered in mud. He looked as if he had been half trampled to death.

Playfair made for the top left-hand corner of the long hut and sat down with his back to the wall, his buttocks on a thin skirting board that could be described as the only furniture. As he sat down he noticed for the first time a line of bullet holes climbed all the way up the wall on his right, ending in a couple of splashes of blood. It was dry and turning brown, but was probably only a few days old.

Something made him turn and peer at the wall behind him. He had not noticed when he walked up the cell. But now he saw very clearly. Someone had sprayed bullets against this wall too, head high as he sat on the floor. One hole was as big as a fist. More blood had splashed upwards, some of it reaching the ceiling. Playfair felt sick; he put his head on his knees and half closed his eyes. On his left the bundle of muddy rags groaned. The other occupants were quite still, as if too frightened to move. Playfair had suddenly realised where he was. C19 was quite clearly a death cell. One, no doubt, of many execution chambers which General Kadongo's tribal mercenaries were now using to liquidate their opponents. For the first time, he felt really frightened, and in his desire to live his thoughts turned to Arabella, and clung to her, as a drowning man clutches at a spar.

9

Playfair must have dozed off, his chin resting on his folded arms, his knees drawn up, and the skirting board cutting hard through his thin trousers. He lifted his head as the door was unlocked at the other end of the cell. A group of men came in, stooping under the weight of a body. As they dumped it unceremoniously on the concrete floor, Playfair saw that most of the back of the man's shirt was covered in blood. He lay there limply on the floor, obviously badly hurt.

Another figure who looked like the NCO in charge, appeared in the doorway. Playfair lowered his chin on his arms and pretended to be asleep, but kept watching through half shut eyes. The NCO stared for a moment at Playfair and then gave an order. The four men who had brought in the body and who were probably prisoners themselves, bent down, lifted it off the ground and carried it outside again. Then one of them came back into the hut with a brush and a bucket and disappeared into the showers at the far end of the hut. He returned a moment later, swilled a bucketful of water over the floor and brushed blood and water furiously out of sight. When the concrete finally shone clean, the NCO snapped another order and the prisoner with the brush went quickly out of the door. The key turned and for a moment there was silence.

Playfair stopped pretending to be asleep and surveyed his companions. The muddy bundle on his left was still sunk in painful semi-consciousness. The two soldiers at the far end who had lain quite still when the wounded man was brought in now sat up, and spoke together in low voices. The three civilians lay rigid and unmoving apart from their eyes. The tap at the far end dripped noisily. Then a new sound penetrated from outside.

There it was again, a heavy thump, thump. Like a hammer striking something soft. Playfair suddenly went cold. He could feel the sweat drying on his body, and a chill spreading up his back and touching his neck. He gave an involuntary shudder.

Thump, pause, thump, pause, thump. Then silence. He waited, breathing quietly and shallowly. After perhaps a minute a new sound filtered through the walls of the hut. The metallic ring and scrape were unmistakable. Someone was using a shovel to dig a hole, and by the sound of it, the earth was hard. The digging continued for about ten minutes. Playfair lost count and drifted off into another short doze. When he jerked awake, the digging had stopped. He could hear voices, very faintly, some distance away. Otherwise the entire camp seemed to be asleep in the afternoon heat.

Perhaps an hour later, keys rattled and the door opened again. Playfair and his fellow inmates watched apprehensively to see what this new interruption would bring. Two guards came through the doorway and said something which made the rest of the prisoners sit up. Playfair soon understood. A packet of hard, round biscuits came skidding up the smooth concrete floor towards him. The aim was good. The African civilians got the same rations, the two soldiers near the door did better. They got some sort of tinned beef, and a couple of packets of cigarettes each. One of the guards even went to the length of giving each one of them a cigarette and lighting it for him. To the others it seemed an enviable mark of favour. Playfair wondered if they were really guards masquerading as prisoners. The door banged shut again and the prisoners fell to munching their hard tack. Playfair managed to swallow one biscuit but it was so dry and tasteless he left the rest of the packet untouched. In any case all hunger had departed. The heat, silence and monotony returned. He tried to turn his mind away from the macabre pattern of bullet holes and blood that zigzagged up the otherwise smooth wall. But his eyes kept straying back to it, drawn irresistibly like the tip of a tongue that keeps going back to an aching tooth. He moved to ease the cramp in his muscles, and the soreness of his back. The heat seemed to press on the roof of the hut. He began to think that he could smell the slightly over-ripe aroma of blood, and of death. It was at that point that he began to pray; something he had not consciously done for a very long time, and in praying he fell asleep, his head on his arms.

It was much later, or so it seemed, that the killers arrived. They must have opened the door quietly, because Playfair did not become fully awake until they were nearly all in the cell.

There were ten or twelve of them, but the two who appeared to be in charge were officers, captains or majors, Playfair could not make out their badges in the half dark. One of them walked down the line of five prisoners hitting them with his swagger stick, cursing them methodically. Behind him came three or four NCOs. They carried no swagger sticks so they kicked the prisoners, idly, like footballers warming up for an unimportant match. Playfair gripped the muscles of his upper arms, waiting for the blows to come. But, unexpectedly, the officer who was in front veered to the right and made for the bundle of rags in the other corner. The swagger stick whistled through the air and hit flesh. The bundle gave a scream of protest. A big corporal started to kick at it with his heavy boot. The prone figure screamed again and was then jerked more or less to his feet. He turned out to be tall and thin, rather stooped, his uniform completely hidden and saturated by a thick layer of mud. The captain shouted something and shoved the thin man so hard that his head snapped back. He stumbled, was pushed upright and made to run the gauntlet to the showers, kicked and punched until he finally fell through the door and collapsed on the floor. Playfair saw him being dragged off and heard his yells as he was pushed under a shower and the water turned on. Then they turned their attention to him.

Playfair got to his feet quickly, his height and presence giving him a slight but sensible degree of protection. The captain, broad-shouldered, not very tall, and with a scrubby beard, faced him. He had a swagger stick under one arm, a torch in one hand and in the other a piece of paper which had on it, Playfair could see, a list of names.

'You, what's your name?'

'Alastair Playfair.'

'What's your job?'

Again Playfair told him while the others crowded round. He could feel their breath on him, as he stood with his back to the wall, almost like a man waiting for the firing squad. Apart from the captain, they were all armed, he noted.

More questions followed. Apparently his name was not on the list.

'Write your name here, quickly.'

A pen was thrust into his hand and Playfair wrote, with

difficulty, against the wall. The captain took the paper away, shone the torch on it and said: 'Play – Fur? Is that how you say your name, eh?'

'Playfair, Alastair Playfair. Yes.'

There was a shout from the other end of the room. The small knot of soldiers opened to reveal a soaking wet figure, his now clean khaki fatigues clinging to his body. Water dripped off the end of his nose, the point of his chin, down the back of his neck. Someone gave him a shove and he went staggering like a drunk up the room towards his corner. It happened so quickly that even Playfair who was so close could hardly follow it.

The noise in that confined space was shattering, although the fact that there were fifteen or twenty people in the cell must have deadened it slightly. The tall soldier in his dripping uniform was caught as if by a whirlwind and thrown precisely to his destination. He must have spun round in midair because he fell with his back to the wall, facing his executioner, who stood grinning, holding his Uzi casually, a slow curl of smoke sliding out of the barrel. The thin soldier gave a couple of coughs. Curiously Playfair was reminded of a leopard: it was the same sort of deep grunt. Then his head fell right forward, and there seemed to be more blood than water on the floor. The small, tight group of soldiers who for a moment had seemed frozen in place began to move. The captain started issuing orders.

A couple of men ran forward, and each taking a bare foot, dragged the wet corpse over the smooth cement. It left a reddish mark, like a wounded snail. Then Playfair could hear them shouting outside. The door slammed. His legs were trembling so much he was forced to sit down, and found himself being sick into the corner.

In the fading twilight, the thin man's congealing blood grew darker, but no one came to clean it up. Playfair told himself this was a bad sign. If they did not bother to wipe up the blood, it could only mean that they intended to kill the rest of them. The slight chill from the concrete floor after the heat of the day made him shiver. He could feel goose pimples rising on his skin. The other prisoners were slumped hopelessly on the floor. He glanced again at the bullet holes on the walls. The handful of new ones across to his left looked white in the dusk. Again his nostrils took in the smell of newly-spilt blood. If I have to die, he told himself, I will stand up and face them. I don't want to be shot in the back like an animal. If I have to die, I might as well do so with some dignity. Playfair felt sick again, and turned his head to the wall. His stomach retched painfully but nothing came up. Only the taste of bile fouled his mouth. Somewhere high above he heard the strange mewing call of a kite. He could imagine its right-angle wings sharp against the dark blue of the evening sky as it quartered the ground, two or three hundred feet up, its penetrating eyes searching for prey, or carrion. Yes, there must be plenty of carrion in Kawawa at the moment. The thought of the bird's flight filled Playfair with a desperate longing to be free. One of the other prisoners coughed, spat and lit a cigarette. It was almost dark now in the cell, and the end of the cigarette glowed as the man drew on it. Vague noises told Playfair the life of the camp was going on outside the cell, but otherwise they might have been on a desert island. And then worn out by nervous tension and strain he slept. He dreamt that he was floating out to sea, and just as panic was taking hold, he saw a lighthouse. Its beam beckoned and then dazzled him. He woke to find that someone was shining a torch right into his eyes.

'Come out!' The stocky captain's English was basic but comprehensible.

They led him out, past the recumbent bodies of the other prisoners, the whites of their eyes big with terror as the torch swept over them, and Playfair thought: 'This is it. They are going to execute me somewhere outside.' As he walked rubbery-legged, he had a moment of self-pity: he thought of ski runs in the Alps, the excitement as the cold air stings your cheeks; the silky feeling of swimming in the Mediterranean, the crunch of heather under your foot on a Scottish mountain . . . He stumbled and they half caught him, half pushed him through the door. Outside the night was warm and fragrant, the red earth only slightly stony under his bare feet. He breathed deeply and gratefully, holding himself erect. He saw that the soldiers were all armed. In the dark they looked even more sinister. Someone put a barrel against the small of his back, the steel cold as a tomb, and the captain said: 'March.' He pointed down the hill. This was the way he had run up with that devil behind him, just a few hours before. His back gave a twinge in painful memory. The party started to walk down the slope. A truck was going by on the main road, its lights slicing through the night to their left.

Where, wondered Playfair, is the execution place? Would it be in the middle of the camp, out in the open like this? Or in another killing cell? Or somewhere else, where they would have to drive? Some unknown clearing beside the river, and afterwards they would dump his body in the river, for the crocodiles to mangle? That thought was almost worse than the idea of being shot, the terrible jaws of the great, obscene predator coming up out of the depths . . .

'Stop here.'

The party halted and the captain began muttering to some other officer. Perhaps they would shoot him here? Get it over with? Playfair waited for the first bullet to strike his back. The first would be the worst. After that, presumably, you would feel only a dull pain. It would all be over very quickly. He wanted to be sick again. Finally the captain seemed to have made up his mind. He gave an order and they started to move again, into a dark hollow. Playfair began to steel himself, clenching his fists as tightly as he could. At the bottom of the dip, they stopped again, and one of the guards went forward to the door of a hut which Playfair now noticed for the first time. The guard fumbled with a bunch of keys for several minutes and then turned to the captain. He appeared to be indicating that he could not open the door. There was another debate and then the captain pointed farther down the hill, to another hut, the last one in the row. Playfair's numbed mind was registering a new thought, that maybe this was not the execution squad, but that he was being taken to a new cell. They were stopping again, the guard gesturing with his automatic. The captain went round to the end of the hut and this time, the guard had the right key. The door swung open and a flood of warm yellow light spilled out into the night.

'Go inside, quickly. Go!' Playfair did not need more urging. He stepped lightly, his feet careless of the stones, to the doorway and then in. The room seemed full of people, warm and immensely friendly. His eyes took a moment or two to adjust. As he was beginning to glance round, a voice from the other side of the room called: 'Hallo there, Alastair, when did they pick you up then?' It was the Cockney photographer, Jimmy Jarvis. Trust him to be in trouble too.

'Shh,' someone else said.

An African, Playfair could see now, was speaking in a low voice, reading in fact. It dawned on Playfair that he had walked into the middle of a prayer meeting.

A man, a white man, hissed at him, and pointed to the floor. As Playfair sat down, the man pushed a mug of hot tea into his hand, and whispered: 'Welcome to VIP Lodge!'

Playfair looked round slowly. By the door sat two Africans, who were obviously conducting the prayers. One of them was reading from the bible, in a gentle mission-trained voice. The other sat, his eyes on the ground, wearing the expression you see on the faces of Christian martyrs in early Italian paintings. Playfair's eyes moved to the man who had given him the mug of tea. He was a stocky middle-aged European, in shorts and a rather grubby shirt. He looked like a local resident, but Playfair had never seen him before. On his left sat Jarvis, two Europeans, whom Playfair vaguely knew, another unknown white face, and then a large, fat and rather frightened-looking black man. Finally, on the opposite side of the hut from Playfair, seated slightly apart, was Rahman, the Indian industrialist. His face was grave, composed, his white dhoti immaculate as usual. He gave Playfair a tiny nod of recognition. Jimmy Jarvis was leaning over and whispering: 'Are you alright, Alastair, old son? They didn't knock you about too much, did they?'

The African with the martyr's face looked over reprovingly at the disturbance and his mouth made a silent 'Shhh'. The other African finished his reading, put down the bible on the mat in front of him and closed his eyes.

'Let us pray,' he intoned.

'Our Father, which art in heaven . . .' The rest of the hut took up the prayer, rather raggedly, as if they were a little out of practice . . .

10

Arabella had had a bad day. Sir Harry, usually so agreeable if a little wet, had been poisonous. He really liked pottering around on a Sunday in his tropical aviary, fiddling about with the water and sugar mixture for his humming birds. The names reminded Arabella of a set of Happy Families cards they had at home: Topaza Pella, Heliothrix Aurita . . . she could not remember the others. To have to abandon his tiny, delicate, jewel-bright charges for the uncertain horrors of doing business with General Kadongo made the High Commissioner unusually bad-tempered. Throughout the night London had bombarded him with a salvo of telegrams about the arrests of journalists and other British subjects; and because he was rich and influential, they were also fussing about Rahman, who was technically a Kawawan citizen.

For once, Arabella's fresh beauty failed to move Sir Harry. She put the folder of telegrams on his desk.

'The Minister seems to be taking a personal interest in the reports of press arrests.'

The High Commissioner smoothed his thin silvery hair in a gesture of irritation.

'Wretched press! If only they'd mind their own business, they wouldn't cause themselves and us all this infernal trouble! I've never seen so many telegrams at a weekend!'

He sighed petulantly and started to read. The Minister was indeed taking an interest. No doubt he had been pestered by some of the proprietors, and, aware of the political reper-cussions, had instigated a flurry of messages. The High Com-missioner swore under his breath. The last message was marked 'Top Priority' and said: 'I need to know urgently what steps you underline you are taking for the release of imprisoned British subjects.' It was signed Secretary of State.

Arabella seized her chance. 'They have arrested all the jour-nalists staying at my hotel, including the *Worldwide* correspondent, Alastair Playfair whom you know.'

'Ah, yes,' said the High Commissioner rather testily, 'your friend. Do you know why they were arrested?'

'For no particular reason. That's the point. Kadongo sent his thugs round and they have all been hauled off to God knows where. I think we ought to demand an explanation, . . . Your Excellency.' It sounded like an afterthought.

Sir Harry struck his desk in a feeble explosion of anger. 'My dear Arabella, we have to proceed with due attention to protocol.' He gave a little shuffle to the pile of telegrams in front of him. 'After all, General Kadongo may have a perfectly sound reason for arresting these people. Who knows what they have been up to . . .?'

Arabella's voice shook slightly. 'Your Excellency can't really believe that. The man's obviously a lunatic. The announcement on the radio about the place being crawling with British spies is enough to convince anyone of that, if they still need any convincing.'

The High Commissioner held up a hand. 'Now, now, Arabella, don't get all excited. Ask James to ring the Foreign Minister for an appointment as soon as possible.' James Ritchie was Head of Chancery and Sir Harry's number two.

'Don't you want to talk to the General yourself?' Her voice was cold.

'No, not at the moment. I don't think that would necessarily do any good . . .' Sir Harry pretended to be busy at his desk. When Arabella still did not move, he cleared his throat: 'Go and give James that message, and then come back and help me draft a reply to the Minister, there's a good girl.'

Arabella strode down the corridor to James Ritchie's office, trying to control her temper.

'James, the High Commissioner is so wet he refuses to talk to Kadongo direct and wants you to see that twerp in Foreign Affairs.'

Ritchie was a cynical and comfortable civil servant who was entirely satisfied with his own indolent mediocrity.

'Now, now, young lady. That is not only a disrespectful way to talk about your boss, but you are also insulting a member of an allegedly friendly government. Pray, who is the twerp in Foreign Affairs that H.E. wants me to talk to?'

'Morombo, or whatever his name is. The so-called Minister.'

Ritchie observed Arabella's figure with pleasure. He shifted comfortably in his chair. 'How is H.E. taking his heavy fan mail from London?'

'Not at all well. I must go back and help him to draft a reply to the Minister. But James, this is serious. A lot of these journalists have been arrested, we don't know how many, and we don't know where they have been taken. They may be in extreme danger. The only thing to do is to go to see Kadongo personally. Can't you persuade H.E. to do something dramatic?' She turned the full voltage of her personality on Ritchie, but she might as well have tried to ignite an iceberg.

He lifted a palm towards her. 'My dear Arabella, I absolutely share your view, but this is something entirely for the High Commissioner to decide, and who knows he may well be right. If we get on the wrong side of Kadongo it may make things a lot worse for the people inside, including your friend . . . Playfair.'

There was an oily smirk on his face which infuriated Arabella.

'James Ritchie, you're a twerp too, a gutless, spineless, twerp.' She spun round in her rage and slammed the door. Something dropped heavily to the floor in Ritchie's office. Good, she thought, I hope it was the picture of him shaking hands with Kadongo. And I hope the glass is broken.

The High Commissioner looked up nervously as she walked in. 'Good gracious, Arabella, was that you slamming doors down the corridor? You'll bring the High Commission down around our ears if you carry on like that. Tst, tst . . . You must control yourself. Now, can we do this telegram to the Secretary of State? Mark it "Priority". "Making strenuous representations to Kawawa Ministry of Foreign Affairs on behalf . . ." '

Arabella's pencil skated over the page making the arabesques of shorthand, but two words kept running through her mind. 'Bloody cowards,' she thought, 'they're all bloody cowards.'

Two hours later, telegrams dispatched, desk tidied, and a dab of lipstick applied to her lips, she drove back to the hotel, a plan taking shape in her mind. By the time she had changed out of her working clothes, the plan was ready to be put into action.

There is something about a beautiful and determined woman in a temper that makes most men quail. The Kawawans were no exception. As she sent her yellow Mini racing up the hill towards the residential part of town, the traffic police and other motorists gave way. The soldier on guard at the main gate leading to the General's headquarters was so overcome by her appearance, that he opened the gate without any hesitation.

'Where are you going?' he asked her simply in Swahili, and she replied in the same language, in the accent of the country: 'To see the *Bwana Mkubwa* (Great Master) General Kadongo himself. I am expected,' she added untruthfully but convincingly.

The sentry saluted and waved her up the hill to the front door. As Arabella drew up, the officer of the guard stepped forward into the gentle evening sunshine and saluted smartly. He presumed that since she had got through the main gate without difficulty her mission must be approved. 'Yes, mistress,' he said politely, 'in what way can I serve you?'

'You may take me to your Great Master,' she replied firmly. 'He expects me.'

The officer walked to the front door, which was closed, and rang a bell. Arabella could see at least two armed guards in the bushes beside the house. The door opened and a man in a dark suit looked out suspiciously. When he saw Arabella, he became slightly more friendly. The officer explained in a dialect which he could not have known that Arabella understood. 'This young female says she has an appointment with the Great Master. Is she one of the special ones who is allowed to come in?' The man in the dark suit turned and gave Arabella another approving but rather doubtful gaze. Then, sharply, in Swahili: 'Who are you, and on what authority do you come here, to the house of the Great Master?'

Arabella, her amethyst dress covering but in no way hiding her striking figure, looked straight at the man: 'My name is Miss Arabella Cavendish, and I am an official of the British High Commission. I come as the personal secretary of the High Commissioner, Sir Harry Crumb, with an urgent message to your Great Master, General Kadongo.' Her Swahili was perfect. The security man swallowed, hesitated, and said: 'One moment.'

Arabella waited. The officer, out of his depth, stood discreetly at what might have been attention, looking with pre-

97

tended fascination into the middle distance. In a few moments, the man in the suit was back, more sure of himself. He crooked his finger. 'Come this way, please. As a special favour the Great Master will see you now.'

He turned and led the way, past two more bodyguards just inside the door, across a hall and down a corridor. At the end, he knocked deferentially on the door and waited, head cocked for a reply. Arabella could hear a deep voice rumbling inside. There was a pause, another rumble, and the door was suddenly thrown open.

As she stepped into the large, pleasantly bright room, Arabella's eyes met an arresting sight. At the far end, standing in front of the picture window, looking rather like a cardboard cut-out, towered the huge shape of the Great Master himself. If Arabella was nervous, she did not show it. She stopped a few paces in front of the still unmoving figure and said in a loud, clear English voice: 'Good afternoon, Your Excellency, I am Arabella Cavendish. I come on behalf of the High Commissioner, Sir Harry Crumb.'

A slow grin parted the heavy features, showing a lot of white teeth. General Kadongo's handshake left Arabella's fingers crushed together. 'I am delighted to make your acquaintance, Miss . . . er, Cavendish, is it? Yes? Ho, ho.' The laugh sounded theatrical but appeared to be natural.

General Kadongo was wearing British battledress uniform, the sheer weight of medals on his chest stretching the fabric. Arabella was still studying the purple ribbon of the General's recently-purchased Victoria Cross when she realised he was waiting for her to speak. She gave a small cough. Her eyes held the man's easily: 'General, His Excellency the High Commissioner sends his warmest greetings and hopes you are well. He hopes that the cordial relations between your Government and ours will continue to exist and flourish. But –' She paused and a tiny frown creased the General's massive brows. 'His Excellency is extremely concerned at the news that a number of British subjects have been arrested, and he asks me to communicate to you that he expects them to be charged within twenty-four hours as the law requires, or else promptly released.'

The General, his face still half in shadow, moved slightly, his size thirteen shoes creaking. There was a long pause, and then the deep voice rumbled: 'I do not need the High Commissioner to tell me what the laws of Kawawa are. I also consider he is meddling in the internal affairs of my country. But, Miss Cavendish, since he shows me the courtesy of sending such a beautiful young envoy,' he gave a low chuckle, 'I am prepared to overlook his, er, impertinence. Come, Miss Cavendish, let us sit down and talk this over in a friendly fashion.'

He put his enormous hand on Arabella's arm and propelled her to a sofa. As he sat down, the sofa tipped like a see-saw, hoisting Arabella up at one end, and almost flinging her into Kadongo's lap.

'Tell me, Miss Cavendish, you say you are the personal secretary of the High Commissioner, how is it we have not met before?'

'I was at the New Year's Day reception given by the late President, King George.'

It was delivered matter-of-factly, but it was a barb and it went home. Kadongo moved slightly, making the sofa groan, and the blue-black features set in a frown. Arabella was acutely aware of the man's great bulk leaning towards her, almost threatening. It took a conscious effort of will to refuse to be intimidated.

'Why exactly have you come, Miss Cavendish?'

'Because, General, the High Commissioner is very anxious about the safety of the British subjects who have been arrested. He would like assurances that they are being properly treated, and asks why they have been arrested.'

Kadongo's eyes stared back at her basilisk-like.

'That is an . . . er . . . administrative matter. It is under investigation. Do you know any of them?'

'Yes, some of them are journalists, as Your Excellency knows, and one of them is a friend of mine, Mr Alastair Playfair. Perhaps you know him? I can personally guarantee he is not a spy!'

The General gave a slow smile of comprehension. 'Ah, now I understand, Miss Cavendish.'

He threw back his head and gave a bellow of laughter. The sofa trembled and bounced. His expression became crafty.

'Would this . . . journalist . . . Playfur be a special friend of yours, Miss Cavendish?'

Arabella tried to fence.

'The point is, General, not that I know him quite well, and that the High Commissioner knows him too, but that he is not a spy! Don't you see?'

'Oh, I see, Miss Cavendish, alright. But this is really a private visit, isn't it, to plead on behalf of your . . . friend, eh?'

Arabella kept her eyes straight and her voice under control. Kadongo's huge presence seemed to have come closer.

'No, it is an official visit, but I must confess I would be very grateful personally if Your Excellency could do something in this particular case . . .' She fluttered her eye-lashes.

'Ahhh . . .' It was a slow double bass exhalation.

Arabella sat waiting tensely for the next move. It was not long in coming. The General put out a hand and closed it over one of Arabella's.

'What a pretty ring, Miss Cavendish; did you get it from an admirer?'

Arabella tried to draw her hand away. But General Kadongo held it firmly. She gave a nervous little laugh.

'Oh no, it was left to me by my mother . . . It's an amethyst.'

'Amethyst, eh?' The General studied it. 'Very beautiful, Miss Cavendish . . . it's the same colour as your eyes . . . that was very clever of your mother.' Kadongo let go Arabella's hand and moved his fingers up her arm.

'You know, Miss Cavendish, I like you. I like you very much. Not only are you very pretty, but I admire your courage in coming here and . . . what do you say . . . bearding the lion in his den . . .? After all, not everyone in your position would dare to do that. Would they? You must like this friend of yours . . . Playfur . . . very much, eh?'

Arabella tried to lean away from the overpowering presence. The man's musky smell was strong in her nostrils. Just like a lion's cage, or den, she thought.

'I do, General. He's a very . . . honourable . . . and good young man. I am sure he would never do anything in any way criminal against your country . . . like spying. That is why I appeal to you to release him and all the other journalists. Please!'

The General's hand was still on her arm. He leaned closer.

Arabella began to feel claustrophobic.

'I will look into the whole matter. I promise you that, Miss Cavendish. Immediately. But you can help too. If you show a little co-operation, that is.' He looked cunningly at her with his large, slightly-bloodshot eyes. 'I would like you to come to my house, Miss Cavendish. In the country. It is very simple, but it is where I was born and grew up. I am going next week. It is near the Nile and you can go for a sail on the river. You can see lots of elephants and crocodiles . . .' The word rang ominously in Arabella's ears. 'And afterwards, there will be dancing and everyone will drink beer.'

'I would love to, General,' Arabella said. 'If I could bring Mr Playfair along too.'

Kadongo's eyes grew hard for a moment and then he smiled, showing all his very large white teeth.

'Well, we must arrange it, Miss Cavendish. Leave it to me.' His huge hand squeezed her thigh. Arabella stood up quickly. She felt as if she had been holding her breath under water too long.

'If your friend, what's he called, Playfur – turns out to be what you say he is, I will see that he is released. For your sake, Miss Cavendish.' He squeezed her arm again, towering over her.

'Thank you, General. You have been very kind, and I shall pass on all you said to His Excellency. Goodbye, General.' She slipped out of his clinch and side-stepped towards the door. It opened before her. The security man had obviously been standing just outside.

'Goodbye, Miss Cavendish . . .'

The deep rumbling voice pursued her down the corridor like a would-be caress. Arabella shivered and hurried on.

II

MacGregor was getting impatient. So were the rest of his men. It was now three days since Gibson and MacNab had returned from Kawawa, and still no word from Thompson. What they all wanted now was some action, and their money. MacGregor walked over to the window. Between the hotel and the lake, parked under the blue gums, stood the ambulance and three Land-Rovers, their black and white striped paintwork cutting the shadows into queer shapes. 'Mechanical zebras,' one of the men had called them. Each one had 'Mombasa Safari Tours Ltd.' stencilled neatly on its doors. They had stowed the sporting guns in the racks behind the front seats, and hidden the heavy stuff in special compartments at the sides.

Then there had been the briefings, kept as simple as possible, with full details only for the section commanders: Gibson, Wagner, and the Sergeant-Major. All they were waiting for now was the exact location of the stuff, he thought, as he stared out at the vast expanse of lake, sparkling in the brilliant sunshine. On the shore, in front of him, the casuarinas bent like dancers, their tresses trailing in the wind.

MacGregor's reverie was interrupted by a knock at the door. Gibson's head appeared.

'He's here!'

'Who's here?' MacGregor asked crossly, but he already knew.

'Ginwallah, sir, with a message from Thompson.' MacGregor's face lit up.

'That is good news! Show him in then, Gibson, don't hang about!'

Gibson opened the door wide, and MacGregor could see behind him a young, smooth-faced Indian. The Indian smiled and held out his hand.

'Colonel MacGregor? Maurice Ginwallah.' He had a soft, well-educated voice.

'Jock Thompson sends you his regards.'

'Been wondering about you as a matter of fact, thought you'd got lost.'

The Indian laughed.

'Well, we've had some excitement in Kawawa as you probably know, and it was difficult moving about for a few days. So I decided to postpone my trip until things were quieter.' MacGregor nodded:

'Are they quieter?'

'Yes, the atmosphere is much calmer. The army has stopped searching everyone on the road, as they were doing.'

'Come and sit down.' MacGregor offered the Indian a seat with a view over the lake. 'Like a drink? Gin, whisky, beer?'

'I'd like a glass of beer, to lay the dust. The road from the border is very bad.'

MacGregor poured beer for Gibson and himself as well.

'Here's to your trip – and ours.'

They all drank and then the Indian said in his quiet voice: 'I have a message for you. Jock Thompson said it was very important. He made me memorise it.'

MacGregor sat forward on the edge of his chair. Gibson put down his glass and picked up a pen and pad from the table beside him.

'The gold is in the Bank of Kawawa, vault number one, opposite the front door, but one floor below. You take the staircase to your right and the entrance to the vault will be facing you when you reach the bottom. It is a one-ton treated steel door with a Prie-Duboeuf combination lock, timed to be opened between nine and ten a.m. – Mondays to Fridays. The alarm system comes into operation if you try and open it outside those hours. The vault is approximately eighteen feet by ten, and apart from a few safe deposit boxes, contains the permanent reserve of two million shillings in new notes.'

MacGregor looked at Gibson. 'Got all that, Jeremy?'

Gibson finished writing and nodded.

'One thing, how do you spell that lock?'

The Indian spelt it without hesitation.

'Apparently it is a fairly old model, and should not present a reasonably competent safe-blower with any problem.'

'Another beer, Mr Ginwallah? I think your message calls for a little celebration.'

'Thank you. Now that the dust is laid, I will enjoy the taste more this time.'

'Did Jock say anything about security?'

The Indian wiped his lips with a silk handkerchief.

'Yes. There are two other messages, what Jock called protocols to the main communiqué.' Ginwallah obviously enjoyed the Englishness of the joke.

'I didn't know that Thompson was such a bureaucrat,' MacGregor murmured. 'Go on, please.'

'Security is light. During the day, there are two soldiers on the front of the building. They leave at six and come again at six next morning. Nothing at the back. No other soldiers in sight of the bank. Inside, there is always one commissionaire on the front door, and one on the floor below by the vaults during business hours. At night there is one watchman responsible for the whole building. He uses the front door commissionaire's office and tours the building every hour, on the hour, until about midnight when he normally falls asleep.' Ginwallah took a long swallow of beer: 'The other message is shorter, and it goes as follows: Timing. I suggest you plan your operation for this Saturday-Sunday. The big boss is due to be away over the weekend making a tour of the north. There are no military guards on the bank after midday on Saturday until six a.m. Monday morning.'

'This weekend,' MacGregor said. 'Nothing could suit us better.'

'One last thing. Jock suggests that you take the old north road into town. Less traffic, and it takes you past the farm where he will be waiting for you. I've drawn you a map of how to get there.' He handed a folded piece of paper to MacGregor.

'If that's clear, I'll leave you gentlemen. I have a lot to do before I go back.'

He got to his feet.

MacGregor's eyes were bright with excitement.

'Tell Jock all is understood, and that we will pick him up at the farm about dark on Saturday. Okay?'

Ginwallah nodded, and held out a hand to MacGregor.

Every prison has its own hierarchy and the Military Police hut in which Playfair found himself was no exception. The two Africans who had been leading the prayers when he arrived were the oldest inmates, and were treated with deference by the rest of the occupants. Their eyes had a distant look as if they did not expect to see the outside world again. The other African, the fat man, was from the West Coast, and had been arrested, it seemed, by some ridiculous error. Playfair spent the night in Rahman's cell. He was assigned there by the scruffy-looking European, Peterson, who seemed to be a self-appointed cell leader. Rahman, ever courteous despite his predicament, apologised to Playfair that he would have to sleep on the floor like everybody else, while he, Rahman, enjoyed the luxury of a camp bed. When he turned back the rough army blankets, Playfair gave a whistle of surprise: 'Good Lord, sheets!' He turned to Rahman. 'How on earth did you manage that?'

The Indian laughed. 'One has to maintain certain standards.'

Jarvis put his head round the door. 'Cor, look at those bleeding sheets. Been sucking up to Rahman, then, have you?' He gave his cheeky grin.

A few minutes later, the lights were switched off and Playfair lay down on his three short mattresses. It reminded him of National Service. He looked up at the small window set high in the wall. Through it drifted the night noises of Africa, the odd soldier's shout and once a laugh. Someone was playing a radio. He was quickly asleep . . .

They were woken at six thirty by the guards banging on the bars of the cell door at the end of the hut. Rahman and Peterson went forward to see what they wanted. Playfair noticed that Rahman took a couple of packets of cigarettes with him, and handed them discreetly through the bars. There was a brief conversation and then Peterson came towards him.

'They just want the names of the new arrivals. That's you and Jarvis.'

Playfair and Jarvis wrote their names and organisations out in block letters on a scrap of paper torn from an exercise book and passed it back through the bars. The soldiers looked at the names suspiciously, folded the paper and departed.

Half an hour later, a huge urn of lukewarm tea arrived, and a dustbin full of hunks of bread. That was breakfast. Playfair wrinkled his nose.

Rahman was standing on his head, his ritual each morning for five minutes.

'Don't worry,' he said from his upside-down position. 'Something better will be arriving shortly.'

At eight o'clock an improbable figure appeared at the cell door, immaculate in white ducks, carrying a Fortnum and Mason picnic hamper, the kind that contains a nest of mess tins stacked one above the other, with a strap round them and a handle at the top. Rahman spoke to the man in a jovial, familiar way, as the tins were passed through the door. A guard looked on casually. Rahman waved his hand: 'Alright, chaps, come and have some breakfast.' He opened a series of steaming dishes, full of eggs, succulent vegetables, bread, honey and yoghourt. There was also a thermos of tea.

Playfair could not hide his surprise. Rahman laughed. 'Well, you see, they know me quite well and they let me bring in my own food. I am a vegetarian, you know, and can't eat their food.'

'No one in his right mind could,' Peterson grumbled.

'So I have told my wife there are lots of us here and to send in plenty of food. Here, help yourself.' He passed round plates and knives and forks.

'Fortnum's think of everything,' said Playfair appreciatively, scooping up a forkful of scrambled eggs. 'But tell me one thing. How is it that they allow your servant into a place like this?'

'Ah,' said Rahman, 'a good question.' He smiled. 'He's the same tribe as all these people, you see. They may not like the fact that he works for me. But when he starts to speak to them in their own language, well, they let him in. The tribal bond is very strong among Africans. He comes three times a day.'

'Fantastic,' said Jarvis, his mouth full of bread and honey. 'Just as well Mr Rahman's here to get us organised. Otherwise we would starve to death . . .'

After breakfast, Playfair and Jarvis were sitting near the door on the floor, when Peterson came over.

'You were joking about starving to death, a few minutes ago,' he said to Jarvis, 'but I can tell you something that will really make your hair stand on end.'

'Don't bother,' said Jarvis, 'we were just having a nice quiet chat about Fleet Street and some of our mates . . .' But Peterson was leaning forward, his finger poking at Jarvis's chest.

'Never you mind about your chat. There's something I'm going to tell you that will interest Fleet Street a bloody sight more than anything else you can tell them at this stage.'

'Do you mind?' Jarvis's tone was unmistakably hostile, but Peterson seemed to be oblivious.

'Listen.' He lowered his voice and looked round to see if any guards were in earshot. 'Last night, when you lot were fast asleep, a lorry drove in through the main gate and parked over there behind the guardroom. I couldn't sleep so I got up to see what was going on. And let me tell you this . . .' he paused for effect. 'That lorry was full to the brim, with stiffs . . . dead bodies . . .'

'Oh, for Christ's sake, leave it alone, will you,' Jarvis made as if to get up.

Peterson was agitated. 'Alright then, you close your ears if you want to, but I'm telling you the truth. There must have been between thirty and forty stiffs on that lorry. I could see the arms and legs sticking up all which ways. They were parked just under one of the floodlights. And then they started dragging them off and dumping them on the ground like sacks of potatoes . . .'

Jarvis was on his feet and pushing Peterson out of the way.

'I've told you, I don't want to hear. If I want to hear your stories, I'll ask, alright? Now just leave us alone . . .'

Peterson was offended.

'What's wrong with your mate? He's all het up. I thought he was a journalist. Doesn't he want to know what's going on?'

Playfair shrugged and also got up. Peterson stood in front of him.

'I swear to you, I saw it with my own eyes, they were all as dead as mutton, killed by Kadongo's men. And do you know how they're killing them? With twenty-eight-pound hammers. It doesn't make any noise and it is cheaper than shooting.' Peterson laughed a mirthless laugh, showing his yellow teeth. 'Yeh, that's what the Africans will tell you if you care to ask them. Twenty-eight-pound hammers, and some say they make the prisoners kill one another. Saves them having to do it, see? Like the Germans made the Jews kill one another. Oh, yes, this man is a black Hitler, make no mistake . . .'

There was a rattle of keys and Peterson stopped short. It was the orderly officer making his daily inspection, accompanied by two sullen-faced guards.

'Stand in your cell,' Peterson whispered, and made off. The inspection lasted only a few minutes. Then two or three more officers came in. Together they studied a list of prisoners and muttered among themselves. They asked Playfair and Jarvis their names and checked them against the list.

As he stood there, waiting at his cell door, watching the guards, Playfair found himself thinking of Peterson's words. The thought of being killed by a twenty-eight-pound hammer made him shiver, despite the heat in the cell. He thought back to yesterday afternoon, in C19, and the thumping noise he had heard after they had taken the prisoner out . . . the ring of the shovel on the hard ground . . . Peterson could be right after all. He looked across at the officers. They had finished going through their list and were now talking to Rahman. Playfair got the impression they had really come to see the Indian million-aire, to gloat over the régime's richest and most influential pris-oner. Rahman was dignified and calm, and after a few minutes, the officers departed. The clang of the cell door closing came as a relief. It was strange, Playfair reflected, to enjoy being locked up again, and left, if not in peace, at least in seclusion. Seclusion after all meant safety.

The rest of the morning passed quietly enough, punctuated by periodic rattlings at the door, as the guards appeared on some obscure errand.

'Why do they keep coming to the door? They don't think we are going to vanish into thin air, do they?' Playfair grumbled to Peterson.

Peterson tapped his nose with a long and dirty finger. 'Haven't you noticed yet? Whenever they change the guards, the new ones come over to the hut. They pretend they are checking, but if you watch, you'll see that someone, usually Rahman, gives them a packet of cigarettes. They expect it as part of their perks.'

'Ah, I see. A whiff of corruption even in the inner sanctum of the Military Police.'

Peterson showed his yellow teeth.

Rahman's white-suited cook appeared punctually and serious-faced at seven with dinner. Afterwards, Peterson came over to where Playfair was reading, clasping a mug of tea in his hand. He squatted down on the floor and began in his conspiratorial voice: 'Know what I was telling you about those stiffs I saw last night . . .?'

Playfair looked up from his book impatiently. 'Yes.'

'Well, I'm told that there will be more coming tonight. I'll wake you up and you can see for yourself.'

Playfair put his book down.

'Who told you that?'

'Ah, I have my sources, don't worry about that.' Peterson looked crafty.

'But unless the guards are confiding in you, I don't see how you can get any information in here.'

'You don't believe me, do you? Think I'm making it up? What, to impress you and Jarvis? Not on your life. I am telling you the truth, Mr Playfair, and if you don't want to believe it, that's your affair.' He got up, clearly upset. Playfair picked up his book. 'Alright, if there is something to be seen, I'd like to see it. If I'm asleep, wake me up.'

Peterson nodded and slipped away. Lights went off at nine and by nine thirty the cell was dark and quiet, except for the soft sound of the two Africans praying and the rumble of someone snoring at the other end of the hut. Playfair lay awake for some time, thinking about Arabella and wondering when release would come. His mind revolved like a tired skater until eventually he fell asleep.

He woke to a strong whiff of tobacco and stale sweat and knew it was Peterson.

'Thought you'd never wake up,' Peterson growled.

'What the hell's the matter now?'

'Like I said, they've brought in another load of stiffs. Come and see but don't make any noise. They wouldn't like anyone watching.' His rank odour retreated into the dark. Silently, his bare feet feeling cautiously for the cement floor, Playfair followed Peterson up the central aisle between the cells to the door. He looked through the bars. Two floodlights on the side of the main guardroom, about fifty yards away, burned a bright hole in the darkness. There were some bushes which partly obscured the view, but Playfair could make out the shape of a lorry, and as he watched, two men walked past it carrying something. It looked heavy. As they walked under the light, an arm swung down and trailed along the ground.

'See anything?' Peterson's voice in his ear made him jump.

'They've just carried a body from the lorry. There's another one . . . Who are those men, prisoners?'

'Yes. They come with the lorries from the other prisons. They bury them somewhere over the back. They've been coming every night now for a week. Do you believe me now?'

Playfair could feel Peterson's breath on his neck. He strained his eyes into the dark. Another corpse was being unloaded, almost slipping to the ground before the prisoners got a proper grip. A sentry appeared from behind the lorry. He was carrying an automatic loosely under his arm, and seemed to be looking for a moment straight at Playfair. Playfair knew he couldn't possibly be seen at that distance but involuntarily, he drew back slightly.

'What's the matter? Lemme have a look.' Peterson squeezed past him and sucked in his breath. 'Christ, they're still carrying the buggers off. Must have been at least twenty already.' He watched in silence for a few more minutes, then: 'That's the last one now, I think. Yes, they're climbing back on the lorry. There goes the guard . . .' They heard the tail-gate being slammed into position and then the engine coughed and started.

Still watching, Peterson continued his commentary.

'Another bunch of poor bastards written off – to satisfy the blood lust of the . . . Black Hitler.' He turned to face Playfair in the dark. 'That's what he is, a mass killer!'

Playfair felt spittle on his face. He stepped back. They heard the noise of the lorry die away in the darkness. Outside, the camp was quiet again. How many people had been killed like that, like animals, like cattle with foot and mouth? Hundreds certainly. Peterson was smoking a cigarette outside his cell, the red glow lighting up his chin, nose and jutting eyebrows.

'How many do *you* think he's killed?' There was a pause and the cigarette glowed.

'I'm told by my African friends that the total runs into many . . . thousands.' The voice was hoarse. 'And my guess is that there will be many more before he's finished. Or before someone finishes him!' The words hung like a menace in the air between them. Playfair shivered. The night suddenly seemed chilly. He felt for the dark doorway to his cell.

'I'm going to bed. Goodnight.'

The only reply was the red glow from Peterson's cigarette. Out there in the darkness, Playfair thought, they must be burying the latest arrivals.

12

It was one of those marvellously limpid African mornings, which are the rule rather than the exception in the highlands. At dawn, the air was like chilled champagne, and the country smelt of dew and wood smoke. The light was soft and the colours of the grass and acacia scrub pale and misty. It was just after six when the MacGregor safari moved off, the peaks of the Mountains of the Moon showing up like sharp teeth among the wisps of cloud. For about five minutes they turned a tender pink, and then the sun climbed and you could see the distant green sheen of the ice. MacGregor took one last look.

'I'm sorry we never had time to climb up there.'

'Aye,' rumbled Jock MacLean. 'It reminds you of the old country. They say the giant heather is verra impressive. Right, surr, we're all set.'

'Let's go, then.'

MacGregor sat huddled in the passenger seat, wearing a wind-breaker over his bush shirt and goggles to protect his eyes from the red dust. By the end of the day, they would all be covered in the damn stuff. It would be up their nostrils, down their throats and in every crevice of their bodies. MacLean drove and behind, on lateral seats, sat MacNab, Lorenzo, who was dressed as if he were a rich Italian industrialist rather than an impe-cunious mechanic, Hendriksen, equipped with a Dutch pass-port, and Stavros the Greek. Behind, in the second Land-Rover, were Gibson, with Sergeant Wagner at the wheel, and in the third Land-Rover Commandant René Thoreau, the senior of the two Frenchmen. His partner, Commandant Claude, was in charge of the ambulance, which brought up the rear.

They climbed up the escarpment road which Gibson had taken on the day of the attack on Bomi, past the spot where he had had to shoot the big cow rhino, and then instead of taking the turning for Mutukulu, they kept straight on, the road getting much bumpier and narrower. It continued to climb, so that they left the bush behind and were once again in rolling open country.

Looking back, Gibson could just see the lake glittering under the early morning sun, until the dust blocked it out. They headed north for about two hours, making not much more than fifteen miles per hour, before reaching another crossroads. There was no signpost, but after consulting his map, MacGregor, standing up in the front of his Land-Rover, pointed to the right, and they started to bump downhill.

'There's a bridge over the river about fifteen miles from the turn-off, according to my map, and that's the border.'

Sergeant-Major MacLean, who for once had agreed to forego wearing his kilt, only grunted. He had both hands full, as the vehicle kicked and plunged through the potholes. The passengers in the back swayed and jolted uncomfortably.

'This is the worst stretch,' MacGregor shouted reassuringly. 'It's much better on the Kawawa side.'

After an hour, the country started to get greener, the trees bigger and eventually even the road improved. Huge baobabs, their bloated trunks making them look as if they suffered from an arboreal form of elephantiasis, edged the road like sentries. Finally, they reached the floor of the valley, and saw between the clumps of bamboo and elephant grass, the muddy, brown, fast-flowing current of the Kawawa river. The bridge was an old Belgian cast-iron single arch, badly in need of a coat of paint.

The convoy bumped slowly over, like a herd of limping zebra. The checkpoint was on the other side. It looked very little used. An elderly African in a khaki uniform made for someone else came to the door of the Customs hut. He looked surprised to see quite such an elaborate expedition arriving on his doorstep. MacGregor and Gibson went forward to greet him in Swahili. Gibson, in his role of courier, carried cigarettes and the passports. But the Customs and Immigration man obviously wanted to have a good look at this amazing safari. There followed a flow of Swahili from the old man.

'Where you go on this safari, bwana?'

'We go to Kawawa Town to see Bwana Minister.'

'Ah, Bwana Minister!'

'Yes.'

'Ah.'

'Mm.'

'Mmmm! And what do you do in Kawawa after you have seen Bwana Minister?'

'Safari go to see Sittatunga antelope and then to study plains game. After, we take the bwanas on safari to shoot some elephant and buffalo down at Kabolo.'

'Kabolo? Ah, I used to be game ranger at Kabolo. Very good place, I very good guide. I have General Eye-Shower come one time, and Prince Burn-heart and one time too Mr Thirst who American bwana, much, much money . . . oooooooohhhhh.' The old African laughed.

Gibson laughed too and his Swahili grew more fluent. This was terrain he knew well and so the conversation flowed on. Life in Africa, as he had learned a long time ago, goes at a more leisurely pace, almost in slow motion, like a waterfall seen from a distance. But MacGregor did not enjoy this sort of palaver. He could barely contain his impatience.

'For God's sake, can't you hurry him up?' he muttered.

'Not a chance,' Gibson whispered. 'He's enjoying himself too much. Leave it to me. Why don't you have some breakfast while we're waiting?'

MacGregor walked away stiffly, clenching and unclenching his fingers in the effort to restrain himself, and gave orders to Jock MacLean.

'Tell the men to have some grub, and behave like gents, until this damned ape has stamped all the passports.'

'Verra good, surr. I'd like to throw him and his bloody stamp in the river, but it's better the way the Major's doin' it.' MacGregor leant against the bonnet of the Land-Rover, chewing the sandwiches which Madame Boenens had made for them her last act of culinary service, and looking with unseeing eyes down the road that led to Kawawa and his objective. He had that tight, sick feeling in his stomach. He always had it before an operation, but this time it was worse, much worse. He ate slowly, waiting for Gibson. If he had any nerves, he never showed it. Thank God for Gibson. His mind was busy with the details of the coming operation when Gibson's shadow fell in front of him.

'Cheer up, Colonel, it's all done. We're free to proceed.'

'No snags? Splendid! I thought we might have to stick a gun in his ribs. Been a damn sight quicker.'

Gibson smiled and waved to the African whom he had bribed generously.

'But it would have been a mistake. He's happy. I've "dashed" him very nicely. I'll follow you, Colonel.'

The peace of the river scene was abruptly broken by the roar of four engines starting up. They swung away in a spurt of dust and impatience, MacGregor's eyes staring towards the venture ahead.

It was three hundred miles from this remote border post to the capital, but the road was tarmac all the way, so say seven hours, or eight with stops. MacGregor looked at his watch. It was just after ten, so with luck they should be at Thompson's farm around dark. He settled down in the passenger seat, and listened to the even hum of the big tyres on the tarmac. The road ahead of them was straight and empty. These drives across Africa were a bit like a voyage, he thought. The road, it was true, was unalterable, although there was nothing to stop a Land-Rover turning off the made-up surface and taking off across the *bundu*. To begin with the country was much the same as Gibson and MacNab had travelled a few days before. Later it became wilder and lonelier, with hardly any villages, the landscape un-rolling itself bare and baked under the huge dome of the sky, empty except for the slow-turning circle of the African vulture. As they got closer to Kawawa, they passed through two or three straggling villages, with small children and pye dogs wandering in the dust beside the road. Big Jock MacLean drove with care. He did not want to involve the convoy in a careless accident at this stage.

'Very little military activity, surprisingly little, really.' MacGregor looked at his watch. It was a few minutes to six. He switched on the radio. There might be a news bulletin. The tribal music faded down, there was a short pause and then the Kawawa National Anthem started up in all its tuneless wonder. This gave way in turn to the voice of the announcer.

'The time is six o'clock. Here is Kawawa Radio with the latest news . . . A spokesman for the President of Kawawa, His Excellency General Edward Chaka Kadongo, has just an-nounced that a sneak attack has been launched against our country by our enemies in the south. It is believed that the invaders are led by some of the supporters of the former King, the traitor who was tried and executed by order of the Supreme Military Council recently . . .'

MacGregor turned the volume up slightly.

'. . . General Kadongo himself has taken charge of the military operation to crush the invaders and already victory is assured . . . The population is urged to remain calm and to listen out for further orders . . . here now are other items of news . . .' MacGregor switched off.

'That could be good news for us or bad. Depending on how many troops are diverted to the south and for how long. Jock, pull over on to the shoulder here and I'll brief the others.'

It had been easier than driving from Bristol to London. For one thing, there was far less traffic and the only military activity they had seen was a squad of men in singlets and shorts out on a training run. There was no sign of Thompson at the entrance to the farm, only a gate with a sign: 'Braemar Farms, J. Thompson and Co. Ltd.' They drove down the rough farm road. On the right a herd of Friesian cattle, great black and white statues of placidity, stared back impassively at the black and white shapes of the Land-Rovers.

MacGregor, relieved of the strain of reaching his first rendezvous, saw the funny side of the confrontation. 'Thompson's cows look a bit surprised to see us.'

Sergeant-Major MacLean laughed. 'They must be wondering what sort of milk this bloody herd produces.'

They coasted down the slope to the house, a low bungalow, with the usual verandah running round three sides, and the barns and outhouses beyond. It was six thirty and the sky was deep gold behind the tin roof of the farmhouse.

The front door opened, and Thompson appeared looking, Gibson thought, even scruffier than the last time he had seen him, in Kawawa. His grin as he came forward, hand outstretched, looked a bit nervous, but still managed to be jaunty.

'Welcome to Château Thompson. The Missus is expecting you.' A large black lady appeared on the verandah dressed rather like a Roman senator in a toga. She moved with superb grace, her hips undulating under the loudly-printed cotton like a heavy swell on a summer's day.

'Come here, Black Beauty.' Thompson beckoned imperiously. 'Come and meet some of my . . . er . . . safari friends.'

Black Beauty's face seemed to be all white teeth and whites of eyes as she glided forward, gurgling with delight at the sight of all these strange white men. She gurgled especially loud when she came face to face with Sergeant-Major MacLean, impressed by the fact that his bulk was even greater than her own. Finally, Thompson shooed her off and she departed, swaying gracefully down the length of the verandah.

Thompson spoke confidentially to MacGregor and Gibson.

'Come and see our latest toy. It's just over here. Or would you like a drink?'

'No,' said MacGregor. 'Let's get the business done first and we can drink later. But I would like to get the men out of sight. Jock, see to it, would you?'

'Surr! Leave it to me.'

'This way, Colonel.' Thompson, his baggy shorts ballooning out as he walked, was full of enthusiasm. They rounded the back of the house and followed him towards an old barn. The Friesians were being brought in by the herd boys. Even here, only fifteen miles from the centre of Kawawa, you often got a prowling leopard. In fact, Thompson remembered when a leopard had got into the garden of his house in Kawawa. That was a long time ago now, before he had the farm. Nowadays, the leopards, like all the other big game, were getting scarcer.

They walked into the barn. In the corner, something bulky was hidden under a camouflage net. Thompson went forward and started to pull the cover off, revealing the dull green paint of a three-tonner truck. MacGregor stepped forward interested.

'What's this, looks like a Pobieda. Some of Moscow's lend-lease?'

'Right.' Thompson grinned.

'How did you liberate that?'

'Ah, you know how these things are. Pal of mine in the army can get his hands on surplus equipment from time to time and he happened to have this old boneshaker in stock. He painted out the insignia, but it still looks fairly official, don't you think?' Thompson slapped the bonnet.

MacGregor walked round it.

'It'll take everyone down to the bank at one go. Good. Then

you can meet us at the rendezvous point with our own vehicles and we'll do a swop. What's the place we're meeting?'

'Flame Tree Motel, on the other side of town. I'll send Karioki with you as a guide.' Karioki, a tall one-eyed African, was Thompson's head farm hand.

In Makonde Prison as the long afternoon began to decline into evening, Playfair ended his constitutional. He had been pacing the cell corridor for about an hour, thirteen strides one way, turn at the door, with a glimpse of the perimeter wire and freedom, thirteen strides the other, turn beside the shower and lavatory, and then thirteen back to the door again. You must not go too fast, he told himself, or else you become dizzy turning. But fast enough to get some impression of exercise.

The others were mostly asleep, or reading in their cells. He stopped and looked outside, through the bars of the door. About fifty yards away, some soldiers were digging what looked like slit trenches beside the outer wire.

'It looks as if they are expecting an attack.' Rahman had come up so quietly behind him that Playfair gave a start.

'I was thinking exactly the same thing.'

Rahman's dhoti was immaculate as usual, his face grave.

'I shouldn't stand watching them too long if I were you. You know how touchy they are. And if there is some scare, it's better that you don't show too much interest.'

Playfair moved away from the open bars.

'You're quite right. It should have occurred to me.'

Rahman shrugged.

'You know, these are small things, like giving them cigarettes. But you have to know how to handle these people. They are very simple, very primitive, you know. They are not like you and me. It is so easy to forget that and it is also dangerous . . .' The voice was still gentle, the brown eyes sombre.

Together they turned, and almost unconsciously, fell into step, side by side, to pace the length of the cell. When they turned next time, Playfair noticed that Rahman did not go too near the door.

13

When Ritchie went in to see the High Commissioner, Arabella was bending over the filing cabinet.

'Go right in, he's expecting you.'

Arabella did not even bother to look up. She was filing the latest telegrams between Whitehall and the High Commission. Whitehall was pressing for more information on the fate of the British subjects arrested, and the High Commission was trying to do its best to conceal that it had no real information. She re-read the last telegram of the morning . . . 'All British subjects in custody believed safe . . . number been released from police custody thanks to our demands . . . others including several members of press still held in army cells . . . exact circumstances not known and awaiting response from Kawawan Government . . .' Which told you precisely nothing, she thought bitterly. Her thoughts went to Alastair Playfair, now gone for a week and in the notorious Military Police headquarters at Makonde.

Her eye was caught finally by a telegram to London from the military attaché, Colonel Gordon, coded and sent out only an hour ago. It was marked 'Urgent and Most Confidential'. '. . . reports from usually reliable sources suggest small' mercenary column (see my telegram 20/2) under Colonel MacGregor, who we understand was hired by the late King George to liberate the "Simba Gold", are about to leave the Ruwenzori area. As mentioned previously they failed to locate the gold in their raid on Bomi, although they did virtually wipe out the remaining Simbas. Our sources say the MacGregor party may head for Kawawa, possibly for the capital itself, the inference being they are going to have a final crack at the gold . . . in which case there could be fireworks . . .'

The Colonel's style was decidedly unmilitary, Arabella thought. '. . . General Kadongo is in the south personally dealing with the incursion by supporters of the King. The mercenaries might therefore be lucky and arrive when the Kawawans' attention is elsewhere . . . on the other hand the group is so small that it is hard to see them achieving anything except their own destruction . . . There remains the worrying fact that any attack by MacGregor on the capital will cause panic and almost certain reprisals against the British detainees of whom a number are in Military Police hands. Those in Makonde would undoubtedly be at greatest risk . . .'

When Arabella put back the file, her hand was trembling.

General Kadongo was on his way to Makonde when he heard over his radio telephone that two of his armoured cars had been ambushed in the south and destroyed by anti-tank weapons. The crews of both had been killed. The enemy were either being reinforced across the border, or else the original estimates of their strength were wrong. By the time his Staff car reached the barracks, the General's rage had subsided to a malevolent glow.

He drove straight to the officers' mess. The CO was a small thickset man with an ingrowing beard. He knew the danger signs.

'How many prisoners do you have at the moment, Colonel? Europeans, I mean.'

'Fifteen, Your Excellency, that is,' he stammered, 'including Rahman, the Indian.'

'He's hardly European, although he's rich enough to buy himself a white skin.' There was obligatory laughter at the joke.

'Who are they?'

'Apart from Rahman, two businessmen, one teacher, one doctor, and ten journalists.'

'Ten, eh?'

'Yes, sir.'

'All British?'

'One American, the rest British.'

There was a pause while the General brooded.

'What papers do they work for?'

The Colonel took a piece of paper from his pocket and started to read out the names. When he got to the BBC man, Kadongo stopped him.

'BBC, eh? What you say was the man's name?'

'Jackson, sir.'

'Hmm. I wouldn't wonder if that man is a spy, more likely.'

The heavy eyes went round the room. There was a chorus of assent.

'Who else?'

The Colonel continued to read '. . . Alastair Playfair from *Worldwide* . . .'

'Playfur, eh?' Kadongo interrupted. He sat frowning. 'Ali?' His ADC came forward.

'Sir?'

'That day of the press conference. Didn't I ask you the name of that one, the tall one who asked a lot of cheeky questions about the King? Was that this Playfur?'

Ali nodded. 'It was, Sir. I made enquiries. Playfur it was. He's a dangerous man.' He leaned forward and whispered in the General's ear. Kadongo looked round the room and smiled at some private joke.

'Yessss . . . He is dangerous, you are right. I have a feeling that Mr Playfur is not so much a journalist . . .' he paused while the Colonel and the rest of the officers waited in silence . . . 'not so much a journalist, gentlemen, but a military spy.'

The word came out quietly, with a soft hiss, and floated round the room like a questing hornet.

'A spy, gentlemen.' His voice was even quieter. Nobody dared speak. He turned to look directly at the Colonel with exaggerated emphasis.

'Colonel, you will examine all the dossiers and put those who might fall under the suspicion of being spies in a separate cell. So that from now on they can spy only on themselves.' He permitted himself a low chuckle. The officers laughed nervously.

The Colonel leant forward and said in a low voice: 'The Indian is waiting in my office . . .'

'Ah.' The General got up with surprising speed. 'Good. Lead the way.'

The CO's office was small and stuffy, although the door was open. An armed sentry stood on guard just inside. When he saw the CO and General Kadongo approaching the soldier drew himself up and executed an elaborate present arms. Kadongo returned the salute.

'Wait outside.'

The soldier went out with a clatter and closed the door.

Rahman stood motionless in his white dhoti, his face showing no emotion. The two men looked at one another for a moment without speaking and then Kadongo smiled and gestured Rahman to a chair.

'Well, my friend, you look well. Are they treating you properly?'

Rahman's expression did not change.

'Perfectly correctly. But no charges have been made against me and I must protest at being illegally detained.' Kadongo smiled again and lay back in the CO's chair.

'The investigation has already started and the Supreme Military Council will be making its recommendations to me as to whether charges should be preferred or not . . .'

He turned his big pink palm over on the table as if the matter was entirely out of his hands. Rahman's face was still stiff and he sat on the edge of his chair.

'I have no idea what such an investigation can possibly be about. I have committed no crime. I would like to know who is making allegations against me?'

'I am not at liberty to tell you . . . after all, the matter is *sub judice* . . .' The smile was smug. 'Of course, you may be entirely innocent, on the other hand, some of your business associates may be guilty. Much money has been leaving the country illegally, as you no doubt know, and the Government is responsible for putting a stop to it . . .' Kadongo's voice was suddenly abrupt.

Rahman did not immediately reply. He knew that he himself was not guilty of any illegal currency deals, but he equally knew that many Indians continually sent money out of the country to their families in India. Finally he said: 'I am not afraid of any investigation. My record is absolutely clear.'

'I am very glad to hear it.' Then in an aside to the Colonel, who had been standing at attention throughout, Kadongo said, 'Leave us for a moment, Colonel.'

When the door had closed, Kadongo leaned across the table towards Rahman and jutted his jaw at him.

'Listen to me, Mr Rahman. Your record may be as clean as a whistle or it may not. It is surprising what these investigators can find once they start digging about . . . and of course the whole thing can be very . . . embarrassing and annoying . . . It seems a pity that a busy man like you should be wasting his time in prison for an indefinite period, doesn't it?' He lay back in his chair and his fingers tapped the table.

'But there is one way I think I could help you . . .' Rahman said nothing. The big man took up a pencil from the tray in front of him and tapped it slowly on the table to emphasise his words.

'If you were to make a generous gesture in some way, say to the Kawawan army, I might be able to persuade those people who are making allegations against you to drop them. Hmm? What do you think of that . . .?'

'What exactly are you suggesting?' Rahman ran his tongue over his lips.

'I am suggesting . . .' tap tap . . . 'that you might like to deposit a generous sum . . .' tap tap . . . 'in some place like Geneva . . .' tap tap . . . 'to finance new equipment for the Kawawan army . . .'

'How much are you suggesting?'

'Oh . . .' the pencil tapped again. 'Say . . . one million pounds . . . would be a nice round figure.'

Rahman sat speechless for a moment, his face the colour of a stale cup of coffee.

'It's impossible . . .' It was almost a whisper. 'One million pounds . . . but all the money I have is here . . . even if I had a million pounds I couldn't get it out of the country . . .'

Kadongo put the pencil back in the tray and pushed his chair back.

'Since it would be a contribution to the army's funds, there would be no problem, my dear Rahman . . .' He got up and stood for a moment, savouring his power.

'Think about what I said, Mr Rahman. One million pounds is nothing to a man like you.' He opened the door and shouted. The sentry performed another present arms. The Colonel came hurrying up.

'Look after Mr Rahman well for me. He is a very precious prisoner. I don't want a hair of his head harmed.' The General's shoulders heaved with laughter at his own wit. The Colonel laughed. Even the soldier smiled. Only Rahman remained stony-faced, his lips pressed tightly together, as he was marched barefoot back to his cell.

With the departure of General Kadongo, the Colonel was able to devote his attention to the problem of the journalists. His method of deciding who was a spy was simple. He gave no one the benefit of the doubt and treated them all as spies. Playfair and Jarvis were ordered to the door of their hut and marched in their bare feet back up the path to another group of huts.

'What are these bleeders up to now?' Jarvis whispered.

'No idea, but it looks as if they're moving us into another of their holiday homes.' Playfair's tone disguised his real feelings.

Their bare feet made no noise on the red earth. Two guards walked behind, their rifles held exaggeratedly at the ready, as though they really believed the two white men might make a break for it. One of them shouted 'Stop' in Swahili.

He prodded Playfair lightly in the back. The suggestion of the steel was enough to make him wince.

'Inside.'

Playfair and Jarvis shuffled forward into the unwelcoming darkness of the new hut. They could sense a presence, faint stirrings inside as somebody moved. The door closed. Then an unmistakable hoarse voice demanded: 'Who's that? Looks like Alastair's long spindle shanks.'

'Bill, you old bastard, Jimmy and I thought we would pop in and see how you were getting on.'

'Ha, ha,' Broadside wheezed. 'Not very well is the answer to that. The nicest thing about this place is the rats. They at least are relatively friendly. Got any cigarettes?' Playfair could make out the tousled shape of Bill Broadside more clearly now as he advanced across the cell floor. Jarvis offered him a cigarette.

'Who else is here then, apart from scroungers like you?'

'Old Man River, Straight that is, is somewhere around, probably having a kip. That's his normal occupation . . . oh, no, here he is awake for once . . .' Straight's enormously tall silhouette loomed up beside them.

'It's bad enough being locked up by these buggers but when you have to put up with bloody Broadside as well, you really deserve your danger money.'

'Who else is here?' Playfair wanted to know.

'Half a dozen very frightened coppers, who obviously think they're going to get the chop, and are probably right.' Broadside pointed to a separate cell at the far end of the hut. 'We've also got three of our lads here, and three next door.'

'How are they?'

'If it's like this, pretty bloody awful. The food is uneatable. The meat we had tonight was absolutely filthy swill. You look alright, though.'

'We've been bloody lucky. We've had Rahman in our cell, you know, and his cook has been keeping us all supplied with grub from the Rahman house.'

'Jammy buggers. Trust you two! Anyway, since they're here, we might as well do the honours. What do you think, Roger?'

'I think there's a drop left. Might just be a mouthful each.'

'Christ, what's this, a home from home?' Jarvis, who had been investigating the confines of the cell, came padding back.

'No, whisky, you fool.' Straight pretended to hit him. He handed out their one glass.

'How did you manage to smuggle it in?' Playfair's voice was full of admiration.

'Washbag.' Broadside took a sparing sip. 'They never looked. Too busy searching between my toes for radio transmitters. Bloody fools . . .' He laughed harshly.

They drank in turn in appreciative silence. Suddenly they heard voices outside and a torch flashed through the bars.

'Keep back,' someone cautioned. The door opened and three more prisoners were marched in. It was the three journalists from the next-door cell. They stood uncertainly, their eyes trying to fathom the dark. Once the guards had gone, Broadside took charge and dispensed the last of the precious whisky.

One of the new arrivals, the *Guardian* man, seemed to have trouble standing.

'Hallo, mate, what's wrong with you?' Straight asked him. Mitchell coughed and pointed to his stomach.

'One of the guards kicked me in the guts for not standing up quickly enough.'

'Why have they herded us all together?' the BBC man demanded.

'Maybe to release us,' someone said.

'Well, safety in numbers,' said Broadside.

Playfair, finishing his whisky, wondered about that. He thought the explanation could be more sinister.

14

At midnight the central square of Kawawa was deserted, the street lights making a chain of yellow puddles round it. The big Pobieda with the ambulance close behind, cruised slowly past the old Parliament and crept towards the building in the far corner. MacGregor sat hunched forward peering through the windscreen. He could detect no movement at all. Two stone lions guarded the flight of steps that led up to the impressive portals of the Bank of Kawawa.

'Just a little bit farther and stop in that piece of shadow, Jock.'

The Sergeant-Major applied the brakes. MacGregor and Gibson got out of the front, and Sergeant Wagner and Piet van der Merwe, who spoke Swahili, jumped down from the back. Each member of the party had blackened hands and faces, and wore camouflage uniforms. As prearranged, MacGregor and van der Merwe started to walk along the path that skirted one of the stone lions and led to the watchman's office on the left of the main entrance. They could see a light inside.

MacGregor went right up to the door and knocked. At the same time van der Merwe said in Swahili: 'This is the Army. We've had a breakdown. Can we use your telephone, please?'

There was a pause and then a voice from inside said hesitantly: 'Who is it?'

'Second Armoured Regiment, on night exercises. Our vehicle has broken down . . . the Colonel would like to use your telephone to call headquarters.'

'Wait a moment . . .'

They could hear a chain rattling and then a key being turned. It occurred to MacGregor that this office was not on the bank's alarm system. The door swung open and released a flood of light on to the path. MacGregor stood slightly to the right of the door and the Afrikaaner slightly to the left, partly in shadow. The night watchman took one step half out of the door and then, to get a better look, another step. As he did so, MacGregor moved in behind him and pushed the barrel of his Smith and Wesson .38 against his ribs.

The watchman gave a gasp of surprise: 'What do you think you're doing . . . Ah . . .'

MacGregor jabbed the revolver hard into his back.

'Tell him to keep his mouth shut and nothing will happen to him. Otherwise . . . Right, inside, you . . .'

A single bulb hung from a flex in the ceiling of the room which was small and bare, with a rickety wooden table in the middle and a cane chair behind it. Piet pushed the frightened African on to the chair and started to tie him up. MacGregor looked around the room. There was a telephone on the table and a folder. He opened the folder and leafed through the papers inside. The top one was headed 'Tour of Duty'. It had a list of times on the left-hand side and a check list on the right. The second page had a list of telephone numbers and addresses of various bank officials. MacGregor turned it over and looked at the third page. It was a plan of the building. He bent over to study it.

As Thompson's man had reported, the main vault was in the basement, opposite the foot of the stairs leading from the ground floor. It was marked vault A, and there were two smaller vaults, one on each side. A small inset diagram gave the details of the operation of the time clock and the alarm system. There was a master control switch somewhere. MacGregor's finger moved along the red line showing where the alarm wiring ran, and finally stopped at a small square. It was right here in the watchman's office. His eyes went round the room. That must be it – a thing like a fuse box just behind the door that presumably led into the bank. MacGregor walked over and tried the door of the box. Locked. The watchman's keys were lying on the table. They were marked with small labels. MacGregor chose 'Alarm' and it fitted. Inside was a two-way switch. Big white letters said 'ON'. MacGregor reached up and pushed it hard. It snapped up to read 'OFF'. MacGregor turned to Piet: 'Got the medicine?'

The African watchman, tightly tied to his chair, watched them with scared eyes. MacGregor lifted his revolver casually and pointed it in the general direction of the man. He spoke in kitchen Swahili.

'What's your name?'

'Mwango, bwana.'

'How long you worked for Banki of Kawawa?'

'Ten years, bwana. Please do not shoot me, bwana.'

'I will not shoot you . . . if you tell me one thing, and you tell the truth . . .'

The old African licked his lips and looked anxiously from MacGregor to Piet and back again. On neither face did he see any sign of mercy.

'What is it you want to know, bwana?'

'Where is the gold? Which vault?'

The watchman licked his lips again and rolled his eyes in an agony of decision.

'I do not know, bwana . . .'

MacGregor lifted the revolver slightly so that it was aiming right at Mwango's heart. With slow deliberation, he removed the safety catch. It made a tiny snap. The sweat began to run down the watchman's face and into his eyes. He shook his head despairingly.

'The gold, bwana . . .?'

'That was brought in secretly the other day! Come on!' He jerked the revolver impatiently and stepped closer.

'I will give you ten seconds . . . One . . . Two . . .'

The old man broke down and started to babble.

'Bwana, bwana, do not shoot me, please, bwana, I will tell you. But all I know is that the secret money is in the big vault downstairs.'

'Which vault?'

'Vault A, bwana, the biggest one. I swear . . .' MacGregor smiled and turned to Piet. The Afrikaaner, who had been standing waiting, scowling, while this exchange went on, had a cup of water and two outsize red pills in his hand.

'Open your mouth,' he ordered.

The African, completely terrified, obeyed, swallowing the pills with difficulty.

'And drink this.' He held out the cup. Half of it ran down the man's chin.

'Right,' MacGregor said. 'Get the others.'

They came like shadows in single file, leaving two men on

guard outside. The vehicles were parked round the corner of the building. Only someone turning down the side street would see them. MacGregor opened the door into the bank and the men filed through it without a word. They all knew exactly what to do.

Two of them lifted the drugged watchman on his chair and carried him bodily into the main lobby, where they deposited him in a corner facing the wall.

MacGregor led the way below, torch in hand. The staircase made a semi-circular spiral and ended in a smaller lobby beside a lift. MacGregor's torch beam came to rest on a big metal vault door with a large combination lock in the centre. He walked towards it, stopping close enough to read the maker's name and the word 'Paris' underneath. Lorenzo, who was following close behind, put down what looked a plumber's tool-bag and inspected the lock carefully. He spun the dial back and forward listening intently.

'Quiet, everybody,' MacGregor called, 'while Lorenzo listens to the music.'

They stood not moving for perhaps two minutes, listening to the gentle clicking, until Lorenzo announced: 'No good, *mon Colonel*. It might take 'alf an hour, and it might take tree hours. I t'ink we use da lance.'

'Okay,' MacGregor nodded. 'Make it snappy.'

Lorenzo bent down to his toolbag and pulled out an object about the size of a cricket stump, wrapped in a cloth. With MacGregor holding the torch for him, he unwrapped the cloth, spread out the pieces and started to assemble them. When he had finished, it looked rather like a gun. In fact it was a thermal lance, which uses a laser beam, invisible to the eye but so powerful it can cut the finest steel in a matter of seconds. It was the latest weapon in the bank robber's arsenal. MacGregor had bought it through a friend in one of the big Johannesburg gold mining houses. It cost a lot of money, but it was worth it. He had considered blowing the lock with plastic explosives, but for this sort of job, they were too complicated and noisy. This method was completely silent. Lorenzo donned goggles and went to work. Holding the lance like a giant pencil, he traced a slow and meticulous circle round the combination lock. Mac-Gregor had counted to fifteen under his breath when Lorenzo switched off the lance and turned to him.

'*Finito*.' he said. 'Watch.' He reached up a gloved hand and grasped the combination. He pulled. Slowly, like a cork coming from a bottle, it slipped smoothly out. Lorenzo dropped it with a thud on the floor, put his hand inside the hole and heaved. Very slowly, the one-ton treated steel door began to swing open.

Like a man entering a haunted room, MacGregor stepped forward into the vault, the mercenaries crowding behind him, their breathing loud in the silence. The torch beam moved jerkily over the floor of the vault and then slowly crept up. Someone behind him let out his breath with a low hiss.

'Christ, there it is . . .'

'By God,' said MacGregor. 'That's the most impressive sight I've ever seen. A ton of gold.'

His torch moved slowly from side to side. The gold was stacked neatly at the end of the vault, close-packed in rows five foot high and about ten feet across. It glowed back dully in the torchlight as if it had just come out of the ground. Handing his torch to Gibson, MacGregor stepped close and lifted an ingot. It was so heavy that he had to use both hands: he raised it above his head and turned to face the mercenaries. The torch followed him like a spotlight. The usually cold face was shining with excitement.

'There it is, boys. The Simba gold. After all these years we finally got our hands on it. It belongs to us now. We've fought for it. We deserve it.'

The mercenaries started to cheer, a deafening sound inside the vault. MacGregor shouted to make himself heard.

'Right! Now we've found it, let's get it the hell out of here. Fast!'

'Right, you heard what the curnel said. I want to see you working like you've never worked before.' Jock MacLean was already stripped to the waist.

Lorenzo had set up two lights by the door of the vault and the Sergeant-Major's shadow was projected across the pile of gold, a giant in a fairy tale.

'Where are those stretchers? Right, come on, Paddy, let's see you bend your bleedin' Irish back . . .'

MacGregor and Gibson had spent hours trying to work out how to shift the gold. Finally, Lorenzo, the illiterate mechanic who had once worked for Maserati, had come up with the suggestion that they should use the canvas stretchers from the ambulance. They were tough and light.

Thompson had provided them with a ground plan of the bank and made a cross against an emergency exit which opened on to the side road where the Pobieda and the ambulance were parked. Gibson had located it and opened the door with a key from the bunch on the watchman's table. Five minutes later the first stretcher-load of ingots went out, with Paddy and one of the big Afrikaaners straining under the weight. They squeezed through the emergency exit and man-handled the stretcher on to the floor of the ambulance. There, the other Afrikaaner, Hendriksen, and Aldo, the big Italian, were waiting to stack the bars.

MacGregor stood outside sniffing the night air and listening. The Pobieda was parked in such a way that it blocked the view from the square. Anyone who came down the street past the Pobieda would no doubt be puzzled as to what an ambulance was doing parked at the side of the Bank of Kawawa, but it was precisely to prevent that that Colonel MacGregor had placed one of the ex-Legion Frenchmen in the shadows at the end of the street.

MacGregor studied the building opposite. It looked like the back of a college of some sort, and appeared to be deserted. No lights showed. The moon was in its final quarter and already down and there were no street lights on this side. Behind him he could hear the muffled thud of the stretcher being dumped on the floor of the ambulance and the noise of the gold being stacked. By two thirty they had moved about two-thirds of the gold bars, working in relays of fifteen minutes each. Inside the vault the atmosphere was stifling, and the sweat was pouring off the faces of Jock MacLean and Stavros the Greek. They loaded ten ingots on to the stretcher, weighing about two hundred pounds, and stooped to grasp the wooden handles.

'Ready, right, UUUPPP . . .'

Stavros swore something incomprehensible in Greek and they lurched off down the corridor.

'This place is like a stinkin' oven. I feel like a roast pig,' MacLean growled. His shoulders were so wide that he had to turn sideways to negotiate the side door. Before he reached it,

MacGregor came hurrying in: 'Drop it, there's someone outside.' He turned and went out again.

The two stretcher-bearers lowered their burden to the ground. MacLean poked his head cautiously round the corner of the door. He looked past the end of the Pobieda, to the square where an army jeep had stopped and a small group of people had gathered. He could see the red tail-light of the patrol jeep, and an officer of some sort standing beside it. He was talking to one of the Frenchmen and Karioki, Thompson's head man. MacGregor was halfway between the bank and the jeep. As MacLean watched, he saw the Colonel draw his Smith and Wesson and heard the click as the safety catch went off. MacLean took out his own revolver and turned to Stavros.

'Go back and tell everyone to stand by for an emergency. There's a patrol outside. But no noise . . .'

The Greek disappeared. The minutes ticked past agonisingly slowly, and then the officer was suddenly climbing back in his jeep and the red tail-lights swung away.

Still holding his revolver, MacLean walked out to join MacGregor, who was waiting for the Frenchman, René, to come back with the African guide.

'It is alright, *mon Colonel*, I think we 'ave convinced him. He seemed 'appy, eh, Karioki?'

The African nodded. He said in Swahili: 'The officer said to carry on and do as the Bwana told me.'

'I say to 'im,' Thoreau said, speaking in his clipped English, 'that we were on a special top secret mission on ze orders of ze President 'imself, *le Général Kadongo*, and zat he had better forget he 'ad ever seen us! 'E seemed quite impressed!' He permitted himself a self-congratulatory laugh. MacGregor was not so sure.

'There's no knowing what the bugger will do! He could go off and report the whole thing immediately to HQ, and they could be down on top of us like a ton of bricks. Not gold bricks either! Sergeant-Major, you'd better post sentries at the front to give covering fire in case we have to make a run for it. Get the machine-gun into position on that corner.' He pointed to the ambulance. 'How much longer until we're fully loaded?'

'About half an hour more should do it, surr.'

MacGregor decided to take the risk. 'Right, get them

cracking. Their lives may depend on it.'

'Surr.' MacLean doubled heavily away.

The mercenaries, aware that time was against them, worked furiously to clear the last of the heavy bars. They hurled them on the stretchers and ran clumsily down the corridor to the back of the ambulance. Inside, Gibson and the other Frenchman, Claude, were now stacking the gold, their bodies and faces shining like wrestlers. MacGregor had gone out to the end of the road to keep watch. He had posted MacNab in a flower bed just beside the angle of the wall, his heavy machine-gun on its tripod, poking through the cannas in anticipation. Nothing moved in the pools of light below the street lamps.

'You'll hear them before you see them, Mac. Don't fire though, unless they come right in. Send our African friend back to call me if you need me.'

MacGregor ran back to the bank. No lights showed, only the dim bulk of the Pobieda, effectively screening the ambulance. It was visibly sagging under the weight of the gold. They had strengthened the floor and the springs, and MacGregor hoped the back axle could take the strain over bumpy roads. As he came round the end of the vehicle the last stretcher-load was being hauled through the side door by the two Afrikaaners, the two strongest men in the group, apart from MacLean. Tiring, they caught the end of one handle on the side of the ambulance and part of the load tipped off and fell. At the sight of the precious booty being scattered on the road, each ingot worth say ten thousand pounds, MacLean raised his fist:

'You two dumkops, I'll have your guts to make a sporran.' Since neither understood they did not reply, but bent stolidly to pick up the fallen gold.

'Never mind the witticisms, Jock, get everyone out and ready to depart,' snapped MacGregor.

Gibson appeared, haggard and soaked in sweat at the door of the ambulance.

'Just these to stack, sir, and we're ready to go.' Behind him the gold bars made a solid wall. When they had placed the last few in position, Gibson pulled down a plywood partition from the roof and secured it to a catch on the floor. Painted on it were a large skull and cross-bones and the words, in English and Swahili: 'Keep out. Danger. Highly infectious disease.'

133

Inside the bank, MacGregor flicked on his torch and made a quick tour of inspection. The night watchman was motionless on his chair in the corner, out cold. MacGregor loosened his gag slightly, and removed his blindfold. It did not matter now.

He took out a large envelope marked 'Manager, Bank of Kawawa', opened it and, holding the torch in one hand, read the note inside again:

'Top Secret.

To Whom it May Concern.

This operation has been undertaken on my personal orders. It is top secret. Nothing must be reported or said in any way about it. All bank employees must be silenced. Burn this letter when you have read it.' It was signed, 'By Order of the President and Commander in Chief, General E. C. Kadongo,' and decorated with an official-looking stamp.

MacGregor smiled a tight little smile. These Frenchmen, he thought, were damned good forgers. They ought to have some fun with that. He sealed the envelope, put it on the watchman's knees and hurried off towards the vault.

As he entered, the Irishman, Paddy, and the Greek were helping themselves to bundles of hundred shilling notes. In their haste, they had scattered some on the floor. MacGregor barked at them: 'Pick up those notes, you bastards, and put them all back. We're here on official business, not as bank robbers.'

They looked at him rebelliously until they saw the revolver. The notes were in thick packets on a shelf. MacGregor re-arranged them.

'Can't do any harm,' Paddy grumbled, emptying his pockets. 'What's a few miserable shillings here and there . . .?'

'That's not the point, you Irish dolt. If we don't touch the notes, they might believe the story about the gold, for a bit anyway. I ordered there should be no looting. You men will be disciplined. Right, outside at the double. Lorenzo!'

'*Pronto, pronto*,' panted Lorenzo. He was just fitting the combination lock back into the neat hole he had cut. Then, with MacGregor pushing too, they swung the heavy door back into position. At first glance, the vault was exactly the same.

MacGregor was still worried about the officer in the patrol jeep. They could be setting up an ambush now. His torch beam leaped ahead of them as they walked quickly to the side door. MacGregor locked it from the outside and threw the keys into the middle of a bush. Gibson came up and reported. 'All ready to roll, sir.'

'Good, I've just completed laying my false trail. It may delay the buggers for an hour or two. All quiet out front?'

'So far. We'll pick up the machine-gun crew as we go past.'

'Right. Bring Karioki up to the cab, he'll have to guide us to the motel.'

The Pobieda, making, it seemed to MacGregor, a terrific noise, turned and roared away up the street, followed by the ambulance. They paused at the corner to allow MacNab and his machine-gun aboard, and then with Karioki sitting between Gibson and MacGregor headed slowly out into the square. They checked their watches. Just after 0315, on schedule. MacGregor was elated.

'Bloody well done, Jeremy. Phase One successfully accomplished. Now for Phase Two, and Goodbye Kawawa.'

Karioki was giving Jock directions. They drove straight across the town and were soon on the main road leading south. They passed a few cars with dipped headlights, but otherwise the road was empty. They had to go a few miles down this road, MacGregor knew, before turning off to the east. Before they reached the turning, they became aware of lights flashing behind. A horn blared. Sergeant-Major MacLean, glancing into his rear mirror, cursed and pulled over sharply to the side.

'What's happening?' MacGregor had his hand on his revolver butt.

His answer came a second later when four big Pobieda trucks crammed with soldiers went roaring past, headlights full on. The last truck past sounded its horn and the soldiers in the back, in steel helmets and full battle kit, waved at them.

Jock MacLean gave a booming laugh.

'First time I've ever had a Kawawan sodger wave to me!'

'I hope the last too,' said Gibson. 'Must be on their way south to deal with the rebellion.'

They reached the turn-off five minutes later. A big neon sign flashed at them. 'Flame Tree Motel – Open.' As they turned into the car park, Thompson was waiting. He grinned up at the cab of the Pobieda, silhouetted against the intermittent flash of the neon.

'Any problems?'

'No. Not so far, touch wood.' MacGregor's face was pale in the hard light. 'We were passed by four lorry loads of the boys going flat out down the main road. Gave us a bit of a turn!'

'They'd be heading for Moto Moto on the southern border where the fighting's still going on. A bit more to it than the radio's letting on, in my opinion. Come on in, I've got some beer laid on.'

The three Land-Rovers were parked among the flame trees opposite the last chalet. They backed the Pobieda and the ambulance in beside them and crowded into Thompson's room. The rest of the motel was in darkness. Thompson had placed a crate of beer on the table.

'Biggest piece of cake I ever saw,' said MacNab, raising a bottle to his lips. 'I can retire now, buy a farm like the Colonel's in the Cape, and get drunk for the rest of my life.'

They all laughed. Even Jock MacLean relaxed for a moment, demonstrating how to drink a bottle of beer in a single gulp. After they had finished the beer, they washed the blackening off their faces, stripped off their uniforms and changed back into civilian clothes. Karioki was to take the uniforms back in the Pobieda and bury them on the farm. Thompson switched off the lights and opened the door. The mercenaries filed out one at a time. Outside the stars blazed down from a cold black sky. Orion's sword belt stood out razor sharp.

15

It was well after midnight when Sir Harry Crumb was woken at home by a call from the duty officer. Young Griffiths from the consular section was so excited that it took Sir Harry a few seconds before he grasped what he was saying.

'General Kadongo wants what? Wants me to go to see him? What, now? You must have made a mistake . . .'

'No, sir . . .' The voice at the other end of the line became more agitated. 'I haven't made a mistake. It was his ADC, Ali. He said the General was at his HQ and had just received a full report of the invasion in the south. He is blaming us and he demands your immediate presence . . .'

Sir Harry allowed himself a rare four-letter word.

'How dare he behave in such a high-handed fashion to Her Majesty's representative . . .'

'Then the General came on the line, sir. I must say he didn't seem to be entirely himself, but he was adamant about wanting to see you tonight . . .'

The High Commissioner gave a weary sigh. He was tempted to have Griffiths call back and say he would go to see the General at a reasonable hour in the morning. But heaven knows what Kadongo in his fury might not do in the meantime. Probably arrest half of the British community. No, damn it, he would have to go tonight, however reluctantly. He swore again.

'Alright, tell them I'll be there in half an hour, and send the car round, would you?'

'It's on the way already, Your Excellency, with Miss Cavendish.'

'Miss Cavendish . . . what on earth . . .?'

'I tried to raise Mr Ritchie but there was no reply. So I rang Miss Cavendish and she said she would accompany you, sir . . .'

Griffiths rang off. What Arabella had actually said was that she would go and hold the old boy's hand, but he could hardly tell H. E. that.

When Crumb tottered into his drawing room ten minutes later, he found Arabella waiting for him with the latest telegrams from London and an encouraging smile.

'They couldn't find James Ritchie, Sir Harry, so I thought I would offer myself instead, on the off chance that a woman's presence might soothe the savage breast!'

'Dear me, Arabella, I don't know what the Office would say, but in view of the extraordinary circumstances . . .' He passed a hand over his rather tousled hair in a gesture of resignation.

They drove in silence to the HQ, Sir Harry rehearsing in his mind the appropriate phrases for what he dreaded would be an embarrassing and possibly humiliating confrontation. He had three years to go before retirement and under normal circumstances this would have been his last post, but he doubted if he would be able to stick out another three months, let alone another three years in Kawawa. He had so longed for some quiet corner like Athens or the Consulate-General in Istanbul, or even Central America, where he could study humming birds in their natural habitat . . . But, no, it had to be an awful hole like Kawawa. He wondered if someone in Personnel had it in for him . . . He sighed. Arabella touched his arm sympathetically.

'We're almost there,' she murmured.

'Ah, yes, my dear, so we are. I'm afraid my mind was wandering.'

The big Austin Princess flying the Union Jack – Kawawa did not rate a Rolls-Royce – strained up the steep hill and made a tight turn towards the floodlit front door. As they drew up, the dark-suited aide Arabella had met on her previous visit appeared. The two sentries on either side of the door came to attention and presented arms, stamping their feet and slapping their rifle butts. They were dressed like British Guardsmen, except that their bearskins were made of leopard skin, the attribute of chieftaincy in Kawawa.

'I've brought my private secretary.' Sir Harry was flustered.

The aide looked at Arabella knowingly, then bowed and led the way down the long hall to the General's office. Throwing open the door, he intoned: 'His Excellency the British High Commissioner and private secretary.'

This time General Kadongo was sitting at his desk on the right-hand side of the room. He rose to his feet as they came in and Arabella could see at once that he was in a rage. His face was swollen with fury, his eyes glaring. He came round the front of the desk and planted himself in the middle of the floor.

'Good morning, Your Excellency,' quavered Sir Harry. The General brushed aside the niceties. Ignoring Arabella completely, he snarled at poor Sir Harry as if he were a new recruit who had trodden on the sergeant-major's toe: 'I have asked you to come here to make a formal and most deadly serious complaint against your country and yourself, as High Commissioner, about what is happening in the south of my country.' His voice rose in anger. 'Yesterday there was an underhand and sneak attack on my forces, an unprovoked and cowardly attack. Because of the bravery and superiority of the Kawawa forces, we beat off the enemy. But that is not the point!' He smashed his right fist into his left palm. Arabella thought he would explode with rage.

'I know the British are behind this attack. These miserable traitors could have never mounted such an operation unless they had the skilled support and advice of the British Army, or officers of the British Army dressed as civilians. We have captured some and they have told us everything. Everything, do you hear?' He pointed to the floor with outstretched finger as if he expected Sir Harry to go down on bended knee like a supplicant petty chief.

'I demand a full apology from Her Majesty's Government and an immediate end to these invasions of our soil. Do you understand, Sir Harry? An immediate apology from the Prime Minister personally, and a guarantee in writing that all damage done, loss of equipment, and compensation to the families of any of my soldiers killed or wounded be paid for by Britain! Or else . . .'

Arabella noted that he was actually frothing at the mouth, and his eyes were red and protruded from his head like some monstrous Pekinese. They waited for the threat to materialise . . . Kadongo suddenly looked at Arabella for the first time.

'Or else I will order the summary execution of all spies my

men have captured, including some who pretend to be journalists and are really soldiers in civilian clothes plotting against Kawawa . . .' The bloodshot eyes glared at Arabella. She desperately wanted to say something, but her tongue seemed to be paralysed. Sir Harry coughed.

'One moment, Your Excellency, I'm sure we can demonstrate to Your Excellency's satisfaction that this . . . eh . . . invasion has nothing to do with Her Majesty's Government and furthermore Her Majesty's Government would be completely opposed . . .' General Kadongo waved him away contemptuously.

'I did not ask for your opinion, Sir Harry. I demand you to pass on what I have just said, every word – your secretary has taken it all down, I see – to your Government and let me have the reply and the apology immediately . . .!' His voice had risen to a shout. He stood swaying slightly in the middle of the room and for one wild moment Arabella thought he was about to throw himself on the fragile figure of Sir Harry. But he dismissed them.

'Now, I must attend to more pressing matters. Good day, Sir Harry, and Miss Cavendish.'

His tone was brutal. As they were escorted back to the front door, Arabella heard a swishing noise behind her. She turned her head and caught sight of the grinning mask of Mulango, the witchdoctor. For a second their eyes met, and she saw in his a madness akin to his master's. Then he turned and scampered, tarantula-like, on bony, bare feet into General Kadongo's office, his monkey skins swinging behind him.

Sir Harry was still trembling when they sat down in the High Commission to draft a telegram. Arabella brought him a glass of water and did her best to soothe him.

'What a dreadful monster that man is . . . how I loathe having to deal with him . . . He's a tyrant.' Sir Harry took out a large silk handkerchief and mopped his brow.

'I think he's stark, staring mad,' said Arabella.

'He certainly was just now,' agreed Sir Harry.

In Makonde, Playfair and his fellow-prisoners felt they were moving towards some sort of climax. The day had started badly with the six policemen who occupied the end cell in the hut being called out and lined up against the wall. Then a tall thin major, called Simi, with the bright unwinking eyes of a snake, had torn the badges and épaulettes from the tunic of each police officer. The policemen had stood mute with shame and fear during their public humiliation. As they filed out of the hut, Major Simi took out his clasp knife, ran his thumb along the blade with exaggerated effect and said in Swahili: 'It won't be long before we finish you off.'

Playfair, keeping well back in his cell, watched the faces of the policemen as they walked past him: he saw terror and despair . . .

The door banged, the keys rattled and they heard the shouts as the policemen were marched away. No one moved for several minutes; it was as if they had all suddenly been confronted with a premonition of their own end.

Jarvis was the first to emerge from his cell: 'Did you see that first bloke's face? He looked like someone who has seen his own death certificate.'

'Do you really think they're going to kill them?' It was the American, Jim Anderson, fresh-faced and bright-eyed. 'How would they do it, by firing-squad or what?'

'Twenty-eight-pound hammer, more likely,' Playfair said.

'What's that?' the New England accent demanded. 'I've never heard of that method.'

Playfair explained.

'Oh, gee, that's terrible. My paper would never believe that kind of story.'

'You write it, they will,' Broadside said. 'There's a lot to be written if we ever get out of this bloody hole . . .' He started to cough. He had asthma. He coughed for several minutes . . .

It was late afternoon when the Colonel appeared, accompanied by Major Simi and half a dozen hostile-looking guards. The ten journalists were ordered to stand outside their cells.

'What's all this then? Another bleeding shortarm inspection?' Jarvis spoke out of the side of his mouth.

Major Simi was on to him like a striking mamba.

'What did you say, you? Eh?' He raised his swagger stick.

'Nuffink. Absolutely nuffink.' Jarvis looked innocent.

'Oh yes you did, I saw you talking. You are being insolent.' The beady eyes never wavered. Jarvis swallowed.

'Oh, I just said it was a bit hot, that's all I said. Honest.'

'Are you sure that was all? What's your name?'

'Jarvis, Jimmy Jarvis.'

'Well, Jarvis. I'm telling you. If you are not very careful from now on, we will teach you a lesson that you will never forget . . .'

'Sorry.'

There was a pause. Jarvis studiously inspected the cell floor. The beady eyes never left his face.

The Colonel said something and Major Simi stepped back.

'Right, line up along this wall when your names are called. Major, would you read out the list?'

The major took out a notebook and gold pen and started checking off his list.

'Broadside.'

'Yep.'

'Jackson . . .'

'Here . . .'

'Mitchell . . .'

'Yes . . .'

Straight was the last on the list. He looked down on Major Simi.

'What paper?'

'*Campaigner* . . .'

'How do you spell that?'

'C . . . like Christ . . . A, M, P, no no no, M for monkey . . . MONKEY, yes that's right, P, A, that's right, I, G, N, E, no E, R.' The Colonel looked up and down the row of white men, all dressed more or less alike in shirts and slacks, all barefoot, their faces drawn, suspicious, afraid. He was enjoying the situation.

'Well, gentlemen. I have orders from our President, General Kadongo, regarding you.'

They waited.

'The President is very anxious to establish who is a *bona fide* journalist and who is not . . . As you know, there are many spies in Kawawa, who would like to overthrow the people's defender, General Kadongo, and restore the old traitors to power. Some of these spies are very clever. Very clever . . .' He rocked back and forward on his feet and rubbed his bristly chin. 'Some of you are very possibly spies . . .'

Playfair thought his gaze rested briefly on him.

'So we must find out who is a spy and who is not . . . Perhaps you are all spies . . . in which case we will know how to deal with you . . . But first, I want all of you to write out a full statement saying exactly what you are doing in Kawawa, who you work for and how long you have been here. Put your name and the name of your employer at the top of the sheet and write clearly in capital letters! Major, hand out the paper!'

Simi stepped forward with a sheaf of foolscap paper and handed out two sheets to each journalist. He gave Jarvis a particularly sharp stare.

'Right,' said the Colonel. 'You have two hours.' He looked at his watch. 'And take my advice, do not tell lies or we shall deal harshly with you.'

They walked out, their heavy boots thudding on the cement floor. The door banged shut, the key rattled, and they were gone.

'Christ!' It was Jarvis who, typically, first broke the brooding silence. 'I don't fancy that bleeder who picked on me. He's a real nasty piece of work.'

'You want to watch what you say to these jokers,' said Broadside. 'They've all got outsize chips on their shoulders and they'd be only too happy to give you a going over.'

The *Telegraph* man was agitated about something else. 'I think it's a load of bloody nonsense . . . Write down what we are doing in Kawawa . . . what the hell do they think we are doing in Kawawa? Anyway, what will they do with these statements . . . read them upside down and decide if we are spies . . .? The whole thing is crazy . . .'

'Well, we'll have to do it, and just hope that it gets to some-one with a modicum of intelligence, and not one of these gorillas . . .' Straight, level-headed, brushed his moustache with the side of his finger.

'But hell,' said the American, 'this is giving in to them. We should refuse to co-operate with them and demand to see our consuls . . .'

'And get beaten up?' snapped Straight. 'Please yourselves, but if you don't write anything, you know the conclusion they

143

will automatically jump to . . . that we're all bloody spies. Our only hope is to insist and keep on insisting that we are journalists and represent powerful sections of the world press. We've got to get that into their thick heads.'

Playfair nodded. 'I think if we give them the slightest opportunity they will make us out to be spies. I'm going to write out a detailed piece, mentioning all the ministers I've interviewed, the Kadongo press conference, without saying that he walked out in a huff . . .'

'You'd better watch it too . . .' said Broadside.

'. . . and make it all as official as possible. That's our only hope.'

Silence fell on the room as the ten men sitting or lying on the floor, began to write. The realisation that they were in a sense pleading for their lives gave their pens a certain fluency.

A guard collected the papers at seven and then brought supper, which consisted of *posho*, a kind of thin porridge made from maize, stale bread and tea. Playfair ate a few mouthfuls and pushed the rest away in disgust.

'Bloody awful grub,' said Jarvis sympathetically. 'Too bad old Rahman can't send his cook up here with his leftovers.'

Playfair laughed. Strangely, his appetite was very small these days. He had lost some weight and felt fit, but if they were on this kind of diet much longer, they would soon start to get weak.

Donne of the *Telegraph* came up: 'It's a bloody disgrace that our offices and the Government haven't got us out by now. They can't be trying very hard . . .' His face was white.

Playfair tried to reassure him.

'This is our eighth day inside, right? A lot of people, including our offices and the Foreign Office must know exactly where we are and what's going on. They'll have put all the pressure they can on Kadongo. But let's face it, the man is a law unto himself, and he won't want to climb down too quickly and lose face. So we've just got to be patient. But my guess is we'll be out tomorrow.' Playfair spoke confidently, more confidently than he really felt.

'Don't kid yourself,' said Jarvis. 'Nobody at home gives a damn about us.'

'We're like those Jap prisoners in the jungles of Sumatra,'

grumbled Broadside. 'The ones who were discovered twenty years after the end of the war with beards down to their knees, who didn't know peace had been declared.'

Jackson, the BBC man, said nothing but looked nervously from one face to another. The conversation petered out. Time was hanging heavy for all of them now. Playfair thought about Arabella. The memory was so intense he imagined he could smell her perfume . . .

They were all asleep when the Military Police returned. Torches flashed through the bars, keys rattled and about a dozen soldiers crowded into the cell. Someone turned on the lights. Playfair, still heavy with sleep, looked at his watch: four a.m. A nice joke by the Colonel to keep them in suspense for so long. But the Colonel was in no mood for joking.

'On your feet, everybody. Major Simi? You have the statements?'

The thin major handed them over, imbuing even that simple action with menace.

Playfair caught a whiff of beer. He expected half of them would be drunk, and that could be dangerous. The Colonel shuffled through the papers, putting them in some kind of order. The guards lounged at ease, their sullen gaze on the prisoners. Finally, the Colonel seemed to be ready. He started to call out names. Those called were made to stand near the door. Jackson, the BBC man, was first, then Mitchell, of the *Guardian*, the American, the Reuters man . . . the little group swelled. Two guards marshalled them at gun point. The Colonel stopped reading. Playfair looked round. Those who had not been called looked a forlorn little group: Broadside, standing grumpily at the other end of the line, Straight, his moustache bristling with contempt for the proceedings, Jarvis, defiantly leaning against the wall, and Playfair himself. The Colonel gave an order, and the two soldiers guarding the larger group jerked their automatics towards the door. The meaning was unmistakable. They were being moved out to another cell, perhaps to be released, or . . .? Playfair looked around at his group. He was sure they were being kept behind, but for what . . .?

'Stand up straight!'

Simi had come forward to stand right in front of Jarvis.

Suddenly, he raised his swagger stick and crashed it down on his head. It happened so fast that Jarvis did not have time to duck and it hit him right in the middle of his skull, making a dry vicious 'thwack'. Jarvis made no sound. Everyone else stood very upright and looked straight ahead. The Colonel said something and Simi stepped back, reluctantly. The room had gone quiet. The Colonel spoke in English: 'You four have written lies . . . your statements are being investigated, but we know enough already to establish that you are British spies.' His voice grew shrill. 'You will be tried and shot . . . that is the fate of foreign spies . . . British spies . . .'

There was a commotion at the door and an officer approached with a message for the Colonel. It must have been urgent for he turned without another word and left the room. Major Simi was now in charge. There was a pause while the group at the door talked in low voices among themselves.

Broadside turned to Straight who was beside him. His face was sweating: 'We must try and get word to the High Commission . . .'

'Silence! No talking!'

One of the guards advanced. He was holding a bottle of soda water in his hand. He flicked his hand and sprayed the group, spattering their faces and shirts. They stood still, the soda dripping down their chins.

'Up against the wall,' he shouted, jabbing with his carbine.

They backed hard up against the wall, standing huddled together, shoulder to shoulder. Playfair's mouth was so dry he could hardly move his tongue. Another guard moved up close. His hand closed on Playfair's gold Rolex, which for some reason he had not had to hand over at the main gate, and tore it off his wrist. The same thing happened to Broadside. Straight had his wallet in his hip pocket. A large hand whipped it out and made it disappear. The crowd of guards moved farther forward. The beady-eyed Simi and his shorter companion seemed to be standing back. But it was hard to see what was happening. Playfair suddenly felt a stabbing pain in his stomach. A guard had lunged at him with the black muzzle of his carbine. He felt the sickness rising up his throat. A stick descended on his head like an exploding grenade. He started to fall, but just managed to push himself up against the wall. There was a lot of shouting.

He saw Broadside lying on the ground and one of the guards kicking him. He started to scream. Jarvis was being clubbed by Major Simi. Playfair could see his arm rising and falling. Jarvis was on his knees as if in prayer. The major was using something heavier than a swagger stick. It looked like a club or a revolver. Playfair realised afterwards that he must have been half unconscious because everything seemed to be happening in slow motion, and the voices were a muffled roar a long way away. He began to slip. Someone hit him on the head again. It felt like a rifle butt. He thought his head had actually split. A red flare exploded inside his brain . . .

He came to with the room careering round him as if he were very drunk . . . and he had a terrible hangover. He stood up slowly . . . his head was hammering. The room slowed down and finally stopped spinning. He became aware of a new sound, the dry rasping bark of a heavy machine-gun firing single shots and then short bursts. Playfair realised the room was empty. The lights still blazed from the ceiling. Broadside was groaning beside him and trying to get up. Straight was flat on the floor like a felled telegraph pole. Jarvis was still on his knees, holding his head in his hands and moaning.

Playfair could hear confused shouting in the camp outside and then, again, the heavy bark of the machine-gun, this time firing longer bursts. There was a pause and then a ragged reply from inside the camp. Whoever was shooting up the camp had timed their intervention very nicely, Playfair thought. Broadside had finally managed to get to his feet, and was walking, swaying from side to side, to the door. Playfair suddenly realised it was open.

Another burst from the machine-gun, and this time it was very close. He could hear the bullets whistling overhead. Then another short burst slammed into the front of the cell.

'Get down,' Playfair shouted to Broadside, who had reached the door and was peering out.

He turned round to face Playfair, still swaying.

'Whatshasay?'

'I said get down before you get killed and switch the bloody lights off.'

Broadside fumbled for the switch and finally turned it. Playfair's head was still pounding, but he clung desperately to one idea: the door was open, they had to get out.

'Hey, come on.' He grabbed Straight by the shoulder and shook him.

Straight groaned and sat up, rubbing his eyes. He had a cut on the temple, and the blood had run down his cheek, giving his face the look of a Picasso.

'What's happening?'

'The door's open, the guards have gone and it's time we got out of here. Somebody's shooting the shit out of this place. Get Jarvis on his feet. Can everybody run, or walk?'

'I think so.' Straight stood up with a groan.

Playfair moved forward cautiously to the door where Broadside was peering out.

'Where's the shooting coming from?'

'Don't know, but there seems to be some trouble down by the main gate. Look out!'

Both of them ducked. A heavy burst of machine-gun fire made them cringe down on the cement floor. This time the fire was definitely coming from the right, going left, in the direction of the main gate. Lifting his head slightly, Playfair saw the red flash of tracer, every fifth bullet. He also saw something else. The floodlights were still on, and under one of them was a big hole in the perimeter wire.

'My God, do you see what I see?' Playfair pointed excitedly.

Broadside was on his feet, peering at the wire.

'It looks like a bloody great hole in the fence.'

'It certainly is. This is our chance, boys. Is everyone able to make a run for it? Okay, here goes.' Playfair slipped out of the door and headed for the gap in the wire. It was only about fifty yards away but it seemed five hundred. About half way across, he heard the dry crack of a shot going over his head. He crouched lower, but kept running. He flung himself down on to the earth as he reached the wire and looked back at the others. They all made sharp targets as they ran into the light, but no one shot at them.

'Let's get through the wire and down to the road.'

'Okay.' Straight's breath was coming in gasps . . . 'But one at a time, and keep ten yards apart.'

Playfair went first, clambering through the hole and sliding down the bank on the other side. He felt naked in the glare of the arc lights and hobbled as fast as he could to reach the shadow of the trees. As he ran for cover, he tripped over a root or dead branch and came down heavily on his side. As he struggled, half winded, to get up and warn the next man, he heard a voice say: 'Alright, laddie, take it easy, that's my machine-gun you tried to kick over . . .'

16

The mercenaries left the Flame Tree Motel while it was still dark and drove with dipped lights along the main road south. MacGregor was worried about running into Kawawa army traffic on its way to or from the battle front, but there was none about. Thompson sat beside him in the front Land-Rover to point out the turning which would take them south-east towards the border and the great plains.

'Only about another mile to the fork, and then it should be plain sailing,' Thompson announced.

The road-block came as a surprise. The Sergeant-Major was the first to see the light in the middle of the road.

'What the hell's this?' He started to brake.

'A bloody road-block,' snapped MacGregor.

MacLean flicked on his headlights and lit up two sentries and a long pole that barred the road.

'If I jump it, surr, we'll get through but I dinna know about the rest . . .'

'No,' said MacGregor, 'hold your horses.'

A sentry had walked into the middle of the road and was signalling to them with his automatic to stop. MacLean did so. The sentry flashed a torch into the cabin, keeping the muzzle of his M16 aimed at the occupants. Thompson spoke first. 'We're a safari party, on our way to Lake Malolo, with permission from the Bwana Minister,' he explained in Swahili.

'Safari? There are no safaris now, there is a war,' the sentry answered. 'Show me your papers.'

Thompson turned to MacGregor. 'He wants our papers.'

'Show him these.' MacGregor produced some fake documents made up by the French.

The sentry began to peruse them laboriously, hampered by his torch and the bulky automatic. There was a shout from farther down the convoy and the first sentry shouted back.

'What's he saying?' MacGregor's voice was tense.

'Something about a check. I'm not sure, he's talking some local lingo.'

Someone began to fire single shots.

MacLean poked his head out of his window and looked back down the convoy.

'The other sentry's firing in the air, surr, I think to attract attention from whoever's behind those trees.'

'That's the Makonde Military Police barracks,' Thompson said. 'The main gate is just up the hill, about two hundred yards away. We couldn't have picked a better spot.'

The sentry with their papers pointed his gun at them and shouted an order.

'He wants us to get out, quick!' Thompson translated. MacGregor, who was next to the door, jumped out. He spoke over his shoulder: 'Right, let's take him . . . but keep him talking.' Thompson stood in front of the man and demanded to know what was going on. The sentry waved the safari papers and pointed up the hill.

'An officer will come down and check all you people. Everyone get out of the trucks and stand in the road . . .!'

MacLean hit him with a karate chop on the back of the neck. The sentry fell forward against Thompson, his M16 clattering on the road. MacGregor had just picked it up when the other sentry came running up. As he appeared from behind the Land-Rover MacGregor fired a short burst straight at him. The impact threw the man backwards into the ditch beside the road. For a moment, there was silence, then a long burst of fire came from the direction of the camp, the bullets droning over the Land-Rovers.

'High,' MacGregor said automatically. Then raising his voice: 'Take cover, everybody . . . Sergeant-Major, take a couple of men and see if you can knock out that damn Bren. It must be somewhere near the main gate.'

MacLean lifted up one of the bench seats in the Land-Rover and took out a heavy Chinese-made machine-gun, a copy of the Russian AK58. He told Hendriksen and van der Merwe to follow him and ran across the road and up into the trees. They could see the perimeter lights of the camp about a hundred and fifty yards in front. The main gate was floodlit and MacLean climbed steadily, carrying the machine-gun over his shoulder as if it had been a 12 bore, until they were above it, and about fifty yards from the camp wire. They could see the tracer from the Bren cutting through the dark towards the Land-Rovers. Hendriksen clipped on the ammunition belt and MacLean sighted on the muzzle flash of the Bren.

'Right, here goes . . .'

He fired three, four, short bursts, each on target. There was a dull explosion and some smoke drifted under the lights. The machine-gun beside the main gate fell silent. They could hear shouting. MacLean gave them another couple of bursts.

In the road below, MacGregor decided it was time to move. He cupped his hands and shouted up the hill. 'Right, Jock, let's go.'

MacLean was about to stand up when he saw some figures climbing through the perimeter wire. They were lit up by the powerful lights, as sharp as cutouts. MacLean began to swing the machine-gun towards them, but big Piet stopped him.

'Christ, man, don't shoot. They're whites . . .' They watched Playfair running awkwardly on bare feet towards them, and finally tripping over the machine-gun. MacLean helped him up and waited for the others. They came one by one, Broadside last, stumbling and cursing. Playfair explained who they were and how they had escaped.

'Lucky for you,' MacLean said. 'Right, let's get down the hill. You'd better come and meet the curnel.'

They found MacGregor leaning against his Land-Rover. His first reaction was frosty.

'I don't want any prisoners. Get rid of them.'

'They're journalists, surr, from the camp. They were getting beaten up when the shooting started and the guards ran away.'

'Bring them round here, where I can see them.' MacGregor's voice was still unfriendly.

The four scarecrow figures were shepherded round to the side of the Land-Rover. MacGregor switched on the inside light.

'Hallo, Colonel MacGregor,' said Playfair, holding out a hand.

'We last met in the Congo. Thank God you came along when you did.'

MacGregor recovered from his surprise. 'I must say we didn't expect the press out in strength, did we, Jeremy? Trouble is we don't have much room for passengers . . .' He was interrupted by a crackle of small arms fire. Bullets whistled past them, several striking the back of the ambulance. MacGregor put one foot inside his Land-Rover and shouted to the rest of the convoy behind him in the half-light.

'Let's get moving, everybody.' MacGregor turned to the four journalists who were standing indecisively in the road, still dazed from their beating-up and escape. 'In the back you lot, quick.' MacLean let in the clutch with a jerk and the front vehicle followed closely by the ambulance and the two other Land-Rovers, all with their lights out, started to roll towards the main gate. When they got to within fifty yards, MacLean accelerated and MacGregor, leaning out of the window, fired a magazine in one long burst at the guard room and empty sentry-box. In the back, a machine-gun loosed off half a dozen deafening staccato bursts, knocking out the few remaining floodlights. It was impossible to tell if they drew any return fire. Ten seconds later MacLean switched on his headlights and held his foot on the floor until they were doing seventy.

Ahead of them the road was empty, and the sun was coming up on their left in a splendour of red and gold. Ten miles from Makonde they turned off on to a dirt road, and drove fast for two hours. Just before eight, MacGregor stopped on a slight rise and looked back over the rolling bush, his eyes searching for the column of dust that would mean pursuit. But the pale sky behind them was empty.

'Brew up and refuel,' he told MacLean. 'Only fifteen minutes. Oh, and find some shoes for our passengers. They may need 'em.'

MacGregor and Gibson were standing, mugs of tea in hand, looking at a map when Playfair and Straight walked over in their newly-acquired gym shoes.

'We'd like to thank you again for rescuing us from rather a nasty situation this morning.'

Playfair's hair was still matted with dried blood and he had an ugly bruise over one eye where the rifle butt had landed.

MacGregor waved his thanks away. He was full of bounce after the success of last night's operation.

'That's okay. Lucky for you we happened to run into the road-block at that precise moment. Just you boys remember it when you write us up next. We're not altogether the shits the press likes to make out, are we, Jeremy? But frankly, I'm not keen to have four passengers on this particular expedition.'

'Precisely what kind of expedition are you on, Colonel?' Straight asked.

'Ah, that I'm not at liberty to tell you, yet, although the news will soon be public property. But I can tell you one thing, it could be risky. That's one reason I would be glad to get rid of you gentlemen as soon as possible. Nothing personal, you understand!'

'Do you expect the Kawawans to come after you?' Straight insisted.

'They might, yes.' MacGregor looked at his watch. 'Alright, Sergeant-Major, get everyone back in the vehicles and ready to move. Where do you blokes want to get to?'

'Well, after last night we certainly don't want to fall into the tender clutches of those boys again.' Jarvis had come up. 'Christ, I've got a lump on my head as big as a cricket ball. That bloke wot was leathering me had a bloody strong arm!'

'You could drop us on the border, but we have no passports so I don't know how we would get across,' Playfair said.

'I'd rather drop you off at the pub in Dodoma, as we go through.' MacGregor climbed into his seat and sat looking at them speculatively. 'The only thing is that you would all be back inside by tonight. Well, get in. I can't hang about here all day.'

They could feel the growing heat of the sun. In front of them, the great plains stretched away into a brown haze, empty apart from a few herds of thin cattle, scrounging a miserable living off the sparse scrub, and watched over by tiny naked boys with pot bellies, armed against marauders only with a stick. They watched the white men drive past in their strangely-striped vehicles in wide-eyed awe.

*

The news of the break-in at the Bank of Kawawa and of the battle outside Makonde Military Police camp did not reach General Kadongo's headquarters until after the General had left by helicopter for the battle front in the south. After the initial advantage of surprise had faded, the Kawawans, who had twice as many men, had pushed the invaders back over the border, capturing most of their transport and equipment. Only one pocket of resistance remained on Kawawan soil, and General Kadongo had given orders for it to be attacked and wiped out without delay. He ordered reinforcements from the capital and then flew back, happy with his day's work and in a jovial frame of mind. It did not last long after he reached his HQ.

The Chief of Staff started with the news of the battle outside Makonde, and the escape of the journalists, and only then worked his way nervously round to the disappearance of the gold.

'Did Your Excellency give any special instructions regarding the Bank?' he stammered.

'Special instructions?' The General's voice rose. 'What are you talking about, you idiot?'

Silently, the man handed over the letter that had been found on the night watchman. Kadongo read it slowly, his breath coming in gasps. Finally, he threw it on the table.

'You fool, it's a bluff . . . to gain time . . . for their getaway.' He rose menacingly. The Chief of Staff backed away.

'Do you know who the robbers are?'

'From what the watchman says and other information, we think it is the party of mercenaries who attacked Bomi, Your Excellency.'

'The mercenaries, of course . . . Where are they now?' The General's fury was just under control.

'We think they are driving south.' The officer's voice trembled.

'Well, then, don't stand there, send someone after them. The Special Operations Unit. Are they available?'

'I've already given the order, sir.'

The General stared at him.

'That gold must be recovered . . . I make you personally responsible.'

The Chief of Staff fell to his knees in fear, but the General walked round him and out of the room.

Broadside leant over to Playfair and spoke in his ear: 'This is a bloody odd safari, I can tell you that!'

'Why especially?'

'When I was coming back from breakfast, there were two types working on the ambulance. It got shot up last night and they were mending the bullet holes. I just happened to look in and one of them said something like: "If there's more shooting like last night I'm going to get behind this lot of gold!" So I pricked up my ears and said: "What do you mean, is it gold plated or something?" And he said: "Too bloody true, this whole lot is gold!" He said the whole truck was stacked with gold bars.'

'My God!' Playfair gazed out at the old ambulance lumbering along behind them with the French Legionnaire sitting upright at the wheel. Various things MacGregor had said began to fall into place . . . his touchiness . . . his secrecy . . . 'My God, it must be worth a fortune . . . where the hell did they get it from?'

Broadside shrugged. 'Before I could ask any more questions the big Sergeant-Major came up and told them to hurry up and finish the job. He obviously wasn't too keen on me hanging around the ambulance.'

'But where the hell did they get it from? They must have robbed a bank.'

'Or several,' Broadside laughed.

It was hot and cramped in the back of the Land-Rover and the glare outside was now intense. The only thing to do was to try to sleep.

Dodoma was a one-street town with a pub halfway down the left-hand side. The mercenaries looked longingly at the bar signs as they drove slowly past. But MacGregor stopped only at a petrol station to fill up all the vehicles and the spare jerry cans. It might be a long time before they reached the next one. MacGregor's main problem was to decide where to leave the main road and head across country. The Land-Rovers would be able to cope, but he was worried about the ambulance. He did not want a broken axle to add to his other problems. He would settle for a decent second-class road, and get as close to the border as possible. Then they could slip across using one of the game trails. A thought struck him. This was about the time of the migration, wasn't it? He consulted Gibson.

'Yes, should be starting any day now. I've been thinking about that too. Could be useful. Cover our tracks and provide some authentic research material.'

Jeremy Gibson permitted himself a rare smile.

'Where exactly does it run?' MacGregor asked.

'Well, it changes direction a bit from one year to another, but basically it runs from the south-east corner of the Lake in a north-easterly direction right up on to the plains. In other words if when we get about twenty miles from the border we turn east, we should run slap into it. If it has started, that is. It's an impressive sight, I can assure you of that . . .'

MacGregor looked over to MacLean. 'Anything in the rear mirror, Jock?'

'Nothing, surr, just the empty road.'

'How far are we from the border, Jeremy?'

'About two hundred miles. We might make it by noon tomorrow, with any luck.'

'Let's press on then.'

When dawn came, MacGregor's convoy awoke to one of the most remarkable sights left in Africa – the annual migration of the herds of plains game from their winter pastures round Lake Victoria to the sweet spring grass of the Serengeti. Playfair was up early and walked away from the convoy to a small rise. He shivered slightly in the chilly morning air. As he stood looking out over the plain he reflected that for perhaps a million years the zebra, wildebeeste, Thompson's and Grant's gazelles and a host of other antelope had made this trek across the Serengeti, obeying some deep-running instinct, pouring across the plains in their hundreds of thousands like some undammable flood. And now, he thought, man in his greed and thoughtlessness, in his hunger for land and in his carelessness of his natural heritage, might be about to destroy one of the last great wonders of the world.

But on the surface at least, this March was no different from any other on the great plains. The winter rains had been punctual and plentiful and the new grass was springing up succulently. The migration had started, obeying its own mysterious rhythm. To Playfair, trying to impress the whole scene on his mind's eye, it looked as if the entire plain were on the move, the current drifting slowly eastwards, the great mass of wildebeeste dark, almost black in the morning light, the zebra far out on the plain, a skein of marvellously variegated black and white. The herd sentries stood with heads up, nostrils inquisitively nuzzling the air, while the rest of the animals drifted slowly along, grazing peacefully.

Somewhere out there, on the outskirts of the herd, the predators would be waiting: lion, the colour of the old, dry grass, cheetah, that could out-run any antelope; and hyaena, always ready to cut down a straggler. Overhead, the vultures were already circling, their heads poking forward as they quartered the ground waiting for a kill or for a sick animal to die.

He turned and walked back to the Land-Rovers. The mercenaries who had camped in the open, beside the vehicles, were brewing tea and eating combat rations. Playfair spotted Gibson and MacGregor and headed in their direction.

'It really is a fantastic sight. There must be, what – four or five thousand animals out there, visible to us now?'

'More,' said Gibson, 'and think of all the thousands that are in front of them and behind. The migration covers miles and miles.'

'Never seen so much game in my life.' Even MacGregor, hard-bitten in all things, was noticeably impressed.

They drove all morning along and across the route of the migration, the herds parting quietly to let the vehicles go through. Occasionally a band of zebra would take fright and go galloping past, kicking up the dust. But mostly the animals stared for a moment at these strange neutral-smelling contraptions, and then, convinced that they posed no threat, dropped their heads again and went on grazing.

There was no way of telling where the dividing line of the border ran, since the plain looked the same for mile after mile. They had halted beside a slight mound to check their bearings, when one of the lookouts began to point excitedly. MacGregor lifted his binoculars. There they were, two, no three small smudges of dust, just visible on the horizon.

'Have a look, Jeremy.' MacGregor handed over his binoculars.

Gibson studied the dust clouds for about a minute.

'I can't see how many vehicles there are. I'd guess three or four and travelling pretty fast. I'm surprised Kadongo has taken so long to catch up with us. Maybe he's still having trouble in the south.' He handed the glasses back.

The two Frenchmen and Wagner were standing behind MacGregor, Wagner as usual stripped to the waist, his Iron Cross slung round his neck on a thin leather cord.

'How far away, *mon Colonel*?'

MacGregor had another look.

'About ten miles, I'd say, but they're heading this way, that's for sure.'

He turned and gestured across the plain to a blue shadow just visible in the distance.

'You see that *kopje*? That's the best defensive position for a hundred miles around. If we can get there we can hold the bastards off for ever.' He jumped into the driving seat and took the wheel.

'Jock, you look after the artillery. I'll drive.' It was smoother and flatter here and even the old Bedford ambulance made good speed, lurching along like a drunken elephant, under the command of its two French keepers.

It was about five when Kadongo's men caught up with them, and they were still a mile or two from the *kopje*. MacGregor was driving, with grim concentration, while MacLean had taken the outside left-hand seat, cradling the machine-gun in his lap. Then came the ambulance, swaying from side to side but still running strongly, followed by Sergeant Wagner in the second Land-Rover with MacGrath and Thompson, and finally, big Aldo with the two Afrikaaners in the last vehicle. The first burst of automatic rifle fire went harmlessly wide, so did the second and third, but the fourth actually splintered his nearside rearview mirror and caused Aldo to swerve and curse.

'Do something about dat bastard.'

Big Piet van der Merwe, who had been sitting stolidly in the back watching the efforts of their pursuers with an indifference that was almost contempt, took up his RPG or grenade launcher, an ingenious little weapon, made by the Americans, which looked like an overblown single-barrelled shotgun and could hurl a small grenade a couple of hundred yards. It could do plenty of damage, especially with a white phosphorus grenade. The phosphorus would eat into the skin like an acid and application of water merely increased the rate of burn. It would finally eat into the bone, a particularly unpleasant way to die. But Piet was firing high explosive. The first one fell short and wide to the left, making a harmless puff of dust in the grass. The second shot was also wide, the other way, but about the right distance.

'Christ, man, it is impossible with the blurry truck bouncing about like this,' swore Piet. He rammed a new shell into the breach, and fired angrily and almost carelessly into the air. It was a good one. You can just see the grenade in flight, if your eyesight is good enough, and Piet knew it was going to be close. He watched it with mouth open, his blond eyebrows frowning in concentration.

'Smack on, man!' There was a sizeable flash. For a moment the vehicle seemed unharmed, then the front exploded. Lumps of metal went shooting up like fireworks and oily black smoke rose into the air. The truck stopped and started to burn. The next truck, swerving to avoid it, overturned, and the third truck ran into the second. As Piet inserted a fresh shell, he heard the sound of the crash and saw a fresh burst of smoke and dust rise in the air. He turned excitedly to Aldo. 'Tell the Baas that I made a direct hit on their front truck. The second one overturned and the third one crashed into it. Do you hear, man?'

Aldo nodded, picked up the microphone and reported to MacGregor. The radio crackled back. 'Congratulations, Number Three, that's great news. Tell Piet he will get an extra ration of biltong tonight. Keep up the good work. Over and out.'

MacGregor radioed the other vehicles.

'MacGregor to all sets. Destination clearly in sight, approximately five miles. It's now five thirty, so estimate arrival around six. We will *laager* round the Red Cross vehicle, refuel and resupply before continuing towards our ultimate destination. Over and out.'

Broadside had been trying to make notes as they bumped along.

'Jesus.' He wiped his brow. 'If ever I get to a telephone, this will make the best splash we've had since the end of World War Two.'

'You'll never live to tell it,' said Straight. 'Kadongo will be down on us like a ton of shit tomorrow.'

'Ah, piss off,' snarled Broadside, putting his notebook away. 'You always were a pessimistic ponce!'

17

They camped under the majestic vault of the African night. Playfair was lying on his back and gazing upwards, listening to the small sounds of tired men getting ready to sleep. He felt insignificant and vulnerable. The immensity of Africa, like the immensity of the ocean, could have that effect. Far off there was a low coughing grunt and someone sleepily said: 'Lion.' The predators were on the move and some half buried instinct made Playfair give a little shiver of fear. Someone behind him spat and lit a cigarette. It was the mercenary who had been unlucky enough to draw the first turn of sentry duty.

The lion roared again in the distance, but the sound carried clearly. He must be hunting the migrating herds, far away on the other side of the *kopje*. From over there, too, would come the threat to the convoy. MacGregor had set departure for one, when the moon would be up. They needed every mile they could travel before sunrise . . .

It was downhill from the side of the *kopje* into the little rift, and then the climb began to the great flat plain they could not yet see. The stars were going out like snuffed candles and the sky began to turn pale in front of them. They drove slowly and carefully, eyes straining for the unseen pothole that could break an axle . . . The horizon began to glow and the sun came up over it with the dramatic suddenness that only occurs in the tropics.

They had been bumping and rattling their way across the plain for about three hours when MacGregor's radio crackled: 'Number Three to Number One, urgent! Two helicopters flying directly behind at about two thousand feet, range about three miles. Over.'

MacGregor passed on the warning to the other vehicles: 'Helicopters overhead, take evasive action.'

MacLean, who was at the wheel, drove another hundred yards and stopped. The other vehicles were fanning out around them making a loose circle. Playfair looked up. The menacing beat of the helicopters was very audible now. They started to tilt towards them in preparation for an attack, one lined up behind the other.

'Here they come,' shouted MacGregor, 'let them have it . . .'

The heavy machine-guns, three .30's and one .50 opened up, their heavy bark shattering what little was left of the peace of an African morning.

The helicopters steadied and hovered. The first pair of rockets were on them with a whoosh and ear-splitting crack, bursting between Wagner's Land-Rover and the ambulance, kicking dust high in the air.

The first helicopter wheeled away, but its door gunner kept firing. The second one was coming in, and everyone who was not actually shooting was trying to make himself as small as possible. Playfair and Straight had crawled under the Land-Rover and were peering out under the tail.

'Christ, here comes number two,' Straight ducked back and put his hands over his ears. Ther was a roaring noise like an express going into a tunnel, the same deafening crack and a terrific blast. Playfair looked up in time to see Wagner's Land-Rover receive a direct hit. Smoke and flames rose from the exploding vehicle. MacGregor was on his feet. So was MacLean, firing his machine-gun from his hip. It must have been a lucky burst. Just as the second helicopter was turning away, the tail rotor began to break up. The Alouette faltered, hung in the air for a moment and finally spun to the ground. Seconds later the fuel tanks exploded, and thick black smoke rose into the bright morning sky. One or two of the mercenaries cheered but MacGregor shouted: 'Look out, here comes the first bugger again.' MacLean was ready for it. He had his machine-gun on the bonnet of the Land-Rover this time, and started to fire steady bursts at the almost stationary helicopter. Several things happened at once. A puff of smoke, the roar, crack and blast of the exploding rockets, and MacLean's shout of triumph. He was standing there, his hairy torso bare, both hands in the air.

'I got him!'

The helicopter was trailing smoke and losing height. It came straight over them, see-sawing as the pilot fought to keep control.

'Come on, everybody,' shouted MacGregor, 'he's hit.'

He sent his Land-Rover careering up the hill in a cloud of dust. Just over the brow, the helicopter had crash-landed and was leaning drunkenly to one side on its smashed undercarriage.

The door gunner was waiting for them. As soon as he saw the two Land-Rovers come over the hill, he opened up with the heavy machine-gun. Bullets whined off the rocks like angry bees. MacGregor swung the wheel round sharply to get out of the line of fire, but the other Land-Rover was about ten yards behind and unable to stop. The heavy armour-piercing bullets cut through the metal body as if it had been a soup tin. Playfair who had followed on foot, saw the driver, one of the big Afrikaaners, take a burst in the chest and fall dead over the wheel. The vehicle swerved, hit a rock and overturned. Mac-Gregor waved to make everyone fan out.

'MacLean, grab some men and go round to the right and take them from behind. Jeremy, you work your way round to the left and keep that machine-gunner busy.'

A couple of grenades smacked down in the grass beside them and MacGregor moved farther back. MacLean crawled for fifty yards until he was behind a rock and stood up carefully, raising his M16. His first burst killed the officer who was crouching beside the helicopter; his second got the door gunner. One of the mercenaries hurled a couple of grenades into the smoking fuselage. A few more bursts and it was all over. Gibson and MacGregor walked towards the burning helicopter, safety catches off just in case. They counted five bodies, in or near the wreck.

'That must be all of them, but it was quite a sharp little dust-up while it lasted. Hallo, what's wrong with you, Sergeant-Major?'

'Just a bit of shrapnel in the shoulder, surr.' MacLean was holding his wounded shoulder with one hand, his face showing the pain.

'MacNab, over here,' MacGregor shouted. 'Bring your kit and bandage up the Sergeant-Major before he bleeds to death.' He turned to Gibson. 'What are your casualties?'

'Six dead, sir.'

'My God, as many as that?'

'Well, Aldo and the two Afrikaaners ran straight into that machine-gun, sir. The first helicopter scored a direct hit – Wagner, MacGrath and Thompson all killed. They can't have known a thing about it.'

MacGregor's face had gone white. 'How many wounded?'

'Three,' said Gibson. 'Sergeant-Major MacLean, Lorenzo hit in the leg, and one of the journalists, Broadside.'

'Broadside? Badly?' Straight asked.

'No, just a small piece of shrapnel in the backside which MacNab has taken out for him. He's over by the other Land-Rover, standing up.' That got a laugh.

'And equipment?'

'One Land-Rover written off, as you know, one damaged but serviceable, although it looks a bit like a pepper-pot. The other Land-Rover and the ambulance are okay.'

'Right, Lorenzo,' said MacGregor. 'I think it's time you made us a cup of tea, and see if there's any whisky left.'

'No whisky, *mon Colonel*, but some South African brandy I have.'

'Better than nothing. Get it out.'

Lorenzo limped away.

Playfair and Straight walked over to see Broadside. He was leaning against the side of the Land-Rover.

'How's the battle hero?' Straight towered over him.

'Not too bad,' Broadside grunted. He had a glass of brandy in his hand. 'Better after a glass of this. Here, help yourselves. Special medical ration.' He handed over the bottle.

'What happened?' Playfair asked.

'I dunno. I think it must have been a grenade, or else a bit of metal from the Land-Rover they shot up. All I know is that it felt as if someone had stabbed me in the arse. Bloody painful.' He swigged down his brandy. 'I'm going to lie down for a bit.'

'On your front, no doubt?' Broadside made a rude gesture. 'We'll have a look at the battlefield. See you later.'

Jarvis walked up. 'I got some fantastic shots of the action. Bodies all over the place. I've just been over to have a look at them. Not a pretty sight, but you ought to have a butcher's.'

'We're just going,' Playfair said.

'I'll come with you . . . hang on until I get some more film.'

He had borrowed Wagner's camera the day before. Now he would not have to give it back.

They walked through the knee-high grass, towards the burnt-out Land-Rover. The bodies of the dead mercenaries had been pulled out of the wrecked vehicle, laid on the ground and partly covered with a groundsheet. Sergeant Wagner's Iron Cross glittered defiantly in the sun. Between the Land-Rovers and the helicopter were four dead Kawawans. One man lay on his back, the others were face down. The fifth man was the door gunner, sprawled over his weapon. The pilot and co-pilot were still strapped in their seats.

The mercenaries were getting ready to bury their own dead, digging as deep as they could go in a hurry. A few rocks would serve as head-stones. The Kawawans they left where they had fallen.

'The hyaenas will get them,' MacGregor's face was taut with weariness, 'but there's nothing else we can do in the circumstances.'

Gibson nodded.

'By the way, Wagner's Iron Cross. He is still wearing it. Shall we bury him with it on?'

'Why not? He never took it off ever, did he? So why should we take it away from him now?'

They fired one volley over the grave in the grass. Then they moved off, a rather battered and depleted convoy now, heading east for the coast.

When they camped for the night, they had left the plains with their migrating herds far behind and were near the main road that runs to the sea. MacGregor invited the four journalists to a conference over a glass of South African brandy. He looked tired, his eyes bloodshot. 'You obviously have a tremendous story on your hands, the attack on the convoy, your escape . . .'

'And the gold . . .' said Broadside. He squatted, for obvious reasons.

'Ah, you know about the gold, do you? Who told you about that?' The voice was cold.

Broadside shrugged: 'I heard some of your men talking about it before the battle. They said the whole ambulance was full of it. Must be worth a fortune!'

'It is. Well, since the story must have leaked out of Kawawa by now, I might as well tell you about it.'

With some satisfaction, he related the story of the gold, how it had fallen into Kawawan hands, and how the mercenaries had sprung it from the bank.

'One thing is sure. Whoever the gold belongs to is a matter of argument, but it certainly does not belong either to the Simbas or to General Kadongo and his gang. In fact, I consider it a prize of war, and since we prosecuted the war against the Simbas I lay claim to it.'

'Doubt if that would stand up in a court of law,' objected Broadside with a sniff.

'Maybe not, but that is my position and I'm sticking to it.'

'What are you going to do with it?' Playfair asked.

'Now, that's the problem.' MacGregor stared at them slowly in turn. 'If I tell you that, I give my hand away, don't I? That would be foolish, very foolish at this stage of the game . . . So what I propose . . .' he paused and took a swig of brandy . . . 'What I propose is that you tell the story so far – all the basic facts must be out by now – but we shall have to put an embargo on publication for obvious reasons . . .'

'I don't agree with that . . .' Broadside was emphatic.

MacGregor held up his hand. 'Just a moment. I'm merely suggesting this to you as one solution. The alternative would be unpleasant for me, but if you force me then I have no option. I would have to keep you gentlemen . . . as my guests . . . until the operation is completed.'

The journalists looked at one another for a moment in silence. The night was full on them now, the stars brilliant in the great spread of sky. Playfair was the first to speak. 'Reluctantly, I think a voluntary embargo makes more sense than being forced to go to the bitter end of this thing as prisoners – with God knows what kind of outcome.' Everyone started to argue. Finally, Straight cut in: 'I agree with Alastair, as long as we all stick together on this embargo. That means, really, Bill, Alastair and myself, since Jimmy won't be filing copy. But he mustn't radio any pictures until the embargo is off. Agreed?'

But Broadside still wasn't satisfied: 'But we're leaving the story hanging in mid-air. Somebody's bound to try and get their hands on the sequel, and I can see us losing out. Simply because we're tying our hands behind our backs, Queensberry rules and all that crap.'

'Well,' Playfair said to MacGregor, 'that is a point. How long will the embargo be for?'

MacGregor cleared his throat. 'Look, the operation will go like this. We leave you tomorrow morning at Karobe, which, as you know, is virtually the first town of any size we come to. There's not a bad pub there where you can stay. I used to know the owner, a Greek, and if he's still there, he'll look after you. We will motor on and should be at our rendezvous by Friday, but give us twenty-four hours for contingencies, so let's say Saturday. I propose the embargo comes off at noon Saturday. I think that's reasonable.'

'I think that's a bloody cheek.' Broadside's face was red. He helped himself to another glass of brandy. 'Bloody sauce. What the hell are we supposed to be doing kicking our heels in some God forsaken pub in the back of beyond for four or five days? That's the best part of a week. Our offices must be going out of their minds as it is. I just don't think it's on.' He took a large swallow.

MacGregor was angry. 'If you are going to be bloody-minded, Mr Broadside, then you are going to leave me no choice. I'll have to insist that you come with us, as prisoners, and I cannot guarantee your safety . . .! Think it over. I have other duties to attend to. But I expect an answer tonight.' He stamped off into the darkness. As soon as he was gone, Jarvis spoke: 'What did he mean by that then . . .? Can't guarantee your safety . . . I don't like the sound of that very much . . .'

'What he is threatening,' Roger Straight said very slowly, 'is that unless we play along with him, he may feel himself obliged to take rather drastic action.'

'Meaning what?'

'Meaning knock us off.' There was a moment's silence.

'Aw, come off it,' Broadside snarled, 'he wouldn't bloody well dare.'

'Oh, yes he would.' Straight finished his brandy and got up. 'Just think of his position. First, we are the only ones who can identify positively who stole the gold from the Bank of Kawawa. The night watchman knew it was a bunch of whites, but can't possibly know any names or even probably give any meaningful description.

'If we go along as prisoners, but eye-witnesses on the last phase, and something goes wrong, I think he would bump us off to save his own skin. This man has killed lots of people. In hot blood, sure. But his blood might be hot at that particular moment. I think if you refuse his offer you are pushing your luck, and I for one intend to accept it.

'And anyway,' Straight coughed, 'once we are in Karobe and they've buggered off, he will have no further say . . .'

'Crafty sod!' Jarvis laughed.

Playfair was serious. 'I think Roger's right. Remember, it's not just MacGregor, there are a lot of pretty wild characters in this lot. Those Frenchmen would give you the chop as calmly as they would open a bottle of wine. These guys have been through a lot of danger, they are playing for very high stakes, and if they have to get rid of us they will. I'm sure of that. I don't think MacGregor wants to do it at all. Now he's got his loot he's all for the quiet life. But if we force his back to the wall . . .'

'What do you think his plans are?' Jarvis wanted to know.

Straight shrugged: 'I would think he will rendezvous with a fishing boat or some other innocent-looking craft at a quiet spot on the coast – there are plenty of them about – transfer the gold and then simply melt away.'

'He might well go with it,' Playfair chipped in. 'If I was in his boots, I would want to see it safely delivered, and I shouldn't want my imminent arrival splashed across the front page of every newspaper in the world. Come on, Bill, wake up, that's what's at stake for him . . . look out, he's coming.'

MacGregor came up, followed by Gibson. When he spoke, it was clear he was angry, but he had it under control. 'There's been a change of plan. I can't risk you breaking the embargo, not now. We've just heard on the BBC that a warrant is out for the arrest of a person or persons unknown for the break-in at the Bank of Kawawa. You will have to come with us, and I warn you, gentlemen, you will obey my orders or face the consequences. Goodnight.'

The journey to the coast was like a nightmare: it seemed to have no prospect of ever ending. They were only stopped once by an officious policeman in a small town who wanted to see their driving licences. He studied them carefully. MacGregor was convinced that his interest was due to the Kawawa robbery, but after several minutes he handed back the licences and saluted. MacGregor withdrew his hand which had been on the Smith and Wesson under the dashboard, and waved.

'Goodbye, you bastard,' he said cheerfully, 'you were beginning to make me sweat.'

Twenty miles from the coast, MacGregor turned off down a narrow, rutted dirt road that wandered through a string of sleepy African villages, over rickety wooden bridges and through dense banana plantations and mango groves. The heat was intense, the air heavy with humidity. It was like travelling through a lost underwater world.

Playfair, Straight, Broadside and Jarvis, the latter no longer so irrepressible, all travelled in the back of MacGregor's Land-Rover, squeezed together between MacNab and Stavros. The machine-guns had disappeared under the seats, but the journalists knew that both guards carried revolvers and were under orders from MacGregor to use them if they tried to escape.

'I wish this Greek would have a bath sometimes,' Straight muttered, wrinkling his nose. 'He's like one of those people in the TV ads that no one wants to be close to.' The hairy Stavros threw him a dirty look. He caught the drift if not the exact meaning. In front, MacLean had taken over again at the wheel and MacGregor and Gibson spent their time studying the map and talking in low voices. They stopped that night in a clearing only a few miles from the sea, as far as Playfair could judge. The palms and other vegetation reminded him of a place he had spent a holiday in a few years before, about a hundred miles north of Mombasa. It was a pretty wild spot.

'What do you think, Roger, it looks to me like the road to Tanu?'

'It all looks pretty much the same on this coast, but you could be right. We turned north off the main road, and we've come about fifty miles I guess. I shouldn't be surprised if we're near the rendezvous spot.' He dropped his voice. 'Walk over this way a little.'

Then turning his back to the convoy, drawn up in tight formation just off the dirt road, Straight pretended to be pointing up to a heavily-laden coconut palm.

'I have a very nasty suspicion that MacGregor will get rid of us tonight, before or after he loads his gold.'

'Why after?'

'Well, he might want us as hostages if anything goes wrong. Anyway, I can't believe that knowing what we do, he's going to let us walk away from this place, straight to the nearest cable head.'

Playfair looked round casually. Stavros was staring in their direction.

'Stavros has his eye on us. I've come to the same conclusion. I think we ought to tell the others to be ready to make a break for it *if* . . . *if* the opportunity arises.' He gave a bitter laugh. 'And if it doesn't . . . then perhaps we would have been better staying in that bloody jail. Let's go back. I'll talk to Jarvis, you tell Broadside.'

They turned and sauntered back under Stavros' suspicious stare. 'Nice evening,' Straight called to him. The big Greek spat and turned away with slow deliberation.

At about the same time that evening, five hundred miles away in Kawawa, Arabella came back from the High Commission to find Rahman waiting for her in the hotel. He had just been released from jail. Rumour had it that he had paid one million pounds as a ransom. Under his outwardly controlled manner, Arabella sensed his anxiety. She offered him a drink but he declined.

'I am leaving tomorrow for England.' He spread his hands. 'There is nothing left here for us now. I just wanted to tell you that I saw your friend in Makonde. We were in the same cell, Mr Alastair Playfair and myself. He talked about you, so I knew you were friends . . .'

Arabella grasped his arm.

'What has happened to him, and the others? We know they are no longer in Makonde, but no one seems to have any real information . . .'

'Well, I only know that they have escaped alive from the camp. I know that because I was awakened by the shooting that night, and although I did not see them, because they were in another cell, one of the guards told me that they had been . . .

roughed up a bit by the soldiers . . . but then when the mercenaries arrived outside the camp, and the shooting started, they were able to escape. So they got away safely . . . after that I don't know. But I should think they are with the mercenaries, possibly as some sort of hostages.' He kept his voice very low.

'What makes you so sure?' Arabella was unusually pale.

'I hear many things,' Rahman smiled. 'I do not know for sure, but I think the mercenaries must be making for the coast, and that if you want to find your friend, you should head in that direction too . . .'

Next day Arabella asked for a week's holiday. Sir Harry expressed surprise. She explained about Alastair and what Rahman had said. The old man looked at her fondly.

'My dear girl, take a week's official paid holiday. Go down to Mombasa, find out what's going on and keep us informed. You'll be more use down there than moping about here . . . We can always find a replacement for a week. You're not indispensable, you know!' Sir Harry came as near as he ever would to a knowing smile.

18

The two ships had come through the reef and anchored in a small bay. As they drove to the beach, a small headland jutted out into the sea on the left and on the right the pale sand stretched away in the moonlight. A few palm trees leaned over so far they almost trailed their fronds in the surf, luminous with phosphorescence.

One of the ships was a big motor-cruiser, about a hundred and twenty feet long, ghostly white in the moonlight, with a flying bridge, raked back funnel and spacious sun-deck aft.

'Just like Cannes in August,' whispered Jarvis.

'Keep quiet, you,' snapped MacLean. His shoulder was bandaged but he was still very much in charge.

The other vessel was completely different, a wooden-hulled Arab dhow, of the kind that have been plying for centuries between the Persian Gulf and East Africa, running guns and carpets over on the easterly monsoon, and sailing back on the westerly with ivory and in the old days slaves. Neither ship showed any lights.

MacGregor and Gibson walked forward to the edge of the surf.

'Congratulations, Jeremy,' MacGregor said. 'All that planning you did in the Ruwenzoris has paid off. Rendez-vous bang on time and the two ships look exactly right. Let's go on board . . .'

Sergeant-Major MacLean was lining up the remainder of the party.

'You laddies are going to have to do some work for a change,' he growled, looking at Broadside in particular. The ambulance was turned and backed down to the water's edge. The dhow, which had a shallow draft, had drifted in as far as she could, but was still twenty feet from the back of the ambulance and her deck was much higher. Playfair did not see how they were going to tranship the gold.

'It would be funny if they screw themselves at this point, and can't get the bloody stuff aboard,' he whispered to Straight.

They could hear MacGregor's voice giving orders aboard the dhow. Something that looked like a ladder started to come over the side. Playfair could see two seamen – they could have been Greeks but it was impossible to tell in that light – manhandling the thing. But instead of dropping over the side, it angled towards them. One of the seamen jumped into the water, and getting underneath it, manoeuvred it towards the back of the ambulance. MacLean shouted something and two of the mercenaries waded into the shallow water to help him.

'Come on, you scribblers, lend a hand,' roared MacLean, 'grab it and bring it to the tail of the ambulance.'

Playfair was up to the thighs in water when he suddenly realised what it was – of course, a conveyor belt, a black rubberised conveyor belt, on a metal frame. It was just long enough to reach the rear of the ambulance by about a foot. It would hardly have worked if the sea had been rough, but Mac-Gregor's luck was still holding, Playfair thought. MacLean was making the end secure, lashing it to the floor of the Bedford. There must be power of some kind at the other end, because when MacLean lifted his hand to give the go-ahead, the belt started to jerk away from them towards the dhow.

'Right,' commanded the Sergeant-Major. 'You two bonny lads,' pointing to Playfair and Straight. 'Get in there and help Stavros load the stuff. One bar at a time, and be careful you don't drop any in the water!'

Stavros was already inside the ambulance struggling to slide the first bars out of the solid wall in front of him; he panted with the effort. The first bar, a dull lump of metal in that pale, sea-washed light, thudded on to the conveyor belt and was carried away jerkily towards the dhow. The final stage of the operation had begun . . .

It took most of the night to shift the stack of gold. The conveyor belt broke down after a couple of hours, but Lorenzo, still limping proudly from his wound, fixed it after ten minutes.

'Thank God for old Lorenzo,' MacGregor said, looking up and down the shore. 'As long as he has a spanner and not a gun in his hand, he's a genius.'

The ambulance's wheels sank to the axle in the sand and by

the time the transhipment was two-thirds complete, the floor was almost awash. The angle of the conveyor belt grew steeper, and the bars, bouncing on the rubber as the exhausted men threw them down, climbed more jerkily to the dhow. MacGregor went aboard to inspect.

'How's it going, Jeremy?'

'Slow but sure, Colonel.' He looked at his watch. 'Another half hour should see us through, I think.' He wiped his forehead with his hand. They were standing looking down into the hold of the dhow. The conveyor belt poked through a hatch below them, and every twenty seconds or so deposited a golden ingot on to a thick sorbo rubber mat. Two large, powerfully-muscled Africans stood at each side and grabbed the bars alternately as they arrived.

Playfair had taken a risk and come on deck quietly behind MacGregor, without MacLean noticing. He peered cautiously past them and saw that there was in fact a second hold below the first. The two Africans lifted the bars from the rubber mat and put them on a chute which led down to the second hold. Playfair saw that there were at least two other Africans who were stacking the bars right down in the bottom of the boat.

'It certainly makes excellent ballast,' MacGregor was saying. 'What are you going to cover it over with?'

'Gravel, the normal ballast. They'll cover it over with six inches of that. Should do the trick unless they take her apart,' Gibson said.

'Not bad, I must say.'

A European came up and saluted MacGregor.

'Hallo there, Skip, I like your ballast idea . . .'

Skip Race was an old friend of MacGregor's and had handled his boat section in the Congo. He was a former warrant officer in the South African Navy and had bought and fitted out the dhow to meet MacGregor's specifications: range and performance, masked behind an innocent-looking exterior. He had recruited the Africans from the Comoro Islands. They were all fishermen and had been paid to keep their mouths shut.

Race grinned at MacGregor's compliment.

'We hope no one will inspect us that closely. In fact with any luck, no one should inspect us at all. We'll keep a little way off the main dhow route . . . we should be able to slip quietly into

Dhauli's private harbour around dusk one evening – and Bob's your uncle.'

Playfair eased himself gently backwards so that he was hidden by the shadow of the high stern, but could still overhear the conversation.

'Right, now listen carefully, this is how we will complete the final handover, Skip. When you are fifty miles off the Indian coast, you will radio me the agreed message. Okay?'

'Okay.'

'I will then send Dhauli a telex telling him the shipment is ready to be landed. Right? On receipt of that he will deposit the money in Switzerland and when I get confirmation I will immediately radio you to proceed. But only then. If anything goes wrong between that point and your handover to Dhauli, it is his responsibility. That's part of the deal. I've told him if he can't bribe the local Customs and police, he doesn't deserve to keep the gold. Any questions?'

'No, that's clear enough. But what's Dhauli going to do with all that gold, for crying out loud?'

'Don't you worry about Dhauli. He can look after himself. There are plenty of rich Indians who are desperate to get their hands on some gold and get the hell out of it. Dhauli will probably melt it down and sell it. The maharajahs and their friends will have it made into jewellery and smuggle it out like that. They're up to every dodge in the book and some that haven't been invented yet.'

'And you, Chief?'

'Well, we'll sail this little lot back as planned to Durban. What about the crew? Have you checked them out?'

'Yes, they're all okay. All South African. Of course they don't know anything about the gold. All they know is that you've had some difficulties with the local authorities and so you want to leave discreetly. She's a nice boat, you should enjoy yourself.'

'One thing,' said Gibson. 'Won't anyone be suspicious of all the modern equipment you've got on an old dhow like this?'

Skip laughed. 'Now that ivory is fetching astronomical prices, especially in India, lots of people in the business have diesels in their dhows. No, quite okay.'

'Fine.' MacGregor looked at his watch. Just on three. 'I'm

sending Major Gibson and Jock MacLean with you, in case you have to quell a mutiny. Major Gibson will be standing in for me. If you have any problems, consult him.'

'Right you are, Colonel.'

Skip knew that MacGregor really meant that the two would be keeping tabs on him and the gold. MacGregor did not take any chances.

'They'll be welcome aboard. Dhauli can fix them up to fly back.'

'Good.' MacGregor turned to look towards the shore. Playfair edged farther back into the shadow. He knew they would shoot him if they caught him now.

An African voice from below shouted something to Race. He translated.

'They've finished. Stacked the lot. Do you want to inspect, Colonel?'

'I certainly do.' MacGregor turned to Gibson. 'And then we'll have to deal with that other matter – our four friends.' He went down the ladder.

Playfair shivered despite the stickiness of the night. He swung over the side of the dhow, dropped into the surf and waded ashore, slipping past MacLean who was busy at the back of the now-empty ambulance. The others were standing a little apart, by themselves.

'Where the hell have you been?' Jarvis hissed at him.

'Tell you later. We've got to get out of here, they're going to bump us off. I've just heard MacGregor say so.' They crowded round him.

'How do you know? What did he say? When?'

'Now. He told Gibson he was going to deal with us right away – our four friends, he said. Come on, we've got to get cracking. Make a run for it.'

'How, through the bush?'

'Any way. Where's MacNab?'

'He's buggered off somewhere.'

'Let's go then, for Chrissake. But not all at once.'

Straight waited until MacLean and the rest of the mercenaries were busy around the dhow. He walked carefully, almost sauntering to the edge of the deep shadow under the palms, away from the brightness of the sand and the dim light inside the ambulance. Playfair and Broadside followed, about ten yards apart. Finally, Jarvis, after a careful look around, ran silently over the sand.

'Right, let's get down the road as fast as we can.' Straight broke into an easy jog trot and the rest followed him. Within fifty yards they could no longer see the beach over their shoulders, and after a hundred yards, the beat of the surf was faint. After four hundred yards Broadside dropped back to a walk, gasping.

'Christ, I can't fucking well . . . huh, huh . . . run all night . . . shit . . .'

They had walked for about twenty yards when they heard faint shouts behind them, followed by the dry crackle of an Uzi sub machine-gun.

'Christ, they're after us.' Jarvis broke into a run. He, Playfair and Straight were all fairly fit. But Broadside's asthma made running for more than a few yards a torture.

'Go on,' he gasped. 'Carry on without me . . .'

'Don't be bloody silly,' snapped Playfair, 'we're all sticking together.'

They walked and ran and walked again. There was another burst or two of gunfire, but clearly they were shooting at random. Straight called a halt and held up his hand.

'Listen . . .'

There was no sound except the soft swish of the wind in the big trees and the stealthy movement of the African night. A fire-fly shone suddenly green above the road.

'They must have gone by now!' Playfair finally broke the silence.

'How do you know they're not following us?' Jarvis demanded.

Straight shook his head. He had fought in the Malayan jungle and the others deferred to his military knowledge.

'I don't think so, but what we'll do is sit over here behind this big mango for ten minutes and rest. If they are coming down the road, we'll hear them.'

They moved off the road and sat down gratefully.

Broadside was still panting.

'Where the hell do you think we are?'

'No idea,' said Straight. 'What do you think, Alastair?'

'I still think we are somewhere near Tanu, and this is the main coast road, such as it is. If we keep going we will come to something – a crossroads, a signpost, a village, or something.'

'You're a bloody optimist.' Jarvis laughed. 'There's nothing here but miles and miles of fuck all.'

'Well,' said Straight, 'we can't sit here all bloody night. It's more than ten minutes since we stopped, and there's no one behind us.'

They listened for another minute, but there was no sound of pursuit.

'Come on then. Let's keep a good steady pace . . . Bill, give us a song . . .'

'Piss off. I need all the breath I've got.' They fell into step, the road a pale blur in front of them, the jungle a dark mass on either side. The moon had set, so they only had the faint glow of starlight to help them. Luckily the road was fairly smooth. They walked briskly, in silence.

After a few miles, Playfair had hardly any feeling in his feet. They had gone numb. But the farther you walked the more you were able to develop a rhythm, and the less conscious you grew of distance.

There seemed to be no habitation of any sort, no villages, not even a house. After perhaps five miles, they saw a tiny, shaky point of light coming towards them wavering about from side to side.

'Hallo, what's this?' Broadside stopped. 'A search party?'

It turned out to be a solitary bicycle.

'Which way to Tanu?' Straight called.

But the African gave one terrified glance at the strange posse of white men walking through the night and sped on.

Conversation died after that. Everyone was concentrating on keeping his legs moving. From time to time they rested but they were beginning to stiffen up, and it became increasingly difficult to resume the march. Broadside was starting to hobble.

They must have covered about ten miles, Playfair estimated, when from somewhere in front of them an unmistakable rattle approached. It came closer. Then round a bend in the road two flickering headlights appeared.

Jarvis gave a faint cheer.

'Maybe they'll give us a lift.'

They stood in the middle of the road, blocking it. The car stopped and a scared African face appeared through the window.

'Can you take us to Tanu?' Straight asked in Swahili. 'We are all very tired. We'll pay you well.'

The African swallowed nervously. 'Tanu is that way, the way you are walking, bwana.'

'How far?'

'Eight miles, bwana.'

'Well, if you turn round and give us a lift there we'll give you a lot of money. Fifty pounds!'

There was a pause. The African licked his lips. He was obviously impressed.

'It's not that, master. The car is very old. She will go downhill to my village. But I don't think she will manage to go uphill, not with four passengers. I am sorry, master, but it is not possible.'

There was a longer pause. The car indeed was very ancient. The engine coughed and wheezed like an elderly patient with TB.

Reluctantly, the four tired and footsore men accepted that their path lay uphill, and that they would have to negotiate it under their own steam. As the old crock rattled off down the road, headlights flickering weakly, they turned without a word and resumed their painful progress.

It was dawn when they finally saw the outskirts of Tanu, a small fishing village with a Portuguese fort gazing peacefully over the harbour. All of them were so stiff and sore, they could hardly complete the last half mile to the Fort Tanu Hotel. It was one of those pioneer African hotels which scorned modern plumbing. The shower was worked by a boy who carried buckets of water up to fill the tank and the actual shower was a watering-can rose. Most of these old places had disappeared, and been replaced by impersonal, air-conditioned boxes, in which the innocent traveller was trapped like a fly in a bottle. But Fort Tanu still flourished in all its eccentricity. The sight of four footsore tatterdemalions arriving at breakfast-time did not seem to surprise the aged English proprietor: nor the fact that they went straight to bed as they were, without a shower. They were all so exhausted that they made a mutual pact to sleep first and file later.

Playfair woke first. He looked at the window, saw it was late afternoon, and then at his watch. It read five thirty. For a moment he had that disorientated feeling that comes on waking in a strange room, then he remembered the events of the previous day. He tried to swing his legs over the side of the bed. The pain made him groan. He looked at his feet. They were badly swollen. It was those damned gym shoes. He walked to the door, his calves feeling as if they were encased in iron. He walked slowly to the window and back again, and the stiffness began to ease slightly. Playfair stopped in mid-stride. The full impact of the situation had just struck him. MacGregor and the rest of them had something like fourteen hours' start. They were getting clean away with it. And here they all were sleeping it off like drunks. He swung open the door, and found himself in a dim corridor. Which rooms were the others in?

'Roger . . .? Bill . . .?'

He heard a muffled voice reply, and steered towards it. Number 24. He opened the door. Roger Straight was sitting up in bed, naked to the waist. He had obviously just woken up.

'Christ, I'm stiff. Aow! What time is it?'

'Half past five – in the evening. Do you realise MacGregor and that dhow have been under way for about fourteen hours now? Getting right away with it? While we've been in bed?'

Straight flung off the bed clothes and stood up. He gave a yelp of pain and tried to walk.

'Listen, we've got to decide what we're going to do, and do it fast. Do you agree?'

'Yes, but what?'

The noise of their voices had woken the others.

'What's all the noise about? God! My legs are bloody sore!'

Broadside came into the room limping and rubbing his eyes. Jarvis was obviously the fittest. His step was still fairly springy.

'Have a seat,' Straight said to no one in particular. 'Now that we're all here, Alastair and I were just saying that we have a decision to make. MacGregor and Co have fourteen hours' start on us. They've been sailing the Indian Ocean in comfort, while we sweated our way through last night.'

'So what's the bloody decision?' Broadside growled.

'He does a good impersonation of a grizzly bear, doesn't he?'
Straight grinned at the others.

'It's this,' Playfair interrupted. 'Do we now all sit down and
write our pieces?'

'Yes!' snapped Broadside.

'. . . and leave the story there, for other people to follow up in
India, South Africa or wherever . . . or . . . or do we try and
follow it up?'

'What do you mean exactly by "follow it up"?' Broadside
asked.

'Well . . . if we were to tell, for example, the Government or
the local authorities, now, we could possibly stop the gold
reaching India, and . . .'

'How can you interfere with a cargo on the high seas?'
Broadside interrupted.

'I don't know. I'm simply thinking aloud.'

'And what do you mean by the Government? The British
Government?'

'Yes.'

'You must be joking,' said Jarvis. 'They've never been known
to do anything positive if they could possibly avoid it.'

'Just a minute.' Straight held up his hand. 'An old chum of
mine, Jimmy Brander, is one of our spooks at the Embassy
here. I could ring him up and give him the story.'

'What would be the advantage of that? He'd probably tell
you not to print it. You know what they're like.' Broadside was
still sceptical.

'Well, I still think it's worth a try,' Playfair said. 'It
might have to go as high as the Foreign Secretary, or the
Cabinet. But if we give them chapter and verse, and our papers
carry the story too, they might well act, I think. After all,
clearly there has been a major robbery, not of private money,
but of state funds, in some shape or form – whether they belong
to the Belgians, or the Congo, or Zaire. It's the sort of thing
that could go before an international court . . .'

'Precisely.' Broadside was still unconvinced. 'You'd look
bloody silly if you forcibly boarded a ship on the high seas –
which is piracy – and then failed to prove that the gold is being
transported illegally.'

'That's simple, surely. All you would have to do is to show

that the gold never left the country legally. It came in illegally from Kawawa, and went out illegally . . . and there is a warrant out for MacGregor, as he told us himself the other day . . .'

'Person or persons unknown . . .'

'So he's arrested on suspicion of being that person. In other words you get MacGregor and the gold in one.'

Straight lifted the receiver by his bed.

'Hallo, operator? Get me the British Embassy in Nairobi, would you? Urgent press call. Yes, urgent press. How long will it take? One hour . . .? Ask the exchange if they can give me priority, would you? Thanks.' He turned to the others. 'He'll do his best, he says.'

'Well,' Broadside rubbed his nose and sniffed, 'we're not exactly at the centre of affairs in this bloody place. Let's have a drink.' He got awkwardly to his feet and rang for the room boy. When he appeared, Broadside ordered in his gruff voice.

'Two whiskies, please. One gin and tonic. Make them large . . . and one beer.'

The operator must have been unusually efficient. The call to the Embassy came through in less than half an hour.

'Must be an all time record,' Straight muttered. 'Hallo, British Embassy? I would like to speak to Mr Brander, please, Jimmy Brander. Can you put me through to him?'

In the silence of the room, they could hear the Embassy exchange quite clearly.

'Hold on, sir, I'll see if he's in . . . who's calling?' Straight told him. In a moment, another voice came on the line.

'Brander here.'

'Roger Straight here, Jimmy. I'm speaking from Tanu.'

'Good God! What a pleasant surprise. What are you doing in Tanu? Holiday?' The voice was thin, but clear. Straight looked at his three weary companions and winked.

'Not exactly. It's a long story. Have you got a couple of minutes, and I'll tell you . . .'

'Fire ahead . . .'

A minute later, the voice at the other end broke in . . .

'Hold on . . . I've got all that, and perhaps it'll surprise you, perhaps it won't, but we know something about this one. Quite a lot in fact. Look, Roger, I don't want to say too much on the open line for obvious reasons, but we have been asked to help. I can tell you that . . . and we are about to try and do something about it.'

There was a brief pause.

'I'll tell you what, Roger, I'll have to consult the Ambassador, but I think we might be able to get you out to the scene of the crime tomorrow, if that suits you? Would you be interested?'

'We certainly would!' Straight looked at his friends. 'More than interested!'

'Yes, well, I thought you might. We were going to leave tonight, but the Navy has some problem, so we'll be setting off about ten in the morning. Why don't I send up a light aircraft for you at, say, eight – bring you down to Mombasa and we'll set off together? We'll need you anyway as material witnesses . . . identify the dhow and so on . . .'

'Sounds perfect . . .' Straight looked round the nodding faces of his friends . . . 'Yes? Surprisingly, for once we're all in agreement.'

'I'll call you back as soon as I can, what's your number there . . .?'

'Right,' said Broadside, after Straight had rung off, 'I'm off to do my journalist of the year award piece. This Navy thing's a bit of luck. Not that we've had too much of it lately. By the way, how long is it going to take to get through to London?'

'I don't know. I'll ask.' Straight got the switchboard again and asked the same helpful operator. He put his hand over the mouthpiece. 'About two hours, he says, if the circuit is good.'

'Ask him to get my number, would you?' Playfair and Broadside both spoke at once. Straight laughed. The competitive urge was always there, but sometimes it revealed itself more nakedly than at others. Now that each of them had a scoop, and a particularly glittering one at that, the bonds of friendship were coming under exceptionally severe strain. Only Jarvis, unable to do anything about his pictures, was relaxed.

'I'm going to have a drink at the bar,' he announced. 'The sound of your typewriters will be sweet music in my ears.'

'Typewriters?' said Broadside. 'What bloody typewriters? There's only one typewriter in this hotel, and I've already borrowed it! Everyone else will have to print it out in capitals!' He went off triumphantly.

'Trust him to get in first,' said Playfair. 'But when the hell did he manage to grab the typewriter?'

'Don't worry,' said Jarvis. 'The housekeeper has a portable and I'm sure she'd let you borrow that.'

'Hey, wait a minute, how do you know she's got a portable . . . ?'

'I saw it in her room . . .'

'When were you in her room . . .? Oh, never mind . . .'

'She's a nice bit of stuff,' said Jarvis. 'Comes from Tunbridge Wells . . . See you boys later.'

Playfair and Straight sat looking at one another.

'Christ almighty! What are we doing looking after these two shits?' Straight fingered his moustache crossly. Then he laughed. 'We'd better get that portable before bloody Jarvis and the housekeeper retire for the night.'

'I'll toss you for first go,' said Playfair.

They had all filed, and been greeted by their offices with that mixture of cloying congratulation and calculated self-interest that marks the news business, when Brander finally called back.

'Hallo, Roger – Jimmy here again. I've managed to track the Ambassador down at some Upper Volta cocktail party and he agrees, but on one condition . . .'

'What's that?'

'That you don't publish until the operation is over . . .'

'We've already filed the story about MacGregor and the gold getting to the coast. You can't embargo us from using our own material.'

'No, no quite. But we don't want any leak of the Navy operations, that's all. And, as soon as it's over, we'll get you back as quickly as possible, probably chopper you back in fact. Okay?'

'Sounds fine.'

'One other thing. I've fixed the plane. It will be an *Air Tiger*, six-seater Cessna, and he'll be there in time for you to leave at eight. I'll see you down at the dock. Good luck.'

19

The Cessna bumped over the grass strip, gave a lurch and they were airborne. Playfair looked at his watch. One minute after eight, not bad. They turned and headed south, flying just inside the shore line. To their left, the Indian Ocean was a huge expanse of cobalt blue, veined and seamed with aquamarine close inshore. Playfair looked for the gap in the reef where the dhow and the cruiser had moored the other night, but it could have been any one of several small breaks. The reef itself was a thin line of dazzling white foam, but inside the lagoon, the shallow water was like a Hockney painting. To their right, the coastal fringe of palms and mangoes made a thick green mat to the horizon. After half an hour, the deserted beauty of the coast began to give way to roads, hotels and finally the docks and dirty white go-downs of Mombasa. They circled the town and came down on the tarmac, rolling to a stop among a clutch of other light planes. The airliners were parked a few hundred yards away.

'We'll have to walk over to the terminal. No buses, I'm afraid,' the pilot apologised.

'Don't worry, mate, we like walking.' Jarvis was his old chirpy self.

But they didn't have to walk all the way. A black Ford, flying a Union Jack, came cruising up. A rating put his head out of the window.

'Mr Straight, sir? Mr Brander is expecting you.'

They drove through the main airport gate, down a long avenue lined with palms and into Mombasa itself, past the Governor's residence, the old colonial buildings waging a losing battle against the new concrete, and finally reached the docks.

A sign read: East African Naval Headquarters. No entry. The driver said something to the sentry on the gate and the barrier swung up. At the end of the dock they could see the

long racy shape of one of Her Majesty's destroyers. At the top
of the ladder, Brander was waiting for them.

'Nice to see you again, Roger . . . you boys do look as if you'd
been sleeping rough for a couple of weeks, but come and meet
the captain – he's a bit anxious to cast off.'

The captain was small and very much in command. He
wanted all the information they had about the dhow and the
cruiser. After they had told him what they knew, he led the
way over to a big chart of the Indian Ocean.

'We're here,' he put his finger on Mombasa, 'and we reckon
that our friends in the dhow should be about here.' He moved
his finger to a spot well out to sea, north-east of Mombasa.

'How far's that?' Straight asked.

'About three hundred and thirty miles, three hundred and
fifty maximum. We reckon the dhow does about ten knots, and
what you've told us about her would tend to confirm that. Now,
we do forty knots when at full speed, so we should reach their
current position about six p.m. However, they will have gone
another ninety miles or so in that time, so we wouldn't catch up
with them until about eight p.m., when it will be dark. No
doubt our friends will be travelling without lights, so the
chances of finding them will be zero.' He looked at Brander.
'What I plan to do therefore is to reduce speed to ten knots
when we've reached what we calculate is their position and
wait for first light . . .' He glanced out of the porthole.

'We're on our way, gentlemen.' The harbour installations
were slipping smoothly past the side.

'Let's go up on the bridge, you'll get a better view from
there.'

They were picking up speed fast, the bows cutting through
the glassy blue water and sending up two smooth white arcs.
The ship began to tremble slightly like a greyhound on the
leash, as the engines drove her to full speed. Ahead of them the
Indian Ocean stretched away, empty and serene.

The captain looked at his ragged guests as if noticing their
true state for the first time.

'My God,' he said to Brander. 'You'd better take them below
and get them some clean kit. I'll see you all later.'

Half an hour later, fitted out in a variety of naval cast-offs,
they headed for the wardroom and a briefing by Brander.

'The first thing we knew was what we read in the local papers – that someone had broken into the Bank of Kawawa and made off with a lot of loot. At first, the Kawawa papers did not mention gold. That came out down here. They were a bit careful too, saying that it was believed a shipment of gold bullion was involved.'

A steward appeared and Brander ordered pink gin all round.

'It was all very garbled but we ferreted around and more or less got the facts – I want to check some of them with you in a minute. Then we got an official request through the people here, on behalf of the Kawawans, asking us to intervene . . . This had to go to London, where they chewed it over for a day or so, but obviously a request like that from a . . . friendly . . . government has to be acceded to, if it's humanly possible. So we set up this operation . . . luckily the Navy happened to be passing by, and then up you came out of the blue . . .'

Brander took a sip of his drink and consulted his watch.

'We have an hour or so before lunch – the captain has asked us to join him – so I want to hear everything from start to finish that you people have been up to. From the moment you ran into MacGregor . . . but first, steward . . . recharge these thirsty officers' glasses, would you?'

All afternoon the destroyer ploughed through the calm blue of the Indian Ocean. They did not see a single dhow. The captain explained that they were outside the traditional monsoon route. Apart from a couple of tankers and one merchantman heading for Lourenco Marques or Durban, they had the ocean to themselves. After dark Captain Mumford doubled the radar watch. He did not want to run the dhow down and send her to the bottom with all her gold. At a quarter to eight, the time when the navigators reckoned they should catch up with the dhow, he rang down for ten knots, and they idled forward quietly for the rest of the night.

The four journalists, still feeling the effects of their imprisonment and long march, went to bed early.

'Call us if anything happens, won't you?' Straight asked Brander.

'Don't worry, I wouldn't dare let you sleep. But I don't think we'll have any excitement until the morning.'

At 0715 the radar operator on the bridge turned to the captain, who had been on deck since dawn: 'I have a trace, sir, about ten miles, sou' sou' east . . .' Captain Mumford walked over to the hooded set and watched the electronic band sweep the dial. As it turned, a rash of green dots flared into life and then died down.

One dot, slightly bigger than the rest, glowed more strongly. Whereas the other flecks on the screen could be waves or clouds, to the trained eye, this was a ship: a small one, but undoubtedly, a ship.

The captain gave orders for the lookout on the mast to be alerted. A message came back almost immediately: 'He says he has her, sir. Looks like a small fishing vessel.'

The captain adjusted course and rang for full speed ahead. He turned to the rating beside him: 'You better tell Mr Brander and his four friends to get up here sharpish.'

When they were about two miles from the dhow, the captain ordered action stations, and told the boarding party to stand by.

'Is that your friend?' Mumford offered Straight his binoculars.

'Hard to say. We only saw her at night. But certainly looks much the same.' He handed back the big Zeiss glasses.

'Well, you'll notice that although she has her sail up, she's really being driven along by quite a powerful engine.' The captain studied her carefully.

'Can't see anyone about, though . . .'

They were within half a mile or so now. Captain Mumford rang down to reduce speed. The destroyer's way was such that she continued to bear down on the dhow, which still showed no signs of life but kept ploughing steadily on.

The semaphore on the bridge began to wink. Still the dhow took no notice.

'I'm telling her to heave to, but she's paying no damned attention. Right, my beauty, I shall have to come alongside.'

The destroyer began to close the gap: two hundred yards, a hundred and fifty, then a hundred yards, and finally fifty. She loomed over the dhow menacingly.

Captain Mumford went out on the flying bridge and raised a loud-hailer.

'Ahoy there, this is HMS *Banshee* . . . I am ordering you to heave to and let us come aboard . . .' He spaced the words out carefully.

Silence, except for the hiss of the destroyer's bows through the water. No movement aboard the dhow.

'That's bloody funny.' The captain studied the dhow through his binoculars again. 'There's no one at the wheel. She must be on automatic . . .' He hailed her again. Still no response.

'Very well, if that's the way they want it. Number one gun, stand by to fire one shot across her bows . . .'

'Standing by, sir.'

'Fire!'

A little puff of smoke billowed out forward, was swept away in the wind, and followed by a sharp crack. Playfair heard a tinny rattle.

'Look out, they're shooting at us!' the captain said casually.

A wild figure had appeared on the deck of the dhow, dressed only in a kilt, bare to the waist, and balancing a machine-gun on his hip. As Playfair watched he saw the muzzle flash and ducked involuntarily. Faint stars appeared on the bullet-proof glass of the bridge.

'Number one, fire single rounds at the wheel house – I don't want to sink her, is that clear?'

'Aye, aye, sir.'

The twenty-five-pounder began to bang shells at the wheel-house of the dhow. The range was absurdly close and it began to break up like matchwood. MacLean was standing in the lee of the wheel-house, still shooting. He was aiming at the twenty-five-pounder, and shouting into the wind, waving one arm in the air and then firing another burst.

'He's gone bonkers,' Straight said, 'he thinks he can take on a destroyer single-handed.'

The twenty-five-pounder barked again and the rest of the wheel-house was blown away.

'Stop firing!' roared Captain Mumford.

There was a pause as the shattered dhow seemed to slow down and started turning in a wide circle. The destroyer shadowed her like a watchful collie.

The jet roar of a low-flying aircraft took them all by surprise. It came over the stern of the destroyer and then right over the dhow at about a hundred feet, so close Playfair got a glimpse of a goggled face, a black face he thought, peering down. It was an old Hunter that must once have belonged to the RAF, but was now painted with the Kawawa colours.

'Stand by air defence,' Mumford shouted. 'Fire warning bursts under him but don't hit him for Christ's sake . . .'

The Hunter did a tight turn and came back heading for the dhow, which was still moving in a wide curve over the placid ocean. Puffs of ack-ack burst just below the Hunter, but the pilot held his course.

'He's going to let her have it . . .' Mumford darted outside on to the flying bridge.

As the Hunter raced low over the dhow, two small bombs detached themselves from the fuselage and hung in the air for a second. Two spouts of water exploded on either side of the dhow, inundating the bows and drenching MacLean who was still straddling the deck with his machine-gun. The Hunter went into a steep climb and turned back into the sun.

Captain Mumford shaded his eyes.

'He's going to have another go. 'It'll be his last chance, he can't be carrying more than two sticks.'

Playfair was also watching the dark speck move across the sun and then turn for his second run. He came down like a *kamikazi* so low that he almost clipped the wave tops.

'Christ, he'll land up in the drink at that rate.'

Captain Mumford ordered his ack-ack guns to hold their fire and kept the destroyer at a safe distance. MacLean, his kilt drenched in spray, still stood on the open deck. Gibson, whom they could see crouching near the bow with a machine-gun over the gunwale, was waving to him to take cover. But MacLean seemed oblivious.

As the Hunter levelled out and came straight for the dhow, MacLean fired a long burst . . . then another . . . The Hunter was so low Playfair hardly saw the bombs fall before a bright orange ball of flame enveloped the dhow. The blast buffeted the windows on the bridge of the destroyer. A secondary explosion lifted the burning dhow out of the water. The Hunter was already well clear of the dhow, and was climbing steeply when it suddenly exploded. It hit the sea from two hundred feet, sending up a great spout of water and a little grey smoke which drifted over the glistening wave tops. Captain Mumford swung the *Banshee* hard about.

'All hands look out for survivors.'

The destroyer cruised slowly through the still smouldering bits of wreckage towards the Hunter. The old fighter was nose down in the glassy swell, its tail sticking high out of the water. Steam curled up from the submerged nose: it would not be long before it sank.

'Hurry up,' Captain Mumford shouted through his loud-hailer. 'Get that ruddy boat into the water . . .'

The chief petty officer had his boathook out and was fishing for something near the cockpit, now awash. After several minutes of struggling and swearing, he hauled a yellow object into view.

'They've got the pilot, sir,' the young officer of the watch reported.

Mumford lifted the hailer.

'Pull him aboard and get away before she sinks . . .' The petty officer and the four ratings in the dinghy had a struggle to get the yellow-suited body aboard. The pilot was exceptionally big and the flying suit had inflated on impact to make him look like a Michelin Man.

They were halfway back to the destroyer when the tail of the Hunter lifted in the air like a swallow diver and then plunged. As the seawater poured down into the still white-hot jet engine, there was a muffled explosion and the water boiled. The tail plane slid out of sight, the surge subsided and all that was finally left on the surface was a patch of oil and what looked like some first-aid packs.

Playfair looked across the sea to where the dhow had sunk. Another of the *Banshee*'s boats was scooping up the fragments, but there was not much left. Certainly no gold floating about. He brought his attention back to the boat that was being hoisted aboard the *Banshee*. Captain Mumford left the bridge and marched aft, the journalists and Brander following him.

The dripping, yellow-suited figure was just being dumped on the deck. Captain Mumford jumped the pools of water.

'Turn him over, chief petty officer,' he ordered, and the chief and a rating heaved together.

With a squelch and a sigh from the deflating flying suit, the body rolled slowly over. Playfair spoke first: 'Good God, it's the General!'

The broad, thick features, although squashed up in the tight-fitting flying helmet, were unmistakable. The General was wearing a battledress tunic with red and gold shoulder tabs and a chestful of medals. Captain Mumford suddenly bent down.

'What's this, the Victoria Cross?' He made it sound like a nasty disease.

'Yes, he awarded it to himself when he made himself up to General.' Playfair's tone was matter-of-fact. The others laughed.

Captain Mumford was on one knee, unpinning the purple ribbon. He turned the medal over in his hand.

'As I thought, won by someone quite different in the Zulu Wars.'

'May I ask, Captain, what you intend doing with that VC?' Broadside tilted his nose up belligerently.

Mumford looked round at them in turn – Broadside, Straight, Playfair and Jarvis, who had just sneaked a picture.

'Identification purposes, that's all, Mr Broadside. Just to be sure it is General Kadongo.'

'It wouldn't be because you resent somebody like Kadongo awarding himself the VC, would it?' Broadside persisted in his gravelly voice.

'Good Lord, no.' Mumford looked at him with eyes that were wide with feigned innocence. 'Whatever put that idea into your head?'

'It is General Kadongo, definitely, sir.' The chief had gone through the dead man's pockets and laid his possessions on a dry bit of deck: a heavy pilot's wristwatch; a gold Cross pen, a lion's claw bracelet, a handful of what looked like official papers, and a handsomely-bound diary with E.C.K. stamped on it in gold. Inside was printed the legend:

'General Edward Chaka Kadongo, VC, MC, DSO, and bar, President for life of the Republic of Kawawa.'

'Right,' said Captain Mumford, slipping the VC into his pocket. 'Take the body down to the sick bay, and tell the MO to stick it in the morgue. No doubt the Kawawans will want the General back so as they can do the full honours.'

'What about the VC?' grunted Broadside.

'Never give up, do you?' Mumford grinned. 'I'll tell you later, if you're lucky. But first of all, let's get a report on the dhow. Where's Lieutenant King?'

'No survivors, sir,' the officer of the watch saluted. 'We've got a lifebelt and one or two bits of wood on board as evidence but there's no sign of any bodies, not even a piece of clothing. They must have been blown to bits, sir.'

'Spare us the gory details, Lieutenant. Right, set course for Mombasa, fifteen knots and make a signal to the Admiralty saying we found the dhow, but that the gentleman in the Hunter got in before us. Kawawa Air Force markings. No survivors. Say nothing about the pilot for the moment, except that he's dead.'

'Aye, aye, sir.'

'My God!' Broadside spoke like a man waking from a long sleep. 'What about all that gold?'

'Gone,' said Mumford dryly. 'Just about the deepest hole in the Indian Ocean. The Americans might get it with one of their deep recovery submarines, but I think it would be a tough job . . .'

'Can I ask you one thing, Captain?'

'Certainly, Mr Playfair.'

'Why did you tell Lieutenant King to report the death of the pilot but not his identity?'

'Well, frankly, gentlemen, I thought we might do a deal.' He glanced at Broadside and continued. 'If you were to forget about General Kadongo's VC or say it seemed to have got lost in the regrettable circumstances of his death, I am prepared to give you gentlemen a . . . er . . . beat, I believe you call it, on the subject of the General's identity. You put it out before the MOD does.'

Playfair, Straight and Jarvis all smiled broadly. Even Broadside raised a chuckle.

'Not bad, not bad at all.'

'And now, gentlemen, I invite you to seal the pact by being my guests in the wardroom.' He turned to Brander. 'Is that okay, Jimmy?'

'It's your ship, Captain,' Brander grinned. 'I wouldn't presume to interfere with an operational decision.' The captain led the way to the boardroom and ordered the drinks.

'Let me give you a toast, gentlemen. I don't know that *we* can say "mission accomplished", but I think *you* have accomplished yours, or will have shortly, and so I drink to your success.'

He lifted his pink gin.

'Oh, by the way, one other thing. We should get you off this afternoon in the *Sea King*. It'll be about two hours' flight. So you ought to be making the wires hum by this evening. I shall give my masters a complete description of the chap we fished out of the drink, but leave the speculation as to his identity to you boys . . .'

'What about the diary?' asked Broadside.

'Oh, we'll find that later . . . But on the VC, nothing more suggestive than "mysterious disappearance", eh?'

Broadside laughed harshly.

'Alright, Captain. If you care to seal that with a pink gin, I'm prepared to buy it.'

The captain looked round. 'Everyone happy with that?'

They all nodded. Playfair laughed: 'I wonder when you'll get a call back on our story, Captain.'

'Not until the dozy buggers read it in their clubs the next day. Or there's a question in the House. Right, that's settled. Fill up these gentlemen's glasses again, would you, steward?'

Playfair turned to Brander. 'Tell me one thing, Jimmy, why was Kadongo mad enough to fly such a mission himself?'

'Well, he was quite a good pilot. He was at Cranwell and then flying school. One of their best African trainees. And when he found out that MacGregor had apparently got clean away, he must have gone wild.'

'He nearly got away with it too,' said Broadside. 'How was he to know that MacLean was such a bloody lucky shot?'

'Yes, but why sink the ruddy dhow and all the gold with it?' interrupted Straight. 'That's the crazy bit that I don't understand.'

Captain Mumford cleared his throat. 'My guess is that he didn't plan to sink them. He thought that MacGregor and the rest of them were aboard the dhow and he was going to give them the fright of their lives . . . leaving us to pick up the pieces and the gold, of course! Instead of which the dhow goes up like a box of matches. Still can't quite understand it. Could have been the diesel tanks, I suppose, but my guess is that they had a whole lot of those Chinese rockets on board and they just went whoosh . . .! What about some lunch, gentlemen?'

They sat down to a typical Navy lunch of thick brown soup and frozen lamb. The peas were of a lurid green that nature had never managed to emulate.

Broadside spoke with his mouth full. 'Aren't we forgetting the other half of the equation? What about MacGregor and his little lot? Why aren't we in pursuit of them now, Captain?'

'Maybe some other destroyer is?' Jarvis chipped in.

'The answer to the first question is that he has too big a start on us now and that our orders were concerned exclusively with the dhow and the gold. The answer to the second question is that the way the Navy is these days, I shouldn't think there's another of HM's ships closer than the North Atlantic. In other words, I think your friend MacGregor has a clear run ahead of him. Right, Jimmy?'

Brander waved away the steward who was advancing with more peas.

'Absolutely agree. We've notified the South African authorities, of course, and it'll be up to them. After all, there's no proof that he has committed any crime – except you gentlemen's stories and he'll deny them like mad. I don't think we can interfere with him on the high seas. The gold was another matter. I expect the South African police will want to have a word with him when he gets to Durban.'

'I can't see him having much trouble.' Broadside gave a sniff. 'You know as well as I do that they'll never prosecute him there for something that happened two thousand miles away in Kawawa. They couldn't care less.'

'He'll get away with it, alright,' agreed Straight. 'He'll settle down on his wine farm and dream of what he would have done with all that gold . . . and plan the next one.'

'The man I feel a pang of sympathy for is old MacLean,' Playfair said reflectively. 'He was a rogue, but there was something grand about him – like a Wagnerian hero . . .'

'Stop being so bloody pompous,' said Broadside, 'and pass the port. Then I must go and write my second award-winning splash . . .'

20

A young officer came up and saluted the captain. 'Sorry to interrupt you, sir, but the *Sea King* is U/S.' Playfair noted his wings and his embarrassment. Mumford looked up.

'U/S? What the hell's wrong with the damned thing? It was okay yesterday, wasn't it?'

The young pilot nodded. 'Yes sir, it was. But it seems to have picked up a stray round or two in the jet intake in this morning's engagement, sir. It would probably be alright, but I can't give it one hundred percent clearance.'

Mumford looked round the table. 'That makes life a little difficult for you gentlemen.'

'What does he mean, in plain English?' Broadside demanded. 'That we're buggered?'

'Just about it.' Captain Mumford turned back to the pilot. 'Any chance of getting it fixed?'

'Don't think so, sir. It'll need a new part when we dock. The only possibility, sir, is to take the bubble, but as you know, it can only take one passenger, and we're just about at the limit of its range.'

Captain Mumford glanced out of the porthole at the bow wave rolling away smoothly over the deep blue of the Indian Ocean.

'Have you checked our position?'

'Yes, sir, about two hundred and fifty miles out. Leave it another fifty miles and I'd be happy about the range. We can fix up extra fuel tanks. But we can't take more than one passenger, sir.'

'Okay, we'll send the bubble. Gentlemen, all you have to do is decide which of you will have the dubious honour of making the run to Mombasa in that little toy of the lieutenant's. Rather you than me. Make up your minds while I go and check exactly how far we are from the coast.'

Straight cleared his throat. 'Well, we'll have to toss for it, unless someone's got a better idea?'

'Throw dice,' suggested Broadside. 'Man who throws the highest number goes in the chopper. Any objections?'

'Between you three then,' said Jarvis. 'I'm willing to stand down provided whoever goes radios my pictures. Those shots of Kadongo bombing the shit out of the dhow, and old MacLean blasting away are worth a lot of money.'

'Right, then it's between us. Who's got some dice?' Playfair looked round.

'Hold on,' said Brander. He went over to the bar and came back a few moments later with a pair of dice and a backgammon board, the inside covered in green baize.

'There you are, chaps, who's going first?'

'Maybe you ought to go on behalf of all of us. Then there would be no argument about copy getting held up,' Playfair said.

Brander shook his head. 'Thanks for the vote of confidence but I'd rather not. As soon as we dock, I'll have to report direct to the Ambassador and then draft a long telegram. I wouldn't want to let you boys down.'

Playfair guessed his real reason was that he wanted to avoid any repercussions about the story getting out before the Embassy and Whitehall knew. If he stayed behind on the *Banshee*, he could avoid that problem.

Playfair reached forward. 'To hell with it. I'm happy to go first.' The dice rolled across the baize, hit the side of the case and jumped back into the middle of the green surface.

'Ten,' shouted Jarvis. 'No, by God, eleven.'

'Six and five, eleven,' confirmed Brander.

'You jammy bastard. You would throw a bloody eleven, wouldn't you?' Broadside was furious. He took the dice, rattled them briefly and threw. They trickled across the baize and stopped.

'Blast!' Broadside turned away in disgust.

'Seven,' intoned Brander, scooping up the dice and handing them to Straight.

Straight lifted the dice high like a barman shaking cocktails and then hurled them down on the board. Playfair saw one dice roll right to the edge of the board and stop on a six. He watched the other, fascinated. As it came slowly towards him it looked for a moment as if it would be another six, and then it swerved and stopped – on a four.

'Eleven beats ten,' said Brander. 'Alastair gets the bubble ride.'

Straight got up and left the table. He turned at the door. 'I'm going to write my piece and if it doesn't get there as soon as yours, I'll break every bone in your blasted body.' He disappeared through the wardroom door.

Broadside sniffed. 'Old Roger really is steamed up.' He hoisted himself out of his chair. 'I'm going to write my piece too. When's takeoff?'

Brander consulted his watch. 'I should think in about an hour, say around three. By that time we ought to be within range of Mombasa. We don't want you coming down in the drink ten miles short of the cable office, and then have to fish you out as we go past. By the way, you know the captain has given you a cabin and a typewriter each to write your immortal prose in? Can you find them?'

'Think so,' grunted Broadside. 'No doubt the sound of Straight's illiterate two-finger typing will lead us to the right spot . . .'

The bubble was a small Agusta Bell 47G helicopter. The pilot climbed in on the right and started moving the control column back and forth, and then from side to side. He extended a gloved finger to indicate that Playfair should climb in on the other side. They sat encased in a plexiglass bowl, except for the metal floor. An AB made sure Playfair's headset fitted properly and that his seat belt was on. They were both wearing flying suits and Mae Wests which would inflate automatically if they had to ditch.

The whine of the rotor blade rose to a shrill whistle and the bubble gave a tiny lurch. The pilot opened the throttle, and, as light as a dandelion seed, they lifted off. Then he put the nose down and they went out over the sea, climbing sharply and leaving the destroyer ploughing along behind them. The speed of the climb gave Playfair a feeling of power and exhilaration. Far below he watched three tiny figures waving from the deck. He patted his inside pocket and the three wads of typed copy that constituted each man's story, plus three rolls of film from Jarvis with detailed instructions printed in capitals.

The headphones crackled as the pilot had a last word with the tower. Then he turned to Playfair and held up his thumb. 'All systems go . . . should be a fairly routine flight . . . not much to see, unfortunately. Zanzibar and Pemba should be coming up in two hours' time to starboard . . . and then we should pick up the lights of Mombasa shortly after that. I estimate we should be touching down just before dark. You sitting comfortably?'

Playfair grinned and nodded. He was getting used to the precarious feeling of seeming to be flying without any visible means of support. The pilot was concentrating on the row of flickering needles and dials in front of him, checking height, airspeed and compass heading.

The beat of the rotor had settled down to a steady, comforting roar. An occasional current of air buffeted the tiny chopper, but it forged on steadily at three thousand feet. Playfair looked down at the blue below, crinkled with white. The fragility of the helicopter made him think of a butterfly which had ventured too far from land. He pictured the *Banshee* pounding along behind them, and how Broadside, Jarvis and Straight would no doubt be propping up the bar and making disparaging remarks about his luck. Playfair began to imagine the headlines in tomorrow's papers. African Leader Shot Down on Bombing Mission – Dhow Goes Down with Ten Million Pounds of Gold – Mercenary Leader Escapes – Our Man Flies out the Story. No, that was too much . . .

He must have nodded off because he awoke with a slight start to hear the pilot saying . . .

'You can see Zanzibar now ahead and to the right – that long green island. And Pemba's just visible to the north . . . We ought to be picking up the coast pretty soon . . . Have a good nap?'

Ten minutes later they could see the faint smudge of the coast and the dark line of the palms reaching down to the water. Mombasa was suddenly below them and they headed for the long line of yellow lights that marked the flarepath.

'Charlie Zulu to control . . . permission to land . . .' Two minutes later they were floating down watching an East African Airways jet climb up into the evening sky with its navigation lights winking red and green. Then they were down with a tiny bump in the military section of the field. The pilot cut the motor and unbuckled his seat belt. He took off his helmet and wiped his face with the back of his hand. It was suddenly hot and sticky on the ground.

'Phew. That was a long haul. Give me a *Sea King* any day. I think there's a car for you. I'll see you later.'

Playfair shook hands, got out and ducked under the swishing blades. Sure enough, the same black Embassy car was cruising over the tarmac. It was the same driver.

'Evening, sir, message for you.' He handed Playfair a sealed envelope. 'Where do you want to go this time?'

'Cable and Wireless, please, as fast as possible.' As they drove through the dusk, Playfair scanned the note. There was just enough light to make out the neat handwriting.

'The Ambassador has sent me down to look after you and your jailbird friends and see that your politer wants are attended to. I've booked rooms for you four at the Coral Reef and am anxiously awaiting your arrival in Room 401. Hope it won't be too long. Love, Arabella.'

Playfair read it a second time. He thought he could detect a slight smell of her perfume on the paper. He spoke to the driver's back. 'How far out is the Coral Reef?'

'Only a couple of miles from town, sir. Very nice too. Best grub in town and right on the beach. You staying there then, sir?'

'Yes. Could you take me there after we've been to the cable office?'

'No problem, sir, they told me to stay with you as long as you needed me.'

The Cable and Wireless office was still housed in one of the old colonial buildings not far from the harbour. Playfair could easily imagine Stanley striding up the steps and sending his famous dispatch about his meeting with Dr Livingstone from the same teak counter. A small grey-haired Indian with glasses came forward and took the copy. Playfair explained that they had not been able to use the proper cable forms.

'Don't worry, sir, we will paste up on to cable forms. This one first, sir?' He held up Playfair's message.

'Yes, then this one, Mr Straight's . . .'

'Ah, yes, sir, I know Mr Straight. Very tall man, isn't it?'

'That's right, and then this one, Mr Broadside's, last.' That was fairest, thought Playfair. In the same order as the dice

'How's the line to London?'

The Indian turned and looked to the back of the big, darkish room, where several machines creaked out the long loops of messages.

'We've had some sunspot activity, and they're just changing the frequency, but I think it will be alright.'

'Okay. If you have any problems can you ring me at the Coral Reef? I'm staying there.'

Playfair wondered if he should call Arabella, and decided not to. He would give her a surprise.

Outside, it was now quite dark, although still warm. It was refreshing to get a breeze from the movement of the car. They left behind them the garish lights of the centre and turned on to a dual-carriageway lined with palms. They were heading south, parallel with the coast. The Coral Reef was at the end of a broad avenue flanked with more palms about fifty yards from the beach. At first glance it looked a fairly modest establishment. It was only three storeys high and the entrance was low and unpretentious. Playfair noticed though that the massive double doors were of teak and studded with huge brass nails like the old Arab doors in Zanzibar. The hall was cleverly lit so that the eye was guided through a series of Moorish arches to a terrace which looked right over the beach. On the right was a swimming pool, now still and empty: and on the left you could sit out at a table with a drink, and listen to the thunder of the surf on the reef, a faint white line in the half darkness. Playfair turned back to the desk, signed in and asked the switchboard for Room 401. There was a short pause and then a familiar voice said:

'Hallo, 401.'

'Arabella, it's me! Not a bad pad you've found.' There was a quick intake of breath at the other end of the line.

'Alastair, darling! Where are you? When did you get here? Are you alright?'

'Hey, just a minute . . . one question at a time . . . I'm in the lobby. Do you want to come down and have a drink . . .?'

But she had already put the phone down. Two minutes later, the lift door opened with a small sigh and a tall blonde girl with a more golden tan than he remembered, wearing a loose white dress, ran across the floor and into his arms. He held her tightly, feeling her supple body pressing against his own, and kissed her a long time right in front of the main desk. But it was a good hotel and the hall porter pretended not to notice. A pair of elderly Americans passing slowly on their way to dinner had to go round them.

'My, they must be in love,' the old lady drawled. The old man cupped his hand to his ear.

'What's that you say, honey?'

'Never mind. Give me your arm,' she snapped. Finally Arabella put her head back.

'Let me have a good look at you. I can't see any war wounds. Your hair's a bit long, but I think that's an improvement. And you're not as pale as a jailbird ought to be. Where are the others, by the way?'

Playfair took her arm. 'Let's go and have a drink on the terrace and I'll tell you.' They walked out under the archway and on to the terrace.

'There,' said Arabella, pointing to a table right at the end. 'We'll be able to look right down on to the beach. Isn't it lovely?'

'What would you like to drink? How about a *margarita*?'

'I don't think I've ever had one. What is it?'

'Let's order and I'll tell you.' Playfair summoned a hovering waiter.

'Well, it's from tequila, fresh limes, a dash of cointreau, and they put a little salt round the rim of the glass. In Mexico, they drink the tequila neat, suck half a lime, and then lick some salt off the back of their hand.' He mimicked the drinking sequence.

Arabella laughed. 'It sounds exciting, but what does it taste like?'

'Like nectar. Tequila is made from a cactus and is said to have hallucinatory – as well as aphrodisiac – qualities.'

'Oh, that's why you suggested it?'

Playfair grinned at her. The waiter arrived and placed the drinks, in frosted glasses, in front of them.

'Here's to you, my darling, and your beautiful eyes.'

As they drank, the sea lisped on the sand in front of them, and the palms creaked gently. The breeze off the sea was deliciously cool.

'They're very good for you, do you know that?' Playfair said after a sip. 'You need the salt in this climate.'

Arabella put her left hand on Alastair's neck. He liked her fingers. They were very gentle.

'You don't have to make excuses for drinking anything as delicious as this . . .' Arabella paused. 'Do you want to tell me about it all now, or later . . .?'

Playfair shifted slightly in his chair.

'Later if you don't mind. It's so . . . perfect here . . . with you . . . tonight . . . I don't want to get all het up . . . and lose it all. Do you mind?'

'Of course not. Let's just relax . . .'

A page from the front desk came up and bowed.

'Mr Playfair, sir?'

Alastair nodded dreamily.

'Telephone call for you, sir.'

'Damn. Why can't they leave us alone?' He got up. 'I won't be a sec. Why don't you order a couple more?' He hurried across the terrace. The page was holding open the door to a booth. He picked up the phone.

'Yes? Playfair speaking.'

'Ah. Mr Playfair, sorry to trouble you, sir, it's Cable and Wireless here.'

'Oh, yes, what's the problem?'

'Bad news, I'm afraid, sir. Very bad propagation and we've been unable to send the messages, sir . . .'

'God . . .' Playfair was almost speechless with rage. 'What, not a single bloody word?'

It was the clerk's turn to stutter. 'Oooooooooohhhhh . . . yes, sir . . . we've s . . . s . . . s . . . sent your message, sir, all but the last page, that is . . . b . . . b . . . b . . . but not the others.'

'Hang on.' Playfair tried to stay calm. 'You say you have sent all of my message – signed Playfair – except for the last page? That doesn't matter too much. But you have not repeat not sent any of either Mr Straight's or Mr Broadside's messages? Is that right?'

'Correct, sir . . .'

'But you will as soon as you can?'

'Of course, sir . . . but we're not knowing when that will be . . .'

'No, no, I understand. I'll tell you what. If I ring in an hour or so, say about nine, will you be there?'

'I'll be here till midnight, sir.'

'Right, thanks.'

Playfair rang off and walked back to where Arabella was sitting. She turned towards him.

'What's wrong?'

'The cable's gone up the spout. That's to say that my stuff got away, all but the last page. But the other two messages are still there in the cable office. Not a word has left Mombasa. Of course they'll never believe there was a fault. They'll be absolutely convinced that I've bribed the clerk to say it was sunspot trouble; that I've done the dirty on them.'

'So what's going to happen?'

'Well, my stuff will be in London now, I should think, and the whole of Fleet Street will know about it in ten minutes. It will all depend on how quickly they get the cable working again. If they do it in the next half hour or so, it won't make much difference. But if they don't . . . then, given the time difference, it could mean they'll miss all editions.'

'Miss all editions? That'll mean you'll have a world scoop, won't it?'

'Yes, it will. It'll also mean that I will have earned the undying hatred of two of my best friends.'

'Well, it's not your fault. Come on, let's go and have some dinner, I'm starving. There's a marvellous crayfish bar down on the beach . . .'

They walked down the steps from the terrace and on to the soft sand. The bar was at the end of the hotel, open on one side to the sea and thatched with palm leaves. There was a long wooden bar down one side, and at the back of the room a big African chef in a white hat was cooking live crayfish over an open fire. Arabella walked over to him and he greeted her effusively.

'You want to sit beach side where you sit last night?'

'Aha,' said Playfair. 'You were here last night, were you?' The big chef winked at him.

'She was, bwana, but she was all alone.' He had a big booming laugh.

'Isn't he divine?' Arabella sat down. Playfair stared back at her without speaking. He thought she had never looked so attractive. They sat for a few moments in silence, looking at one another. The chef brought over the crayfish himself and served them, slitting them in half and pouring melted butter over the white flesh.

Playfair attacked his crayfish. He spoke with his mouth full. 'Wonderful! You can taste how fresh they are. I think this is the best crayfish I've ever eaten . . .' He had lifted his glass to taste the white wine . . .

They had finished dinner and were having coffee and a brandy when the same page reappeared.

'Excuse me, sir. Telegram for you.'

'Ah,' said Playfair, putting down his cigar. 'So the line's working again, is it?' He tore open the green envelope.

'Congratulations your sensational gold scoop which already making headlines around the world. Like you catch next flight London to make full report in person to Chairman and Board. Please acknowledge. Multi-regards . . .' It was signed: 'King.' Playfair handed it to Arabella without a word. She read it.

'Not *the* King?'

He smiled: 'No. Just some joker on the desk.'

'Oh, well, I should disregard it.'

Playfair took it back and very slowly tore it up. He dropped the bits in the ashtray and lit them with the candle.

'The trouble is that if I don't reply they will simply repeat it. Notice the cunning insertion of the words – "please acknowledge".'

'Can't you tell them to get lost? That you need a break?'

'I could. But that would only make them cross.' He thought for a second.

'No. It would be cleverer to out-manoeuvre them.' He turned to the page who was still standing at attention by the table.

'Have you got a piece of paper?'

The boy produced a cable form. Playfair began to write.

'Your correspondent Alastair Playfair is well but exhausted. I am prescribing the patient three days absolute rest before allowing him to embark on the flight to London. I must insist he is not disturbed unnecessarily . . .' Playfair hesitated over the signature . . . 'What on earth shall I call this chap, the doctor?'

'What about . . . Cavendish . . .?'

'Of course. Dr Cavendish . . . how simple and how perfect. You deserve a very special kiss for that . . .' The page was still waiting patiently. Playfair gave him a coin.

'Show the cable to the desk and tell them to send any reply to Room 401; Dr Cavendish.'

'Doctor, do you mind?' Alastair leaned forward and kissed Arabella's half-open lips.

'You taste of strawberries.'

'Not of crayfish?'

'No, strawberries. That should shut them up in London for a while. What a girl you are . . . not only beautiful but brilliant as well . . . the perfect secretary, qualified in diplomacy, medicine . . .'

'Want to go for a stroll along the beach . . .?'

'What a good idea.' Playfair got up. 'I must just ring the cable office first and find out what's happened to those messages.'

They walked across the terrace to the reception desk. Playfair spoke to the switchboard and asked for Cable and Wireless. The same clerk answered.

'Ah, Mr Playfair, is it? You got your message, sir? Unfortunately . . . circuit came back up for ten minutes only, and then went down again. It's still down, and not looking too good, sir.'

'Did you get anything out at all?'

'Only a few words . . . and rather badly garbled. Very sorry, sir, but nothing I can do . . .' His voice trailed off in an agitated squeak.

'Is there no other routing? It's terribly urgent, you know!'

'No, sir. No other routing at all, sir. Nothing to do but be patient, sir.' Playfair swore, and put down the phone.

'Well, it looks as if they've had it . . . absolutely nothing going out at all . . . any chance of getting the Embassy to help?'

Arabella shook her head. 'Don't think there's a hope. The man in Nairobi is said to be even more anti-press than Sir Harry.'

Playfair laughed. 'Just our luck. Well, they'll kill me tomorrow, so perhaps we ought to make the most of tonight.'

She took his hand and they walked back across the terrace, down the steps and on to the sand. Their feet made no sound. The sea was still lapping infinitely gently a few yards away. The

207

lights and voices from the hotel faded into the darkness behind
them. Someone was playing Beethoven and the music floated
towards them out of the darkness. They walked hand in hand
slowly up the beach to where the palms made a pool of darkness.

'Let's sit down here.'

Playfair pulled Arabella gently down beside him. The sand
was still warm. Tiny crabs scuttled away into the darkness. His
fingers found the zip at the back of her dress and gently eased
it open . . . She had no bra on.

'Wait a minute.' Arabella stood up.

'Let me take this silly dress off . . .' He pulled her down on the
sand beside him, suddenly desperate for her . . . as if it were the
end of the world and they would never have another chance.

Afterwards, they lay for a long time listening to the lullaby of
the sea.

Finally Arabella sat up.

'Come and have a swim . . . it'll be lovely and warm and it'll
get all the sand off.'

'You keep making such brilliant suggestions. I love you very
much.' He kissed her tenderly and pulled her to her feet.

They walked in the semi-dark to the faintly luminous edge of
the water.

'Hold on,' said Playfair. 'What about sharks?'

'No,' Arabella laughed. 'Not here. Not with the reef.'

She took his hand and they waded into the water. It was as
smooth against the skin as silk, and like silk, cool when it first
touches the body. Beethoven was silent, and the sea was now the
only music they could hear. They waded out until the water was
up to their chests and then swam, close together, feeling the
water caressing their bodies. Arabella put one arm round
Alastair's neck. They floated in the quiet dark, their bodies
touching. Out on the reef even the surf seemed to be half
asleep. When it began to get a little cool, they swam lazily back
towards the shore and the black mass of the palms. Their feet
found the sandy floor.

Arabella shook the water out of her hair.

'Do you know what I would like to do now?'

'No.'

'Guess.'

'Go back and have a hot shower . . . and then go to bed and

make love for a long time . . .'

'You must be a mind reader.'

Alastair put his arm round Arabella's waist and together they walked up the beach. Behind them the moon was just beginning to climb out of the sea.